VALENTINO McKELVIE

VALENTINO McKELVIE

MICHAEL O'KANE

Michael P. O'Kane

ISBN: 978-1-9993529-0-5
Drombeg Books, Skibbereen, County Cork, Ireland

About the author

Michael O'Kane, is a long-time journalist and barrister who has written a number of
short stories which were published by the late David Marcus in New Irish Writing
in *The Irish Press*. He has had a lifelong fascination with great historical authors like
Charles Dickens, Jane Austen, Catherine Cookson, and especially James Plunkett,
authors who through their great stories gave us such a wonderful insight into how
people lived, loved and died in the latter centuries of the second millennium.

CONTENTS

PROLOGUE

1926

Shemmy McKelvie leaned against the wall of the old stone bridge and fixed his gaze on the sparkling white water gliding through yawning arches below, flowing over boulders rounded by centuries of wear and tear; long strakes of green moss waved over them in the gentle current. He had seen it hundreds of times before, but he looked anyhow for he had nothing better to do. Most of his pals were in orchards picking fruit to earn pocket money; others had been packed off to relatives in the country to keep them out of mischief for the holidays. He was on his own for the day—no one to play with, nobody to talk to.

It was the same every summer. When holidays finally came, life was hectic during the first weeks of freedom doing all the things you wanted but couldn't do when at school; now with time on his hands for something new, some new adventure, his friends were off doing their own thing and he was left on his own. It was such a waste when the weather was so good; in a couple of weeks the holidays would be over, and he would have nothing to look forward to except another year in a stuffy classroom, a leather strap threatening him, homework in the evenings and nights getting longer as another cold wet Irish winter approached.

Shemmy was annoyed with his pals for deserting him. It would not have been so bad if he was allowed to go with them to pick fruit, for he knew they had good fun, not to mention a shiny half-crown in their pockets at the end of the day. The problem was his big sister Jinny. She wouldn't let him pick fruit with the others. He had poor eyesight and she was over protective of him, worried about the others making fun of him, playing tricks. She had a good job in the local mill and could afford to give him pocket money for the pictures a couple of times a week and a fish and chip treat at the weekend. He didn't like it, but she was the boss.

Shemmy was an orphan. His mother died from tuberculosis

while he was still a baby. When he was 7 his father died of a heart attack brought on by the physical strain of heaving bales of flax at the mill. He was only 45 years old and had worked there since he was 15. Jinny and the boy were left to fend for themselves after that. She was fifteen years older than her brother but looked after him as if he was a son.

They lived in Murrinbridge, a town in north-west Ireland with a population of 10,000 people, a community whose only claim to fame was that it had the highest rate of male unemployment in the country. There were some jobs for women in shirt factories and a nearby linen mill, but little work for men. While Shemmy was growing up there in the Thirties it was still a sizeable town, but lack of jobs had robbed its men folk of their dignity and pitched many families onto the poverty line

The stone bridge on which the unhappy Shemmy stood was supported by thirteen high arches and had been built a hundred years before to connect two halves of the town that straddled the river Murrin, from which the town took its name. On one side of the river were streets of shops and offices; on the other rows of terraced houses fanned out from the bridge like spokes on a wheel. The main road from Belfast to Derry ran over the bridge and through the heart of the town, but the streets were so narrow that nobody stopped unless they had business there. Horses and carts fought with motor vehicles for the right of way; on market days tempers flared and traffic came to a standstill as hundreds of animals blocked the town centre while dealers haggled over prices.

Murrinbridge was officially labelled a "depressed town". After school most boys and girls went to England or Scotland in search of work. Those who did not resigned themselves to a life of idleness at home. A few families with means sent their children to secondary school, hoping that education might open the door to a worthwhile job, but the vast majority were lucky to even get a primary education. Farmers' children often had to leave school at ten or twelve years of age to help out on the land.

Like everybody else Shemmy's prospects were not great, and to make things worse, he had an additional problem—bad eyesight, so bad that his sister realised from the time he was five or six years of age that it was going to be a drawback to him all his life. Even with the help of the thickest of glasses it was so poor he was a danger to himself and others. The only hope she had was that she might be able to get him some sort of work at the mill. If she did not, his prospects were dire, for he could never go abroad to find work like other young men.

Shemmy wiped perspiration from his brow with the cuff of his shirt. The intense heat of the sun made the hairs bristle on his back. Hot sweat seared the skin under his armpits. As if the heat wasn't bad enough, his back itched. He knew exactly what it was—a flea inside his shirt. He could feel it in the groove between his shoulder blades. He put his hand down under the collar of his shirt but couldn't reach the spot. He pulled the shirt tail out of the back of his trousers and tried to get at it from below but no matter how hard he tried or how much he cursed he still could not stretch his fingers to where it was biting into the tender flesh.

Shemmy pressed the broad of his back against the bridge wall and slid from side to side over a rough stone. The cold granite felt good against the hollow in his spine. He moved up and down and pushed hard against the uneven surface until his skin ached more than it itched. It gave him some relief, but he knew from experience that the respite would not last long. The little bugger would be at him again as soon as he stopped scratching. He would have to wait until he got back home to get rid of him permanently with a puff of DDT. The white powder had a terrible smell, but it was the only sure way to get rid of fleas.

He rested his chin on his arms on the parapet wall and squinted hard until he was able to make out anglers in the shimmering water. They had waders up to the waist to keep them dry as they edged their way cannily into deeper pools where trout and salmon were lying. The men heaved long rods back and forth through the warm breeze to dry their flies before skilfully dropping the fishing line gently back onto the glistening water in a slow snaking movement. Salmon and trout did not normally feed on bright summer days like this but they instinctively snatched at insects dancing on the rippling surface, and if you got lucky, they would take your fly.

His daydreaming at the bridge was disturbed by a clatter on the ground behind him. Tommy Richardson, the butcher boy, was trying to park his delivery bike against the kerb with the pedal, but it was so laden with parcels it fell over. Eventually he stood it against the wall.

"I hate that fucking bicycle," he said.

"Ye have a right load today," said Shemmy. The square metal basket on the front of the butcher's bike was packed with blood-stained brown paper parcels. Some had fallen to the ground when the bicycle toppled sideways and Tommy picked them up, rubbed the dirt off with his striped apron and put them back in the basket.

"Aye," he said, "I'm still on the afternoon delivery. I'll be killed if auld Hamilton finds out I let his good meat fall on the ground." When everything was ship-shape again he joined Shemmy at the wall.

"Any action down there?" he asked .

"Naw, Tommy. I've been here for a good while and they haven't caught a thing. They won't be having fish for dinner today—unless they get it from the chipper," he added, chuckling.

"There are enough of them—fishermen, I mean," said his companion sarcastically.

The pair ambled to the other side of the bridge to see what was happening upstream; nobody seemed to be having any luck there either.

Shemmy looked down into darker water shaded by the arches from the bright evening sunshine. It was a long drop and he squinted hard. He thought he heard the splash of a fish breaking the surface.

"Look there, Tommy," he said pointing to the spot. "Can you see anything moving down there? I thought I heard one jumping."

"Jesus, there's nothing wrong with your hearing," Tommy said leaning over the wall. "There are a good few fish down there. Somebody ought to tell those bloody eejits they're casting in the wrong place."

Shemmy's eyes were sore from squinting. The glare of the bright water gave him a headache and his neck ached from stretching.

4

When Tommy Richardson moved off to continue his deliveries he rested his forehead on the back of his hands on the wall and closed his eyes to see if it would get rid of the pain.

Now that the itch was gone he felt more comfortable. The cool stone against the hot skin on his chest also helped. His stomach gurgled, and he began to think about going home soon for something to eat. Jinny would make a plate of griddle scones when she arrived from the mill and after dinner he loved to ladle them with butter and jam; they were great with a big mug of tea.

He was looking forward to the evening; it was the best part of the day. His pals would be home from the fruit farms, and once they had something to eat his gang would meet at the end of the street and head for the rushy glen. Courting couples gathered there on warm summer nights and Shemmy and his pals had great fun watching them. The boys had a hiding place in nearby whin bushes from which they could see the lads and their girls rolling around in the tall grass. On a fine evening there could be anything up to a dozen courting couples so there was always plenty to see. The lovebirds wrestled and cavorted in the glen, oblivious to the fact that they were being spied on.

Shemmy could not see anything at a distance, especially in the evening light, but the others gave him an animated commentary on what was going on and his imagination did the rest.

One of the girls who went there regularly—and not always with the same boy—was Minnie Sharkey. He knew her well. She was 16, a friendly, good-looking girl with straight shiny hair that spilled over her shoulders and bobbed up and down as she walked. She wore tight blouses and skirts that made the most of her ample bust and shapely waist and legs.

Shemmy knew Minnie because she often came to his house. His sister Jinny in her spare time was a seamstress who made clothes for her. Minnie was mad to keep up with the latest fashion. She sent away to magazines for mail order patterns and brought them to his sister to have them made. She was always in a panic to get a dress finished for some dance or other. Minnie was a great one for dancing.

When she visited, and he was at home, she gave him a friendly

5

hug and playfully ran her fingers through his hair. He liked the feel of her soft hands on his face and the warmth of her body when she pulled him close.

"This brother of yours," she said to Jinny, "is going to be a right Valentino when he grows up!"

Once she held his face between her hands and pulled him so close that he could feel the softness of her bust and the sweet-scented odour of her breath. He loved to be near her but at the same time was worried she might sense that he was getting excited. His nostrils were filled with the scent of her body long after she left the house.

He had a big secret about Minnie, one he shared with nobody, not even his closest friends. Apart from spying on her in the glen he secretly watched when she came to his house for fittings. When Minnie had to undress Shemmy was sent out to the garden and told not to come back until he was called. But through a finger hole in the back door he had a perfect view of her in the kitchen. Even with his bad sight he was close enough to see everything though the peephole.

She always stripped to her brassiere and knickers before she tried on a dress. When she took the new garment off so that his sister could make adjustments, she stood for ages in the middle of the floor in her underclothing waiting for changes to be made. She spent the time admiring herself in the mirror, turning from side to side to look at her profile, glancing seductively over her shoulder at her bottom. Shemmy blushed as he watched her use her fingers to tuck her white breasts inside the cups of her bra and press her hands flat against her stomach and hold her breath to see how she would look if she lost another few pounds. When it was cold he could see her nipples through the shiny material in her bra. Neither Minnie nor Jinny suspected anything, even though he always seemed to be hanging around the house when she came for a fitting. In bed at night he imagined her lying beside him, his hand squeezing the cup of her shiny black bra or smoothing the wrinkles of the stockings that covered her legs right up to her thighs. It made him feel excited. He wanted to touch her.

He had mixed feelings about spying on Minnie. His pals knew

she was his favourite in the rushy glen and exaggerated what she got up to with boyfriends, just to tease him. He wanted to know what was going on but he was also jealous and angry that she allowed different men to put their arms around her and kiss her. He did not want to share the love of his life with anybody else.

He boasted to his pals that every time she came to his house she gave him a squeeze and ran her fingers though his hair and sometimes gave him a kiss on the cheek. "I think she fancies me," he bragged. "She calls me her Valentino". There were some guffaws among his pals when he told them about his encounters with the pretty Minnie Sharkey, and thereafter they all took to calling him Valentino, a name that stuck to him for the rest of his life.

His reverie was interrupted suddenly by excited shouts from the river. Either somebody had hooked a fish or one of the anglers had stumbled out of his depth into a hole. He lifted his head to see what the commotion was about, but the afternoon sun had dropped low on the horizon and turned the shimmering water into a highway of dazzling brightness; no matter how hard he tried he could not focus his eyes properly through the whiteness.

He took off the glasses and rubbed his eyelids to get some life back into them, but when he put them on again they didn't work; the dazzle was gone but he still could not see the fishermen. He breathed on the lenses, cleaned them on his shirt and tried again, but all he could see was a dark grey screen as if a blanket had been thrown over his head.

It wasn't the first time that he had lost his sight. He sometimes suffered from severe eyestrain and blurred vision, particularly if he read for any length of time. It seemed to happen for no apparent reason—maybe when he jumped out of bed in the morning late for school or nodded off at his desk in the classroom and had his hair pulled by the teacher to wake him up. Usually the problem cleared after he closed his eyes and relaxed for a while.

He opened and closed his eyes several times, desperately hoping the veil would lift as suddenly as it had fallen, but it didn't. He couldn't see anything, not even the wall of the bridge where he was standing.

Panic gripped Valentino. His heart thumped inside his chest and he had difficulty breathing. He began to shiver with fright. His legs felt weak and he had to lean heavily on the wall for support. Beads of cold sweat ran down the pit of his back where the flea had been annoying him a short time before. He took deep breaths and rolled his head from side to side to ease the ache in his neck.

His head was light, and his body felt as if he was suspended under water, drowning. He couldn't see but into his mind came flashing images, pictures of a tall grey-haired priest towering over him at his school desk, long bony fingers threatening, his booming voice warning of the dire consequences of boys touching and exciting themselves, committing the mortal sin of Onanism. His voice thundered: *'If you keep touching your privates you will go blind, and if you die you will go straight to hell!'*

Valentino was a regular offender in that regard. Thinking about Minnie, he often aroused himself in bed, imagining her lying beside him. He knew it was a sin but it made him feel so good that he found it easy to ignore the warnings they got regularly at school. Was he now paying the price for offending God?

With eyes shut tight, he prayed to the Blessed Virgin, begging forgiveness for the impure thoughts he had, for all the times he touched himself, all the times he imagined sliding his fingers under the cups of Minnie's bra and fondling her breasts.

"Mother of God," he begged, "if you lift the veil from my eyes I promise I will never touch myself again or spy on Minnie or go to the glen or steal toys from Woolworths or prog apples from orchards. If I do, may God strike me dead!"

He lifted his head—he was alive, but the veil was still there.

"For Jesus sake, St Patrick," he muttered in desperation, "do something for me. It wasn't me who was spying on the girls in the glen—I couldn't see that far. I was only listening to what the others were telling me. I didn't mean to do anything wrong, to offend God. For Christ's sake, don't leave me like this!"

When his pleading fell on deaf ears and the grey blanket still hung in front of his eyes he made one last desperate effort to bribe St Jude, the champion of lost causes.

"If you get rid of the greyness in my eyes," he promised, "I will put my fish and chip money in your collection box at Mass on Sunday."

He had never been so terrified in his life; he could not stop shaking, nor could he stem the tears that streamed onto his cheeks and dripped from his chin. No matter how hard he rubbed or how much he pleaded with God and his Holy Mother and the Saints it was no good, the curtain still hung in front of him.

Passers-by, hearing Valentino's confused mumblings, wondered what he was up to—talking to himself, swearing at the wall of the bridge when there was nobody near him, running his fingers through his hair until it stood up straight, his eyebrows and eyelids red from continuous rubbing, the tail of his shirt hanging out.

On her way home from the factory Minnie Sharkey stopped at the bridge to see what was going on. Valentino McKelvie was standing at the wall sobbing convulsively, people standing around gaping at him.

She dropped her bicycle on the roadway and went over to him.

"Good God," she said, putting her hands on his shoulders, "What's wrong with you."

He recognised the voice.

"Aw, Minnie," he sobbed, gripping her arm tightly. "Something happened to my eyes. I'm blind as a bat."

Minnie was frightened when she saw the state he was in. She put her arms around him and held him tight. He clung to her.

"Come on," she whispered. "I'll take you home."

Minnie wheeled her bicycle with one hand and put the other around his shoulder, and together they walked unsteadily along the street to his house. He was crying, but the more she tried to comfort him, the more convulsed he became.

"I can't see, Minnie. I can't see anything."

"Don't worry," she said, "Jinny will know what to do. You'll be all right."

But he wasn't all right. Diseased nerves at the back of his young eyes had finally snapped from years of strain and excessive squinting. Detached from the retina, sensitive optical nerves starved of natural light left the 13-year-old to face the future in complete darkness.

9

Jinny was heartbroken by the onset of her young brother's blindness. She promised to save every spare penny she had in the hope that sometime in the future she might be able to buy an eye or pay for an operation to let him see again. Great developments were taking place in the medical world; she had read in the papers that surgeons were able to graft cornea from the eyes of dead people onto those of the living to give them their sight back.

As he sat in his dark world Valentino often thought about that day on the bridge and the fishermen in the river—the day he lost his sight. It was also the day that he fell madly in love with Minnie Sharkey.

The young Valentino McKelvie found it hard to accept that he was permanently blind. It made him angry, bitter, and rebellious. Jinny watched anxiously as he stumbled about the house aimlessly bumping into walls and chairs and people, ignoring warnings to avoid places he was not familiar with, and deliberately crossing busy streets uncaring as to the danger of being knocked down by a car or a horse. He refused to carry a white cane, rebuked people who tried to help him and would not attend training to teach him how to find his own way about safely.

At school he became disruptive to the point where he had to be sent home several times. Since he was due to leave in a couple of months on his fourteenth birthday the Education Authority decided it was best to let him stay at home altogether and provide him with an instructor to teach him the Braille system of touch text.

Thus it was that, six weeks before his birthday, into Valentino's volatile existence and his home came the formidable Miss Alma Carroll who introduced herself as his Special Needs Teacher. He was totally uncooperative, made no attempt to do anything she asked and sat on his hands whistling while she tried to explain to him the benefit of being able to read Braille.

"It will give you confidence, open up a whole new world for you, help you become independent," she told him. "You have to realise, Valentino, that people will make allowances for your affliction for a while, but after that you are on your own. Your sister won't always be here to hold your hand, and if you are going to make a life for yourself you have to prepare now while you are still young."

When he was still unresponsive she threatened him. If he did not co-operate with her and pay attention she would recommend that he be sent to a residential school for the blind twenty miles away in County Derry.

His attitude changed. He had no desire to be put into a home.

When Miss Carroll began to teach him the Braille alphabet, she found he was an exceptionally fast learner. He had an uncanny sense of touch and once he mastered the basics, he read with his fingers almost as fast as he could when he had his sight. Thereafter she introduced him to a world of adventure through novels like *Kidnapped*, *Treasure Island*, *Gulliver's Travels*, *Huckleberry Finn* and *Lorna Doon*. Although he was familiar with some of the stories before he was afflicted by blindness, reading a complete novel with poor sight was slow and laborious. Now he could close his useless eyes, sit back and feel the words and sentences and paragraphs flow under his fingertips. He became so adept that he began to speed-read by using the fingers of both hands for alternate lines. His appetite was voracious; as soon as he finished a book, Miss Carroll brought another. As the weeks passed, he warmed to his teacher and looked forward to her visits, especially when she brought a new book with her.

For his fifteenth birthday Miss Carroll persuaded the League for the Blind to reward his progress by providing him with a wireless set to stimulate his interest in news and music. He fiddled around with the radio for days to familiarise himself with wavelengths and channels and volume and soon learned where to find the more interesting programmes. He liked quiz shows, which were a well of information on all sorts of subjects, and music; he especially loved dance music. He kept the radio on all the time when he was in the house, singing along when he knew the words, humming tunes when he did not.

Jinny was so relieved with the change in her brother brought about by this newfound interest that she bought him a brand-new German radio for his sixteenth birthday and paid extra for the latest *Magic Eye* tuning system. It was the only set of its kind on their street, and thereafter the McKelvies had a steady stream of neighbours and friends calling to the house, eager to hear this marvel of German engineering.

"No more fiddling around with the tuner looking for the best reception," explained Valentino proudly. "Just switch it on and hey presto! the *Magic Eye* does the rest."

Jinny was horrified when she came home from the mill one evening and found her expensive birthday present lying in a tangled mass of wires and valves on the kitchen table.

"My God!" she shouted at him. "What have you done? Do you realise how much that radio cost? It's in bits."

"Don't worry," he said. "Just don't touch anything on the table for I know where to put my hand on everything. I'll get it back together again."

Seeing the mess, she had her doubts that the expensive radio would ever produce another sound, but when he rebuilt it and got it to work perfectly a couple of days later she was quick to brag to friends about the clever young brother she had.

Valentino became so familiar with the apparatus that he acquired a reputation as a fixer of radios and people came with broken sets to see if he could get them going again. If he succeeded, they paid him a few pence for his services. He was delighted to be earning a bit of money working from his own house; and it was also a labour of love.

BOOK I

AN UNHAPPY HOUSE

1939

Sir Kenneth Montgomery did not want to face his wife over breakfast after the tirade of abuse she had hurled at him the previous evening; he had left the house before she got out of bed, told the maid he had an early meeting and, before she had a chance to offer him a cup of coffee, disappeared through the front door to walk to the mill.

It was chilly when he stepped out into the crisp morning air. He pulled the collar of his overcoat up around his neck and plunged his hands into the deep pockets. He could see his breath in front of him as he laboured uphill but as he got into his stride he warmed up. He picked up the pace, took his hands out of his pockets, let his arms swing free and pushed his shoulders back; he smiled—it felt just like the old days in the army.

As he approached the high iron gates beside the gate lodge he could hear the chatter of birds in the tall trees that shaded the garden from the early morning sun. Those creaking oaks were home to thousands of birds of all species. In autumn he often woke to a crescendo of cawing crows squabbling over nest space in the rookery behind the house. It was so bad at one stage that he thought of introducing the local gun club to get them under control, but his wife would not hear of it.

"God made trees so that birds could nest in them," she said. "The world has enough trouble without interfering with nature." That was the last time he mentioned getting rid of the crows or of the rabbits that kept digging holes in their lovely lawn or his idea of putting barbed wire on top of the wall in his orchard to keep local urchins from stealing the fruit. She would not agree to any such measures.

His lungs filled with pungent odours of flowering shrubs and the distinctive smell of bark discarded by eucalyptus trees. The scent of pollen was so powerful that it clogged his nostrils; he sneezed to clear his head.

He let himself out of the gate beside the lodge and walked downhill towards the mill. The only vehicle he met was the early morning bus to Derry, clattering along in the middle of the road to avoid potholes, its noisy engine shattering the stillness and putting birds to flight; diesel fumes from the exhaust poisoned the woodbine-scented air. Cows gathered near gates by the roadside awaiting farmers to bring them to the milking parlour; alarmed by the noisy bus, they retreated a short distance into the field until it passed.

As the joints in his arms and legs loosened and he lengthened his stride, he resolved to make the journey more often on foot. Apart from the exercise and fresh air it cleared his mind and gave him time to think about himself for a change rather than worry about his ailing wife and problems he was having with her. Gradually the frustrations of life at Mill Brae House dissipated into the morning air.

Near the end of his walk he swung off the main road, took the footbridge over the railway and made directly for the main entrance to the mill. It was not his usual route and the porter was taken by surprise when the boss appeared outside his sentry hut. He jumped up from his seat to open the door.

"Good morning, Sir Kenneth!" he sang out.

The smells of the countryside that filled his nostrils were quickly dispelled as he entered dusty noisy skutching rooms where bales of flax were broken open to extract the delicate fibres that would end up as thread to be woven into linen. Sunlight coming through openings in the roof framed the clouds of rising fibre particles. He covered his face with a handkerchief. It worried him that the unfortunate workers were cocooned in this dust-filled area for eight hours a day during which slivers of fibre drifted around like snowflakes in the artificially moist atmosphere. The fibre had to be kept moist so that it could be spun into thread. The men had masks to prevent dust from the damp tow getting into their lungs, but most of them did not bother to use them. He made a mental note to talk to the manager and have him rectify this situation; dust clogging their lungs could be dangerous. It was the same in the giant spinning room where the clatter of fast-moving machines was deafening. The women who worked there had plugs for their ears, but few made use of them. Instead they chattered away to one another while they worked. He nodded to the women tending the noisy machines as he passed, and some smiled back at him while they carried on with their work.

Though conditions in the mill were not ideal, people lucky enough to work there were well paid, and Sir Kenneth was very proud of the quality of the material they produced. He was also proud of his workforce. The mill village where they lived was a very close-knit community and the present workers had for the most part come from generations of the same families employed by the Montgomerys over a period of a hundred years. Despite the dust and noise, the mill workers seemed happy at their work.

Sir Kenneth's business was going well. He had good agents buying flax for him in Ireland and England and was exporting linen to nineteen countries around the world; America was his biggest customer.

He had a hardworking force who appreciated what their pay-packets contained at the end of the week. Sperrin was a picturesque village designed and built to provide a good standard of living for the people lucky enough to work and live there, with shops and schools and churches and playgrounds aimed at fostering community spirit among the mill hands and their families. It should have been an idyllic place to live, and this was largely true during his father's time but despite Kenneth Montgomery's best efforts since he took over, there had been a serious breakdown in relations between Catholic and Protestant factions living there. Political bickering had taken its toll on community spirit and the situation had now been reached where Catholics lived on one side of the village and Protestants on the other. The lovely village which the Montgomery family specially designed to foster community spirit was now just as divided as the wider community in the North of Ireland—Nationalist Catholic on one side and Protestant Unionist on the other.

When he reached his first-floor office in the administration building he took off his coat and hung it on the back of the door. His secretary, Kate Reilly, had already been through the mail and sorted the letters into neat piles on his desk. There were envelopes from France, Belgium, Italy, Spain, England, America, Argentina, and as far away as Australia. Only the stamps were missing. Kate cut them out and gave them to a charity that sold them on to collectors to raise funds for the Foreign Missions.

He went to the office door and called Kate.

"Yes, Sir," she answered.

"Sorry for the short notice, but I'll need you to work a bit late this evening," he called to her. "There's an important letter from London that has to be answered. It'll take me a while to get the reply ready, and I need it typed and posted this evening."

"Very well, Sir," she said.

"Dependable Kate," he mused as he closed the door and returned to his desk. "Nothing is a problem to her." She had been in the office since she was 16 and he had trained her well. She was naturally neat, efficient, never a day ill, and he could not remember a morning when he got to his desk before her. He had given up opening the post because it was boring. He left it to her now. He had come to rely more and more on Kate to deal with administration while he spent his time touring the mill.

More important, Kate was very discreet, and he knew he could count on her to keep her mouth shut about matters that he did not want circulating among the workers. In fact, he put so much faith in her that he was aware it caused jealousy among other staff.

In his post were the usual bills from merchants and farmers for last year's flax crop, cheques for rolls of linen already received and advance payments for orders yet to be filled. There were invoices for electricity, bills for supplies of coal, and demands from the railroad for payment for shipped goods.

He piled everything into a tray for the office staff to deal with and turned his attention to an envelope Kate had put to one side of his desk. It was marked Personal Private and Confidential. A personal letter was a rare item in his post, especially at the mill. He turned the envelope over to read the return address on the back and raised his eyebrows when he saw it was from a former army colleague, Colonel Edward Johnston, with whom he had served for four years in Egypt. He smiled as he recalled the ruddy-faced spit and polish officer who made life hell for the men in his command. His reputation was built on two tenets—that the English upper classes had a God-given right to rule the world, and that the strength of an army in battle depended on the degree of discipline enforced in the lower ranks.

The letter, however, had nothing to do with things military. It was a plea for help. The Colonel divulged details of a scandal involving the youngest of his four daughters. She had got involved in a romance with a soldier who turned out to be an absolute scoundrel. He wanted to get her away from home for a while so that things could settle down, give the girl time to see the error of her ways. Could Sir Kenneth find something for her to do at the mill and a place to stay, keep an eye on her for a while?

He found it ironic that such a great stickler for discipline in the Army, a man's man to the last, had ended up with a family of four girls whom he could not control. Was it some sort of a punishment from God for the hardship he had inflicted on all those young soldiers?

Colonel Johnston was not just a friend; he was a flax agent who procured badly needed supplies for Sperrin Mill. He wanted to help his old friend if at all possible, if only for old time's sake, but he had to consider the situation with his wife. Imagine her reaction if he told her he was bringing a young woman into the house? The more he thought about it the more he realised it was out of the question. In the end he would have to make some excuse for refusing his friend.

Normally Sir Kenneth was a decisive man, but recently because of domestic problems he found himself putting things on the long finger. He placed the letter and photograph back into the envelope and slipped it into the pocket of his overcoat.

At dinner that evening he had another row with his wife. She complained that the soup was cold and the service sloppy and vowed she would not put up with such carelessness from the servants. When he told her to keep quiet and finish her meal, she swept the tureen and soup bowls to the floor. When he tried to restrain her, he got a whiff of alcohol. He had never known her to have a drink except at dinner, but obviously she had been drinking that day. Could this have accounted for her violent outbursts, for the erratic behaviour of late? If she was drinking and taking medication it might explain her paranoia. There had been rows before, but never had she resorted to violence.

Later, he rang the family doctor to ask if her angry outburst could be due to her taking alcohol with her medication.

Dr McFarlane did not think so. "It's more likely her behaviour is caused by failure to take the medication as prescribed," he said. "You will have to make sure she takes the pills every day and if she will not listen to you, have one of your staff do it. She has to take the tablets every single day."

"Part of the problem," said Sir Kenneth "is that she does not trust the staff, not even her personal maid. She thinks they are laughing at her behind her back. And since she has little communication with me, she is living in isolation, almost like a recluse, with nobody to confide in."

"Then find her a companion, somebody she knows and feels she can trust," said the doctor. "Otherwise I will have to commit her to hospital so that her medication can be monitored and see if that will improve her health. If we do nothing, her condition will continue to deteriorate, and God knows what will happen to her."

Sir Kenneth took the Johnston letter from his coat pocket that night and read it again. Could the wayward Emma Johnston be the answer to his wife's problem? The fact that she was English, from a good family and a stranger might make her more acceptable as a companion. It was better than engaging somebody from the village who could not be trusted to keep her mouth shut about things that happened in Mill Brae.

In the days that followed, the doctor visited and gave Eleanor injections to sedate her, and suddenly life at Mill Brae became almost bearable again. His wife seemed more amenable when he talked to her, even gave a civil answer to questions when he inquired about replacing a maid who had left.

In this new calm atmosphere, he took the opportunity to raise with her the letter from Colonel Johnston, saying only that his old friend was anxious to get his daughter out of England in case war came. He suggested the girl might make an ideal companion. She would live in the house and help manage the servants until she herself felt well enough to take on these duties again.

"The girl is English, from a good family and could be a friend and confidante for you," he assured her. "The management of Mill Brae could be shared between you and it would give you an opportunity to get out and about again, spend more time in the gardens, see more of the countryside," he ventured.

"If you found her presence in the house disagreeable, of course, I would get lodgings for her in the village and she would stay there at night," he added.

His heavily sedated wife nodded her head, and although he wasn't sure how much she had understood he took it to mean she would accept the girl.

Next day he wrote the Colonel that Lady Montgomery "would be happy to welcome" his daughter into their home where no doubt she would "be pleasant company and bring new life into the old house". He would keep an eye on her and make sure she was safe in Ireland as long as she wanted to stay. But he warned: "This nonsense with the soldier must be put behind her. Please impress upon her that it is not to be spoken of when she comes to Ireland."

He kept the letter in his pocket for another day, still not quite sure that his wife fully understood what she had agreed to; then on a sudden whim he handed it to Kate as she was leaving the office to go home and asked her to make sure it was posted.

"It will be interesting," he thought as he walked to work next morning, "to see if the arrival of the young girl from Lancashire will change the atmosphere in Mill Brae."

EXILE

It was afternoon when the Heysham ferry docked in Belfast. As soon as the gangplank slipped into position hundreds of people congregated on deck around the narrow walkway, jostling to be first ashore.

Emma Johnston leaned against the ship's rail until the scramble eased. She let her eyes wander along the line of vans and cars and horse drawn vehicles on the quayside. Close to the ship was a convoy of mail vans, doors open to receive bags of post and parcels assembled on the lower deck, ready to be tossed ashore. Her father told her to look out for the Montgomerys' black Austin Princess, and sure enough there it was near the head of the queue with the driver standing beside it. When the gangplank cleared, a porter loaded her luggage onto a hand truck and he followed her down the shaky walkway onto the dockside.

"De ye want a car or a sidecar, Miss?" he asked, anxious to get his tip and be rid of her so that he could get back on board for another job.

"No thank you," she said. "My transport has already been arranged."

"Right, I'll go then."

He dropped her trunk on the quayside and lingered only long enough to get his sixpence before boarding the ferry again to find another customer.

She waved to the driver and he moved the car forward and opened the rear door.

"Miss Emma?"

"Yes," she said. "I'm Emma Johnston."

"I'm Patrick Kennedy from Mill Brae House, sent to collect you," he said.

"Would you like to sit front or back?" he asked. "If you're tired there's more room to stretch your legs on the back seat."

"I am a bit tired," she replied, and he opened the rear door for

22

her. Inside, soft seats with leather arm rests and fur pillows made a welcome change from the hard metal chair bolted to the steel floor of the second-class lounge on the ferry. She snuggled between the cushions and made herself comfortable.

When he had loaded the heavy trunk into the boot, they moved off along the busy dockside, past the Albert clock and into the heart of the city.

"It's not unlike Liverpool," she said.

Once they got away from the centre towards the west, Belfast looked much the same as any Lancashire industrial town. The landscape was dotted with smoking factory chimneys surrounded by streets of red-brick terraced houses. They passed a cemetery and almost immediately the car was in open countryside with fields stretching to the horizon.

She moved the cushions around so that she could snuggle between them and buried her hands in the cuffs of her coat.

"If you are cold there is a heater in the car and I will turn it on," said the driver.

"Not really," she replied. "It's a habit of mine—tucking my hands into my sleeves. It's a very comfortable way to travel."

Emma was suffering more from exhaustion than coldness. She had just four miserable weeks at home waiting to see what punishment her parents had in store for her. Even though she resented what they were doing to her, at least she now knew her fate –an uncertain future among strangers in a country she knew nothing about in order to avoid a family scandal.

On her way to the ferry port from their home in Lancashire that morning, her father had maintained a stony silence, not even uttering a word to his sobbing wife beside him in the car. In the back seat, Emma, resigned to her fate but still defiant, stared blandly through the window at blurred images of people and houses and other vehicles, ignoring her parents, showing contempt for what they were doing to her.

She was sad when she recalled leaving the house without a word to her sisters. They stood stoically in the doorway and waved politely, afraid to show any sign of regret at her departure in case they incurred the displeasure of their father. The two younger girls had tears in their eyes but her elder sister Elizabeth clearly had no sympathy for Emma.

"She brought it all on herself," she said to her younger siblings as she closed the front door. "She deserves to be sent away to teach her a lesson."

There was an awkward moment of silence when they arrived at Heysham. Emma gave her mother a hug as her father unloaded her trunk from the boot onto a porter's trolley. Without another word to him, she followed her belongings up the gang plank to the deck of the Duke of Argyll.

They stood on the quayside until the boat pulled away from the dock. "Not so much to see me off as to make sure I don't go ashore again," she thought.

She gave one final glance back as the ferry moved away from the dock to see they were still there. She went inside the lounge to find a seat and made herself as comfortable as possible as the boat moved slowly down river through the narrow channel to the choppy Irish Sea beyond. She was off to a foreign land, but not on the great adventure she used to dream about at school. She felt more like a criminal being deported to a far-flung penal colony for some hideous crime.

Alone and free at last from the prying eyes of her sisters and oppressive coldness of her parents, she closed her eyes and leaned back on the lounge seat. She would never forget this day, 2 September 1939, the day she was sent into exile to live with strangers in a country she knew nothing about.

'Punishment for falling in love,' she thought bitterly

She closed her eyes and let her body rock with the motion of the ferry, her mind drifting back to a chance meeting with a soldier in Blackpool a month before, a meeting that brought romance into her life for the first time and changed her whole existence.

In the space of a couple of hectic days she threw caution to the wind and surrendered herself body and soul to a handsome soldier, Peter Morrison. She spent a week with him at a hotel in Liverpool, seven passionate days and nights of touching, kissing, embracing, in a frantic cycle of lovemaking that she wanted to go on forever.

Why did Peter not stand his ground like a man and protect her when they were discovered? Where had he gone? For weeks afterwards, she kept a lonely vigil at her bedroom window in the evenings, hoping he would suddenly appear out of the darkness and take her away from all the unpleasantness at home.

When she first learned that she was going to Ireland, she stared defiantly at her father, threatening to run away again. But he was in no mood for threats and kept her locked in her room until eventually the fight went out of her. They were determined to send her away, and she had to accept it.

"Anywhere is better than living in a house where I am treated like a leper," she shouted at her mother.

After three weeks in her room, the door was unlocked, and she was ordered downstairs to be confronted by her parents about her "outrageous behaviour". That's when she first heard she would have to leave home to avoid further embarrassment to the family, that she would travel shortly to Ireland where she would stay with an old friend of her father's. She sat in the parlour with head bowed staring at the floor while her father coldly described to her the consequences of her conduct. She made no response, not giving any indication that she had any interest in what he said, nor that she regretted anything.

"She hasn't heard a word you said! How dare you ignore your father!" Mrs Johnston said as she took her daughter by the shoulders and shook her until she got her full attention. Emma jerked her head upwards, dazed. She roughly pushed her mother away, got up and walked unsteadily toward the door.

She turned around and pointed an accusing finger at her father. "You are trying to destroy everything—my happiness, my future— but I know Peter will come back for me! He loves me, and when you see how happy we are, you will be sorry!"

He raised his fist to hit her, but her mother stepped between them and grabbed the sobbing Emma and held her close, feeling the anger subside as tears tumbled down her daughter's cheeks.

"Read that and tell me more about your wonderful Peter!" the

Colonel shouted, throwing a folder at the two women as he charged past them out of the room. The contents spilled over the edge of the table onto the floor.

Mother and daughter stared at the sheaf of documents on the carpet. One item caught Emma's eye and she knelt down and picked it up. She gasped when she realised that it was an unfinished portrait she had done of Peter. Her father must have found it in her bedroom after she left Blackpool. This is what led to their discovery.

She turned over the folder and picked up another document marked "Private and Confidential". It had a picture of Peter, but the report attached to it was about somebody else, about a "Corporal Matthew Jenkins of Slough, Buckinghamshire, married with a two-year-old daughter and a four-year-old son."

"Lies, all lies," she said as she read it. "That has nothing to do with Peter".

"Where do you think you are going?" her mother said. "I've not finished with you yet."

"I'm going to pack my bags," she replied coldly, venom in her young voice. "Isn't that what you want? To be rid of me?"

After Emma left the room her mother gathered up the documents from the floor. She read the last paragraph of red type in the investigator's report:

"He left Slough owing substantial sums of money to financial institutions and joined the Army. Until I visited her, his wife had not seen or heard from him for more than a year. She did not even know he was in the Army."

Mrs Johnston put her head in her hands and cried.

* * *

On the road from Belfast to Sperrin Mill, the car braked suddenly, and Emma pitched forward against the back of the driver's seat.

Patrick Kennedy switched off the engine.

"Sorry, Miss Emma," he said. "Are you okay?"

"I'm fine," she said settling back among the cushions. "I got a bit of a fright."

"Sorry," he said again. "Some cattle ran onto the road from a field and I had to brake hard to avoid crashing into them. Are you sure you are okay?"

"I have so many cushions around me that I could not come to any harm," she reassured him.

When he moved off again Emma stared at the patchwork quilt of green landscape moving slowly past the car window. Fields were fields, no matter where you were, suitable only for animals and crops. She had no interest in farms or farming and even less in this alien land to which she had been banished. She rested her head on the back of the seat and closed her eyes again. She was feeling very sorry for herself and apprehensive about what lay ahead.

Patrick Kennedy looked at his young passenger in the rear-view mirror. She had her head back, eyes closed, hands pushed into the sleeves of the coat she was wearing. He wondered if she was cold. Surely, she would tell him. When she stepped off the ferry he thought she looked pale and sickly looking, but that could be the sea journey, maybe a bit of sea sickness. If her health was not good, he wondered, why she was coming to live in Mill Brae House as companion to a woman suffering from severe depression?

She seemed a pleasant girl, good-looking, not very tall but cutting a neat figure in her tailored grey suit. The beret she was wearing tilted to one side only covered part of a full head of dark curly hair. She looked the arty type, self-assured, maybe still a student. Sir Kenneth had told him to look out for a 20-year-old travelling alone. She looked younger.

Emma was not in the mood for conversation but was curious about the place she was going to. "Is Sperrin in a town or out in the countryside?" she asked

"It's a village in the countryside but very different from other Irish villages," Patrick answered. "It has a mill, a couple of hundred houses designed and built specially for mill workers and their families. And two churches, of course, one for Protestants and another for Catholics. Sperrin was built by the Montgomerys and is more picturesque than most villages. The houses are arranged in circular streets in the centre of which is a large green with the main Belfast to Derry road—the one we are on now—cutting through the middle of it. And there is a lovely river flowing nearby which adds to the beauty of the place.

"Mill Brae House where the Montgomerys live is on the edge of the village, on land overlooking the river. The big house was built by Sir Kenneth Montgomery's grandfather. It's a lovely spot—I'm sure you will like it there."

Emma began to feel better. Her parents made a point of taking them to visit great houses in Lancashire on many occasions to show them the way real gentry lived. She loved those outings, marvelling at the pristine condition of the buildings after hundreds of years. She especially loved the expansive gardens and their exotic designs, manicured wonderlands of flowers and trees and shrubs. Some had mazes and others replicated the splendid gardens of Eastern dynasties. The Colonel bought her some books on gardening to nurture her interest; one of the last things she did before leaving home was to put them in her trunk.

"I like gardens and gardening," she said. "I'm particularly fond of flowers."

"Then you will enjoy Mill Brae," he said. "It has a tremendous variety of flowers and shrubs and it's a blaze of colour at the moment."

He wondered if he should prepare her for the fact that she should not expect too much by way of a welcome from Lady Eleanor but decided against it. He had learned a long time ago that when you worked for gentry you had to be very discreet if you wanted to keep your job. In any case, she would find out soon enough about the situation at Mill Brae.

Emma was puzzled by large concrete pillars which blocked the main road on either side of towns and villages they drove through. Some were already completed, and others still being built. The pillars were eight or ten feet high and placed so close together that carts and cars and buses had to slow down and pass through one at a time.

"They're to stop tanks using the roads in the event of invasion," he said. "If war comes and the Germans invade England the British Government believes they will come to Ireland too, so precautions are being taken to slow down their advance."

He didn't seem unduly worried about German invasion. "There's nothing here for them," he said, "no coal or oil or gas. Our only problem is regiments of British soldiers billeted here; the Germans might not be happy about that."

"So," thought Emma, "I haven't left the soldiers behind after all. What would my father say if he knew that in Ireland I am still surrounded by men in uniform?"

Apart from the ugly roadside pillars and shabby farm dwellings she liked what she saw of the Irish countryside with its rolling hills, trim fields and dense hedgerows. Although it was nearly autumn the greenery was still at its summer best with trees and shrubs clothed in healthy foliage. Flowers had gone from the hawthorn hedges that divided fields and had been replaced by bright red haws. Ribbons of bushes, branches laden with the red berries, stretched out over the landscape like battalions of redcoats in battle formation. Fields of ripening oats and wheat and pink blossom potatoes stretched as far as the eye could see; on darker green pastures, cattle, horses and sheep gorged themselves on a late flush of sweet grass.

Towns and villages they passed had a dowdy, run-down appearance. People were poorly dressed, streets deserted; offices and shops were unpainted, neglected looking. Many of the children did not have shoes, small feet leaving footprints on tarry roads softened by the hot sun. There were a lot of horses and carts but very few motor vehicles. From time to time they passed rickety buses with hardly anybody aboard. The roads had rough bumpy surfaces and endless bends that kept her swaying from side to side in the spacious back seat.

"How much further to Sperrin?" she asked, breaking the silence.

"Only about ten miles," he said. "We have one more town to pass through; we should be there in less than half an hour."

A WAIF OF WAR

On the other side of Europe, 1,500 miles away from Ireland as the crow flies and a world away from the scandal that beset the Johnston family, colliery owner Stanislaw Walenski had worries of a different kind; and he was having just as much trouble trying to deal with them as Colonel Johnston.

Seen through the rain-spattered window of his office, Poland in the late summer of 1939 did not present the kind of place that might fire the imagination of a landscape painter or a picture postcard photographer. It was early autumn, and the fields still had much of their summer greenery, but the sky was dull, dreary, foreboding. Soon the days would get shorter and temperatures would tumble with the approach of winter. All he had to look forward to were months of snow and ice, disruption on railroads, coal vessels icebound in Baltic ports and absentee miners laid up by colds and flu, and now the threat of invasion from Germany.

"This damn place is making me old before my time," he muttered. "Why the hell do I put up with it?" He turned away from the window and returned to his desk. He intended to tidy up some paperwork before he went home but he was in no mood for the task and pushed it aside. He had more important things on his mind. Only twenty years after the end of "the war to end all wars", the lesson about the futility of mass conflict had been forgotten and Europe was in turmoil again. What would he do if another war started?

He had a son, Krzysztof, whom he needed to get out of the country to a safe place, but his plan was meeting with a lot of resistance from his wife. He was an only child and she could not bear to be parted from him. Should he sell the mine and leave the country and bring his son with him? More resistance from his wife, Justyna.

"I am not going to be driven out of my home by that Austrian barber," she railed, annoyed that her husband would even contemplate leaving Poland to live among strangers because of the antics of

Adolph Hitler.

The Walenski mine was a busy, profitable enterprise which kept the family in comfort and allowed them to amass considerable wealth over a period of nearly a century. But with the mine also came responsibility for a workforce of 200 miners. They and their wives and children depended on the black hole in the earth for their existence. If war came, could he flee with his family and leave them at the mercy of the Germans?

His most immediate concern was the safety of Krzysztof who would be conscripted into the army if war came. If that happened, it would break the heart of his gentle, good-natured mother.

He had another problem that was not going to be easy to deal with either. He had a mistress, Barbara Kubinska, and they had a love child together. He visited them once a week at Barbara's restaurant in the nearby town of Lubiala. The mistress knew all about his wife and Krzysztof, but Justyna was totally unaware of the existence of Barbara and her daughter Maria and the double life her husband had been leading for twenty years. If the Germans came to Poland, life for the Kubinskas would be more difficult than for Justyna and Krzysztof. Barbara was Jewish; she would be in serious danger.

Justyna did not want to be parted from her son, but Stanislaw insisted it was better to have him abroad and safe rather than being forced into uniform to fight a war that Poland could not win. Once the decision to let the boy go was made, his belongings were hastily packed, and his parents took him to Warsaw and put him on a train for Paris. From France he was told to make his way by train and boat across the Channel to London and finally by ferry to Ireland where his father had a business acquaintance who would find him a job. Ireland was in a remote part of Europe and it was highly unlikely that it would be involved in hostilities. He had a letter from his father for Sir Kenneth Montgomery at a place called Sperrin Mill, about ninety miles from the port of Belfast.

Krzysztof Walenski stepped off the bus in the Village Square in Sperrin, County Tyrone, on a cold afternoon in the early autumn of 1939 and in his best English asked directions to the mill. He was told it was "a good way off" and was pointed in the direction of a smokestack in the distance. His back ached and his backside was sore after sitting for nearly three hours on a hard, wooden bench on the bus on the long journey from Belfast. The seats were made from slats of wood, and no matter how many times he changed position, he could not get comfortable; the sharp edges of the wood bit into his buttocks as the bus rattled over bumpy country roads. He had bruises on the back of his legs and his elbows were swollen from knocking off the hard wood.

He felt the stiffness begin to ease as he walked downhill carrying two suitcases. After the engine fumes from the bus the fresh air made him feel better.

Even before he reached the mill he could hear the racket of machinery. He crossed a railway where men were unloading coal from wagons onto horse-drawn carts that stretched in a long line awaiting their turn. He wondered whether this was Walenski coal, all the way from Poland.

Over a door in the main building was a sign with polished brass letters:

Sperrin Linen Mills
Established 1830

Krzysztof went inside and when he saw a door with Office on it, pushed it open with his knee, brought the suitcases in sideways and found himself in a small waiting room with three hatches on one side and a bench seat on the other. He put his luggage on the floor and tapped the glass of one of the hatches.

The window opened, and a girl looked at him cheekily. "We have a bell, ye know, and ye're supposed to ring if ye want somebody, instead of trying to break the glass with yer fist. What do ye want anyways?"

Krzysztof smiled. He had no idea what she was talking about.

"My name is Krzysztof Walenski from Poland and I come to Ireland to find job. I come to see Sir Kenneth Montgomery. He is friend of my father." He spoke slowly, careful to get the words in the right order. He had his father's letter in his hand and she saw it, but he made no effort to give it to her when she put her hand out.

"Ye've come a terrible long way," said the girl, friendlier now that he seemed to have some family connection with the boss, "but I can tell ye there's not a pile of jobs going around here at the minute. Sit down and I'll send somebody upstairs and let him know ye're here."

She closed the hatch. He could hear her whispering to somebody behind the glass and giggling.

A couple of minutes later another girl came into the waiting room, shook hands with him and introduced herself.

"I'm Kate Reilly, Sir Kenneth Montgomery's secretary. Please follow me upstairs."

He picked up his cases, but she motioned to put them down again and rang the bell and asked the girl inside the hatch to look after them for a while.

"Good luck with the job," smiled the girl as she dragged the luggage into her office.

Krzysztof was pleasantly surprised by the secretary from the upstairs office. She was neatly dressed in black skirt and white blouse. Her delicate pale face was framed in a head of tight black curls and a warm welcoming smile. As he climbed the narrow steps behind her he liked the way her bum swayed from side to side. Her skirt was so tight that it crept upwards on her rounded buttocks. He was looking so intently that when she paused to pull it down he bumped into her.

When she turned around he mumbled "Sorry!" and she could see he was blushing.

"Mind your step," she smiled. "These stairs are steep."

Inside an office she took his coat and pointed to a chair.

"It will be a while before Sir Kenneth can see you," she said. "I'll get some coffee." She offered him a cigarette, but he shook his head. He was anxious to get on with his interview.

"I have a letter for Sir Kenneth Montgomery," he said. "It tells why I am here."

She took the envelope from him, went back to work, and waited. A couple of times she inquired if he would like another coffee.

It was a large office for one person. The girl sat at a polished wooden desk with her back to the wall of an adjoining room. There was a separate desk at right angles to the other with a typewriter in the middle. To the left was an alcove with canisters marked Tea, Sugar, Coffee, and a milk jug on a shelf. There was a gas ring with a kettle on it and a teapot and cups and saucers neatly stacked on a tray beside it.

The wait gave him a chance to have a better look at her, but he had to be careful; now and again she lifted her head from her work to smile in his direction and he was afraid she might catch him staring.

Her dark curls were tucked back on either side of her head and held in position neatly by two gold combs. Blue eyes contrasted with pale unblemished skin and she had a slightly turned up nose that gave her a cheeky look. He watched the eyes move from side to side as she scanned shorthand notes and typed at the same time.

When she approached and bent over to offer him more coffee he could not take his eyes off the protrusions on her breasts where her nipples pushed against the white blouse.

Back at her desk she turned to pick up a pencil sharpener and caught him looking at her. She smiled, flattered by his attention.

Kate often had to meet people looking for work but very few of them were afforded the privilege of speaking to the boss himself. This fellow was about 20, well dressed, clean cut, fresh faced and good-looking too. He had no appointment and normally she would have turned him away telling him to write and she would arrange for him to meet somebody at a later date. But he was a foreigner and had a letter marked "Personal and Confidential" addressed to Sir Kenneth Montgomery. She would take the letter to Sir Kenneth when he was free and let him decide whether to meet the young man himself or pass him on to one of the under managers.

"Sir Kenneth won't be much longer now," she told him when she refilled his mug with coffee. "I have given him your letter to read."

The mill owner read the letter twice and looked at Kate and shook his head before telling her to bring him into the office. He was surprised by the arrival of his young visitor from the other side of Europe and annoyed that he had been given no advance warning of his arrival.

"I had to leave Poland in a hurry because of the threat of war," Krzysztof explained before Sir Kenneth had time to say anything.

"I understand your father's concern," said Sir Kenneth. "The problem is that all this talk of war is affecting us too—we are finding it difficult to get supplies of flax. If war starts I may have to cut back on the workforce.

"I understand you hope to study engineering. I'll see if I can fit you in somewhere. In the meantime, we'll find you a place to stay in the village. You will have to be patient, for it might be a while before you hear from me."

When Krzysztof emerged from the boss's office he was disappointed and apprehensive. After coming all this way, he did not get a very warm reception. What would he do if he did not get work?

Kate sensed his disappointment. "Take a seat for a few minutes," she said, and disappeared into the boss's office with some letters for signing.

"I'm sorry for that young man," said Sir Kenneth. "He is very much on his own in a strange country, but I don't know if I can do anything for him."

"He seems a nice fellow," said Kate.

"I've asked him to stay around for a bit to see if we can fit him in somewhere. Would you be good enough to leave early this evening and find lodgings somewhere close to the mill? That's all I can do for the moment."

Outside she made more coffee and sat with Krzysztof while he drank it. She told him not to be too disappointed—she was sure the boss would find something for him. She would go with him to the village later to find a place to stay. She suggested he should go and have a look around the mill and come back to her at 4 o'clock.

Krzysztof would have preferred to sit with Kate rather than tour the mill, but she was busy, so he left. He liked her, and he got the impression that she liked him too.

Later the two of them walked from the mill to the village.

My father is worried about another war," he said. "That's why he sent me to Ireland."

"There's a lot of talk here about war too," she said, "but people in

Ireland think the British are just scaremongering. Herr Hitler just wants back the land stolen from his country after the last war and most people in this country feel he is entitled to it."

"No," he said, shaking his head emphatically. "Hitler wants much more—he wants to be master of Europe. My father is sure he will invade Poland before the year is out."

"Well," she sighed, "let's hope you're wrong. Even though it's not our war, there are still an awful lot of Irishmen in British army uniforms who may never return home alive if the fighting starts."

She found the lodging house and introduced him to the landlady, and when she mentioned he was a personal friend of the mill owner and might be a permanent lodger he was given the most comfortable room in the house. She left the fussy landlady to let him get settled in.

"In a few days I'll show you around the village if you want me to," she said as she was leaving. "Keep your fingers crossed about the job."

He didn't understand what crossing his fingers had to do with getting a job but smiled at her anyhow.

After she left, Krzysztof felt good. He wanted to work at the mill more than ever, if only to be close to this pleasant girl.

"Kate," he said to the landlady after she left, "a pretty name for a pretty girl."

Two weeks later Sir Kenneth called her into his office and told her he had a job for the young Polish lad. With the prospect of war coming, some of the men with army experience had decided to join up again.

"We have a vacancy in the Power House," he told her, "and if he is interested in engineering, he could be the right person for the job. Tell him to report to the manager on Sunday for the night shift."

That same evening, Kate went to tell him the news. After all the worry about his parents and days moping around wondering whether he would get a job or not, he was delighted when she told him.

Before she left, he said: "I don't forget your promise to show me the countryside."

"I can't break a promise, then," she smiled. "Can I?"

BRITAIN AT WAR

When the Austin Princess reached Murrinbridge, the last town before Sperrin, traffic slowed to a snail's pace and eventually came to a halt. It was market day and the narrow streets were crammed with people and livestock. Patrick Kennedy blew his horn a couple of times to see if he could get some movement, but the only response was from cart drivers who hurled abuse at him for being so impatient.

"We're all in the same boat, ye eejit" one shouted. "There's a blockage ahead."

Patrick apologised to Emma for the delay and left the car to see what the trouble was. When he came back he shook his head. "We are going to be stuck here for a while," he said. "There's trouble up ahead. The road is full of people listening to a radio blaring out news from the BBC in London. Apparently, the Germans have invaded Poland, and the British Government says that if they don't withdraw immediately Britain is going to war with them."

"Are you sure?" she asked, finding the news hard to believe. "There was no mention of war this morning when I left home."

"Yes," he replied. "It's all on the news. Everybody is getting a gas mask. The windows of houses have to be blacked out during the hours of darkness in case of air raids and food is going to be rationed." Patrick was out of breath by the time he finished.

"You'll hear all about it when you get to Mill Brae House," he said. "I only got a garbled version from people in the crowd."

She remembered that Peter had told her that war with Germany might be coming. If what the driver said was true, he would be in the middle of it. Even if he wanted to get in touch with her now he would never be able to find her in this God-forsaken place.

Traffic moved forward in fits and starts until the car came within earshot of the radio. It had been placed on the sill of an upstairs bedroom window, and hundreds of people were crowded around below looking up at it, listening to the sombre voices of the announcers.

She rolled down the window. On the fringes of the throng children were running around chanting: "The Germans are coming! The Germans are coming!" Some people were cheering, and fights broke out between them and others who wanted quiet so that they could hear the radio.

"The radio belongs to a blind man called McKelvie," said Patrick. "He has it turned up full blast."

There was no way through, so they had to sit and wait. Patrick decided there was no point in remonstrating with the excited crowd as some of them were in a belligerent mood, spoiling for a fight. He advised Emma it was best to keep her window closed.

Nearly half an hour passed, and the children changed their chant. "The police are coming! The police are coming! Run for it! Run for it!" But nobody moved. Two constables dismounted from bicycles and began to push people off the roadway so that the traffic could get moving again. When some resisted, they drew batons.

More shouts and jeers from the crowd. "The Germans will sort your lot out!" and "Hitler will make mincemeat of your lot, ye British lackeys!"

The policemen didn't want any trouble. They took the abuse hurled at them but doggedly continued to force people off the road onto the footpaths; eventually they made enough space to get the traffic moving again.

The crowd, annoyed at being pushed around, taunted the men in uniform. But the police retained their sense of humour. "You better pray that Hitler doesn't get this far," one of them said jokingly, "for if he does, you lot will feel the toe of his jackboot on your lazy arses. Herr Hitler has no time for layabouts!"

As they moved slowly forward the driver pointed out a red-headed man standing in the doorway of a shop. "That's the blind man, Valentino McKelvie, the one I was telling you about," Patrick said. He's knows all about radios. He once took one apart and put it all together again. He may be blind, but he's gifted in other ways."

Emma had a good look at him. He was quite handsome. "He is a fine-looking young man," she said. "You would never suspect he was blind."

"Blind since his early teens," said Patrick.

"See the fellow standing beside him—his name is Krzysztof Walenski. His father has a coal mine in Poland. He arrived at Sperrin Mill recently with only the clothes on his back, looking for a job. He had a letter from his father and he got a job in the mill. He must be a worried man today. His parents are still in Poland."

Emma perked up when she heard this. Another war waif in Ireland on the strength of a letter! She spotted him right away, a good-looking young fellow dressed in a dark suit and shirt and tie standing near the window, looking bewildered by the commotion going on around him and the arrival of the police.

"From Poland?"

"He's been here for six weeks," said the driver.

Emma was glad when they put the town behind them and eventually arrived in Sperrin. The village was much as the driver had described it, very different from the towns and villages they had passed through on the way from Belfast. As they drove along the main road she caught glimpses of the village green and the circle of houses that surrounded it through breaks in the trees. There were a lot of noisy children about climbing trees, swinging on branches, chasing one another, playing football, girls playing hop-scotch on the footpath.

The houses were single-storey cottages arranged in perfect semi circles on either side of the roadway that bisected the village green. The neat homes had freshly painted white walls but the doors and window frames had alternating colours of brown, red, blue and green and patterns of leaded coloured glass.

It was a quaint place, not unlike the greens in English villages and hamlets, but on a larger scale. She asked Patrick Kennedy to slow down so that she could get a better look.

"It's a lovely village. It must be a pleasant place to live."

When they reached the furthest extremity of the green the car turned across the road and stopped in front of a stout iron gate with the sign "Mill Brae House".

"Here we are," said Patrick. He blew the horn and a barefoot boy emerged from a gate lodge. He saluted and opened the gate.

As soon as they passed through, the main house and grounds came into view. The sun was low in the sky, but long shadows cast by high trees could not mask the beauty of the place. "An oasis," Patrick had called it, and how right he was. It was another world. She moved to one side of the car and wound down the window to get a better view. He slowed down to let her have a longer look.

"It's beautiful, really beautiful," she said. "And the scent from the flowers! It's overpowering!"

"Her Ladyship will be delighted to hear you say so," said Patrick. "She puts a lot of time and effort into her gardens."

From the gate lodge the grounds fanned out into an expanse of verdant lawn, with a driveway of white marble chippings sweeping around on either side until it met in front of the house. A line of tall trees flanked the lawn and driveways. Where the carpet of green ended in front of the main entrance to the house, banks of flowers in sloping beds obscured the driveway.

The house itself was set against a backdrop of high oak trees. Emma recognised the Tudor style but unlike many of the big houses in England there was a lovely uniformity and symmetry about it. Everything was in perfect proportion, perfect harmony. There were no annexes or add-ons to upset the original design. It was not as big as many of the grand houses she had seen in Lancashire and Yorkshire, but big enough in its particular setting. The lovely period building blended with multicoloured flower-beds to give the appearance of a large tapestry hanging against a backdrop of blue sky. The difference here was that this tapestry had been brought to life.

"It's lovely, really lovely," she said aloud, unable to contain her admiration.

When the car crunched to a halt in front of the house two maids appeared and waited until she alighted. Emma stretched her arms and legs a couple of times when she stepped out of the car, then followed one of the maids up the steps.

Lady Eleanor Montgomery was there to greet her.

"Miss Johnston, you are most welcome to Mill Brae," she said.

Before Emma had time to reply Lady Eleanor put her arms around her and hugged her warmly.

"You have a beautiful home, Lady Eleanor," said Emma. "Your gardens are breathtaking."

Eleanor brought Emma through the house to a small sitting-room at the side of the great hall.

"I'm so glad you like the gardens. I put my heart and soul into them and at this time of year I get the reward for my effort. You will have plenty of time to explore in the days to come. Now let's have some tea and you can tell me about the journey from England on that horrible ferry."

"I must confess I cannot tell you much about the ferry crossing," laughed Emma, "for I slept most of the way. All I remember is that it was crowded and the seat I was sitting on was not very comfortable."

Patrick, following with Emma's baggage, was surprised at the welcome. Her Ladyship seemed unusually benign, more relaxed than he had seen her for a long time. He hoped for the girl's sake it would last. He was glad he had kept his mouth shut earlier.

The two women sat by a window where the evening sun shone through, warming them while they talked.

"We might as well enjoy the sunshine while we have it," said her host. "God knows, you will see little enough of it here."

"Well, what are your first impressions of Ireland?" she asked as the maid poured the tea. "I'm sure you think us quite backward after Lancashire."

"The countryside is pleasant, more heavily wooded than I expected. But your home and gardens are splendid and more beautiful than anything I have seen," she said.

"I'm sure you are just being polite," said Lady Eleanor. "We do our best to keep Mill Brae as it was meant to be, and from spring to autumn it's a pleasant enough place but Irish winters are cold and gloomy, and we are forced to spend a lot of time indoors."

"In Lancashire we are well used to dreary weather and long dark nights," said Emma. "And we don't have the luxury of beautiful gardens to spend our leisure time in."

"Let's not talk about winter on a lovely evening like this," said her host. "Tell me about home and your family and what your father thinks about this Neville Chamberlain plunging us into another

41

war. At a time like this your parents should be happy they don't have a son to go into the Army when you think of all the worry it brings."

While Lady Eleanor rambled on about the devastation caused to families by war, Emma wondered how much her host knew about her family. Was it possible she was aware of what led to her enforced exile to Ireland? She hoped not.

"I'm told you have three sisters, all older than you," said Lady Eleanor.

"Yes," said Emma. "We are a family of four girls—Elizabeth, Harriet, Jane and I—and I'm afraid between home and school we lead a very humdrum life. Father is busy in the flax business and mother looks after the family. We don't have any servants."

"And what will your sisters do if war comes?"

"I expect they will spend some time with relatives in Scotland," she replied

"Sadly," Lady Eleanor confided, "we don't have any children, which is a pity when we have such a large house. At times like this, however, I'm glad I don't have brothers or sons to go to war. The worry would break my heart.

"You know," she went on, "my husband's father was the only survivor of three sons who served abroad with Irish regiments. His two brothers were killed in action—both in India. Kenneth is the last of his family. He was in the Army, too, of course, but luckily not in time of war; otherwise there might have been nobody to carry on the business, and that would have been a real tragedy. So many families depend on the mill for their livelihood."

Emma admired the décor of the room, with its delicate French furnishings and paintings. The walls were decorated with light and dark-blue floral embossed papers rising to an eggshell coving with small gold leaves. It gave the room a fragile appearance, certainly not the sort of place where you could let children run free. Over the marble mantelpiece was a collection of ivory statuettes, and on either side of the fire brace larger ivories of rampant lions and tigers. Lady Eleanor obviously had the ability to create beauty within the house as well as without.

"This is my favourite room," she said. "It took a long time to get it right. When sunshine floods in like this, I often come here and sit alone. I find it very soothing, very peaceful."

She stood up abruptly: "I think we have talked enough for now," she said. "Rest a while and get settled into your room, Emma, and we will meet again at 8 o'clock for dinner."

As they walked towards the stairway Lady Eleanor put her hand reassuringly on Emma's shoulder. "It's going to be nice having you around the house, really nice to have somebody to talk to. I have not been well this past year and part of my problem is loneliness. There are lots of people around, but with village people it's more gossip than discussion, if you know what I mean. I hope you and I will find that we have much in common to talk about."

As she escorted Emma upstairs she pointed to architectural features of the house and particularly to the wall space in the hallway and on the upstairs landing which she used to hang pictures.

"I could never see the sense of placing pictures at different levels on a rising stairway," she ventured, "for while you are preoccupied looking at them, you are liable to miss your step and take a fall. Don't you agree?"

Emma paused on the landing to look at some of them, country scenes in varying shades of green, others a myriad of autumn shades that showed off the richness and beauty of landscapes.

A portrait of a younger Lady Montgomery showed a girl of striking beauty with rose-tinted cheekbones, piercing blue eyes and long hair combed to one side and draped over her right shoulder. She wore a dark blue strapless dress revealing graceful arms and shoulders and she had the fingers of her left hand demurely placed around a large sapphire pendant nestling in the cleavage between her breasts. When Emma stopped to look at it Lady Eleanor seemed embarrassed.

"Ah! Once upon a time...." She sighed as she took Emma's arm and continued up the stairway. "Enjoy your youthful looks while you can," she said forlornly. "They don't last forever."

In the bedroom, maids had already unpacked her belongings. It was only when she saw them laid out at the foot of her bed that she realised how little she had with her. Some of the dresses and suits she had packed herself, including the off-the-shoulder cotton one she wore the day she first met Peter on the beach. She had also packed the underclothing she wore while at the hotel in Liverpool, but it was missing—obviously her mother had been through the trunk and removed anything that would remind her errant daughter of that episode. She had hidden some romance novels among her clothing and these had gone undetected. When she unfolded her nightgown, Forgotten Love and Dreaming of You tumbled out.

As Emma surveyed the jumble of items it occurred to her that this was everything she owned in the world. Her parents clearly did not expect her to return home for a quite some time. Even her schoolbooks and painting materials had been sent into exile with her.

Patrick Kennedy heard a sigh in the back of the car as they drove home from the mill that evening. He glanced briefly at the rear mirror. Sir Kenneth had his head back, eyes closed.

"Don't go straight home," he said when they reached the main road. "Take me for a drive—it's been a troublesome sort of a day." He shifted his position so that his neck rested on the back of the seat, closed his eyes and relaxed until weightlessness engulfed his body.

Free of all the chores he had at the mill, this was the only time he had to think about his problems, especially his marriage, which had lost all its sparkle since his wife Eleanor started to suffer from depression. In her present confused state, she was threshing about finding fault with everything, blaming him for her illness. She even accused him of infidelity, of flirting with young girls at the mill. He sometimes got so angry he felt he ought to proposition one of the girls out of spite.

Sir Kenneth was aware of gossip in the mill about a romantic liaison between his secretary, Kate Reilly, and himself, loose talk that had filtered back to his wife and added to his personal problems at home. But there was always talk going on behind backs about somebody—it was harmless for the most part and maybe it helped relieve the boredom of humdrum life in the village.

"More overtime, Kate," said the office manager with a smirk when she was asked by the boss to stay behind while the others left. She felt her face flush and her cheeks burn when they taunted her; she was annoyed for giving them the satisfaction of seeing her embarrassed by their snide remarks.

She knew what they were spreading stories about her romantic links with the boss, and though they were wrong, completely wrong, she never denied the tittle-tattle. Let them think what they like—she would not satisfy their curiosity; if she told the truth they would not believe her anyway.

Nobody could say they actually saw anything going on between Kate and Sir Kenneth in the office but lack of proof of an affair did not deter gossip. If it were not for the discomfort caused by her embarrassment, she might even have enjoyed it.

If she had a boyfriend on her own it might have been different, but there was no romance in her life. The mill boys were a rough lot and she stayed clear of them. So, she was reduced to relieving pent-up emotions with romantic fantasies in the privacy of her bedroom, using erotic magazine pictures to fire her imagination and nimble fingers to excite her body. That way she did not have to struggle with a boy who wanted to go too far or run the risk of producing an illegitimate baby and bear the stigma of a fallen woman for the rest of her life.

When she worked overtime, he dictated letters; she took shorthand notes and typed them. He made alterations and corrections, she retyped, and he signed them; that was all, no touching or groping or kissing.

Some evenings after the office staff had gone home he had a couple of glasses of whiskey from the bottle he kept in his desk. If he was in a mood for more, he ignored the glass and drank straight from the bottle. When he got tipsy sometimes, the spirit loosened his tongue and he confided in her about his troubles with his wife and her illness. He told her more than once how sad he was that he did not have a family to take over the running of the mill when he passed on. The Montgomery name would die with him and he had to accept that one day the mill which his grandfather had built would end up with strangers—or worse, close down altogether.

Although he had misgivings about taking a young refugee girl into his own home, he told Kate he had grown fond of the Johnston girl.

"Which reminds me," he said, "has the young Polish fellow started in the Power House yet?"

"Yes," she said. "He is delighted with the job."

Walking home in the dark after finishing a letter to the Ministry, she was greeted with a chorus of "Overtime tonight again, Kate?" from boys she met on the road. "It's well for you!"

She had a three-mile walk home to Murrinbridge if she was delayed until after the last bus had gone. Sir Kenneth was often still in his office after she left, the bottle of whiskey in front of him. She was concerned at times that if he got too drunk he might fall coming down the narrow office stairs.

One night when he was very drunk, and she was particularly worried about him, she rang Mill Brae House from a public telephone in Murrinbridge to inquire if he had arrived home safely.

Kate was expecting one of the maids to answer but she it was Lady Montgomery.

"Are you the hussy from the mill? You have a cheek ringing this house," she snapped.

Kate quickly put down the phone. She was shocked at the tone of the voice on the other end of the line. She began to cry. It was bad enough suffering the taunts of her friends at the mill without being called a hussy by her boss's wife. She vowed she would never make another call like that again.

"Arrogant witch!" she said aloud, venting her anger.

A BEAUTY IN BLUE

Sir Kenneth's marriage was a shambles and his personal life miserable. How it had come to this he was not sure. Only a few years before he was a contented man with a loving wife, a beautiful home and friends who visited; birthdays and wedding anniversaries and success in business were all occasions for celebration. Then his wife gradually changed, and so did everything else.

She was ill, no doubt, and it was no ordinary illness. She was still the lovely woman he had married, but medication had taken the sparkle out of her eyes and changed her effervescent disposition. Something strange was going on in her head and her physician had no answers.

It was a blow to her that they had no children. It made her feel a failure as a wife and mother. But lots of couples did not have children and managed to keep the flame of love alive in their marriage. Whatever the reasons for the change their relationship deteriorated to the point where she would not let him touch her; lately she would not even tolerate him being close to her.

Sir Kenneth opened his eyes briefly as the car turned sharply at a corner. He closed them again and let his mind wander back to the early years when they were so happy together.

Etched in his memory was a picture that would never be erased as long as he lived. It was of a beautiful woman in a blue gown he saw at a ball in a friend's home in County Antrim when he went to visit in the summer of 1929. He was having a drink with male friends during a break in the music and they were admiring the curved hips and plump backside of a girl a short distance away. While they were laughing, she turned around and smiled at them.

Suspecting that she might have overheard them talking about her bottom, the friends sloped away to leave him on his own. Kenneth was embarrassed. The girl glanced over her shoulder and smiled at him. This made him even more uncomfortable. Obviously, she had heard them talking about her.

When she turned around so that she faced his way, he stared straight at her. Blue eyes complimented the low-cut evening gown she was wearing and the sparkle in them matched the pendant around her slender, graceful neck, a sapphire nestling between her breasts. She was beautiful.

Kenneth wanted to move away and rejoin his friends, but his feet were rooted to the floor. Those eyes and that mischievous smile had transfixed him. He felt like an animal caught in the headlights of a car, mesmerised by the beam of light hurtling towards it, unable to escape its fate. He was still staring at her lovely neck when she turned her head to one side and glanced over her shoulder at him. This time, it was she who blushed, embarrassed that he caught her looking at him.

He started towards her, intending to ask her to dance, but before he got there she was whisked onto the floor by somebody else.

When he sat down to dinner later in the evening, Kenneth found himself on the other side of the table from the girl in blue, far enough away so that he did not have to look directly across at her but close enough to be included when formal introductions were made.

"I feel I know you already, Mr Montgomery," she smiled when she heard his name.

"I owe you an apology, Miss Parker," he replied when she was introduced.

"I'm not so sure you do," she said mischievously, "but you certainly owe an apology to my bottom." His companions could not conceal their mirth at her humorous retort. He saw the humour but squirmed in embarrassment.

After dinner she crossed the room to where he stood with his friends and to his surprise asked him if he would like to dance. It was what he wanted more than anything else. When they began to move to the music he became so flustered by the warmth of the body pressed against him that he didn't know what to say to her.

As they moved to and fro he was conscious of the fact that a lot of men had their eyes on her and he felt pleased that it was him she chose to dance with. When the music stopped he asked if she would like a drink. When she nodded he fetched a bottle of wine and two glasses and they sat in a quiet corner of the room sipping it and talking until the party came to an end. Before they parted that evening, he was so besotted by her that he made up his mind that this was a girl he could spend the rest of his life with if she would have him, a girl he would be proud to have as the mistress of Mill Brae House.

Kenneth Montgomery and Eleanor Parker belonged to a small but influential Protestant upper class that dominated politics and business in the North of Ireland in the first half of the twentieth century—merchants, mill owners, land owners, Members of Parliament and the likes with a sprinkling of lesser peers who had been given estates in Ireland for services to the Crown. Once the couple showed an interest in each other they got all the encouragement needed from wealthy friends to make sure they stayed together. They were the perfect match, the perfect couple.

They married in her parish church in Cushendall, County Antrim, in 1930 and after a month-long honeymoon in Italy he took his bride to County Tyrone, to the house that was home to three generations of the Montgomery family. In Rome he had her portrait painted in the same dress she was wearing the night he first met her, and that was the picture that had adorned the staircase at Mill Brae ever since. He never tired of looking at it.

In those idyllic first years of married life the couple enjoyed to the full their deep love for one another and the frequent company of a wide circle of friends. Dinners and music recitals, poetry readings and balls filled their lives. While he was busy at the mill she spent time in London and Dublin seeking objets d'art to make their home beautiful. On trips abroad, she bought clothes from fashion houses in Paris and Milan. In Dublin she hired experts from the Botanical Gardens to create a beautiful garden for her.

Eleanor Montgomery became just as besotted with her husband as he was with her. She could not bear to be parted from him and when he had to leave on business for a few days she showered him with affection on his return. She had no inhibitions about showing the depth of her feelings for him.

"I think I married a nymphomaniac," he exclaimed when she

clung to him as he came through the door on his return from one absence. "You have to be more careful with the servants around."

"So that's what I am," she laughed, "a nymphomaniac! I don't care what you call me—I need love and sex and more love and sex and even more love and more sex! And babies, God, I want babies too—a houseful of babies!"

There was a lot of love and sex in their lives but, despite the close physical relationship, there were no babies. In the second year of their marriage she went to London to see a specialist to find out why she did not become pregnant. When Kenneth asked her afterwards what they said, tears welled in her eyes as she explained how one doctor after another failed to find the trouble. He consoled her by pointing out that often couples did not have children for years and then suddenly out of the blue it happened. She needed to relax, enjoy life and let nature take its course.

But pregnancy never did happen for Eleanor, and as the months of waiting and hoping lengthened into years, she became more and more anxious. She was persuaded by her mother to travel to a clinic in Switzerland specialising in fertility problems. She spent a lonely month there amid the snow-capped Swiss Alps during which eminent gynaecologists monitored her menstrual cycle and performed tests that left her physically and emotionally drained. Their conclusion was that while she had a slight malformation of the pelvis that might cause a problem when she had to deliver a baby, this in no way interfered with her ability to conceive; she had ovulated normally, and they could not find any physical barrier to conception.

She was advised to return home, try and relax, work with her local doctor to accurately establish her fertile time and hopefully the problem would solve itself. If no pregnancy occurred within a year, she should encourage her husband to have his sperm tested.

Eleanor was impressed by the thoroughness of the examination at the clinic but disappointed at the fact that after all the pain and discomfort she had to put up with they had not been able to get to the root of her problem. The suggestion that her husband was in some way infertile did not ring true for her, for he was a strong, passionate man—a lot more virile than most if she was to believe what she heard about the love life of married friends. She was convinced the problem was hers and she would have to be patient; the doctors were agreed that the greatest barrier to conception was stress.

After another two years, however, during which one period followed another with monotonous regularity, Eleanor Montgomery gradually reconciled herself to the fact that she might never have a child. It began to prey on her mind. She felt inadequate as a wife, unfulfilled as a woman. She still hoped for a miracle but as time slipped by she felt that God was not on her side, was not prepared to give her the child she craved.

Approaching her thirty-seventh birthday, Eleanor had given up all hope of ever conceiving a baby. She began to suffer from headaches, panic attacks, weakness and periods of depression which her doctor attributed to early onset of the menopause.

As she retreated into her dark world of despair, she lost interest in making love, spurning her husband's sexual advances. She had single beds moved into their room so that she could sleep apart from him. When he became desperate and demanded his rights as a husband she threatened to call the servants. Eventually he was forced to move into another bedroom.

Kenneth Montgomery would have loved children—not just one or two as was the custom with wealthy families, but enough to fill the empty rooms of the big house. He had the means to support a large family, and what was the point of owning a mill and a big house and money if there were no children to spend it on, nobody to pass it on to when he died? He envied his workers, especially the women, who regularly produced children without difficulty. And though it was hard to feed a family on a mill hand's wages, children seemed to bring their own happiness. Eleanor wanted a son to carry on the tradition of the family in the mill, but he was not particularly concerned about that. He felt that a child—boy or girl—would light up their lives, breathe warmth back into his wife's cold body and save their marriage.

As her condition deteriorated, he too eventually came to accept that there would be no issue of the union of himself and Eleanor Parker. Harder to bear was the loss of her love and companionship.

If Eleanor's gradual descent into depression could not be cured by conventional means, Dr McFarlane advised him that in time it could progress to the point where it might become impossible to cope with her at home. With no prospect of improvement in their relationship, Sir Kenneth gave up hope of ever resuming a normal relationship with his wife and concentrated on running the mill.

Apart from domestic troubles, Sir Kenneth had been landed with another problem which he knew was not going to be easy to solve. It came in a letter from the War Office in London informing him that under the provisions of the various Emergency Acts, Sperrin Mill was being brought into the front line in the war effort. Specifically, the mill had been earmarked for the manufacture and assembly of parachute packs. It was estimated that 100,000 would be needed when the time came to return to mainland Europe. Linen production would cease for the time being and new machinery installed for the change-over to the manufacture of cotton canopies. The shroud lines and harness would be produced in England and shipped to Ireland, where the finished product would be assembled and packed.

Such a change had serious political implications. Ireland was divided into two parts—the Irish Free State, which had self-government since the War of Independence two decades before, and the Six Counties in the north-east of the country, which were still governed by Britain. The Free State claimed sovereignty over the whole island of Ireland, and its prime minister, Eamon de Valera, decided it would remain neutral in the event of hostilities between the British and the Germans. Not only would the Irish Free State not take sides in the conflict, he had made it clear to the British Government that neither would he tolerate any form of conscription of Irishmen or the production of war materials in any part of the island of Ireland, north or south.

Sir Kenneth was sure there would be trouble with the workforce when it became known that linen making was to cease so that the mill could turn over to the manufacture of parachutes for the British Army. Worse still, farmers would be up in arms when they discovered that flax, their main cash crop, was no longer required.

FIRST LOVE

Resting on the bed in the luxuriant surroundings of her room, Emma had time to think about the events of the previous month which had caused such an upheaval in her life, about the chance meeting with Peter Morrison on the beach in Blackpool when the family were on their annual holiday.

Emma could still remember the strong brackish smell of sea air and hear of surf tumbling on the beach, pushing multicoloured pebbles up and down the ribbon of sand that stretched as far as the eye could see as she tried to capture the scene on canvas.

She used to work on her easel for hours, oblivious to noisy trams clattering on steel rails along the sea front; the hustle and bustle of boisterous holidaymakers thronging the promenade, their chatter competing with the swish of the seething surf. Children played games with waves on the beach, daring one another, squealing as the rolling surf advanced towards them, little hearts beating faster and faster, waiting until the last moment before scurrying ashore to the safety of the dry sand. She tried to capture the happy atmosphere but there was too much movement; the urchins never stayed long enough in one place to let her get them down on paper.

She loved this part of the beach and never tired of the boisterous confusion of it all, sun bathers jostling for space on the sandy shore, hemmed in by the sea wall on one side and rolling brown crested waves coming ever closer on the other.

She had set her heart on being an artist, to make a living from her pictures or from teaching art. She had a natural talent for design but was aware it was not enough. Whatever aptitude she had needed to be developed and disciplined, requiring practice, practice, and more practice; sound training and dedication made the difference between a talented artist and a mediocre one. She was determined to be one of the successful ones.

One morning Emma slung a bag over her shoulder, tucked her

easel under one arm and her little fold-up stool under the other and set off for the beach to stake a claim at her favourite vantage point.

She painted the same scene every day, altering the dimensions, changing colours, experimenting with different brushes, different strokes. She was trying to get the length of the pier into proportion that morning, framing the scene by making a square with her fingers, when the face of a young man appeared in one corner of her view. He wore a peaked Army cap with a red band and was smiling at her through the aperture formed by her fingers. Emma felt colour rush to her cheeks but pretended not to notice him. A couple of minutes later she sensed he was still there, behind her, looking over her shoulder. She was more embarrassed than ever and didn't dare look around.

Corporal Matthew Jenkins, using a borrowed officer's uniform and masquerading as Lt. Peter Morrison, spotted the pretty little artist as he sauntered along the promenade and decided to dally a while to get a better look at her. He liked what he saw—the shapely waist and round buttocks protruding over the tiny seat when she sat down. She was no film star, but good looking all the same. If he could strike up an acquaintance with her she might be nice company for him during the holiday.

He was in Blackpool on the prowl. Jenkins was no amateur—he had picked up lots of women before, so he knew exactly what he had to do to rope in the delectable little artist sitting pertly in front of him on the beach—all bust and bum and rose-tinted porcelain skin. And a budding artist—that would make a nice change

He saw her blush when she caught him looking at her. That was a good sign. A shy girl almost always meant that she didn't have boyfriends; maybe she was even a virgin. If she was he needed to be extra patient, extra careful, to succeed. First, he would strike up an acquaintance with her. Once the ice was broken and he got talking, experience told him the rest would follow naturally. He had done it before; he had perfected the charm and the technique. All he needed was a bit of patience and she was his for the taking.

He moved closer until he was beside her. He had to find out whether she would respond to his advances. He fancied her but had no intention of wasting time if she rejected him. There were thousands of birds in Blackpool at this time of the year ready to be plucked. Before the week was out he would have one of them one way or another.

"You make Blackpool look even lovelier than the picture postcards." He spoke softly. She paused with her brushwork and turned around to face him.

"I have a lot to learn before I can do justice to a scene like this," she said, still not sure how to react to his approach. "There's an awful lot going on in one place."

He was surprised that it was so easy to engage her. "Do you always paint scenes?" he asked. "Do you ever do portraits?"

"Occasionally," she replied, "but I'm not very good at people. I'm still at Art College."

"I thought all budding artists had to do portraits," he ventured. "I had a friend who used to pose at art school. He said it was boring, and very cold work too", he joked. "Do you paint nudes?"

"Well, yes," she said hesitating, "female nudes. The college finds it difficult to get male models."

He continued talking about the weather and the lovely day and confessed he knew nothing about painting, but had a camera and liked to snap landscapes, especially in the early morning or late evening when the light was changing. The longer they talked the more she felt at ease with him.

He excused himself and went off and returned a couple of minutes later with two large ice cream cones, blood-red strawberry juice dripping from them. He offered her one and when she took it he sat down on the ground beside her and introduced himself.

He talked while she licked the cone frantically to prevent the melting mass from dripping onto her clothing. Would she do a small portrait of him, he asked, something to have when he went back to the regiment, a memento from Blackpool?

"I'll pay you something for your trouble," he volunteered. When she nodded between licks he knew she had taken the bait.

The romance developed so quickly thereafter that Emma was swept off her feet by her handsome soldier. She worked on his portrait for two days; that gave him all the time he needed to rope his little filly in.

Emma was happy that her father would approve of her good-looking officer.

"My father is a retired Colonel," she said. "He was a professional army man for many years and served abroad in India and Egypt."

An artist and a colonel's daughter—his eyes gleamed.

The more she talked the more confident he became. He was certain she was a novice with little or no experience of men. All he needed was a day or two and he would have her eating out of his hand.

He had his camera and the second time they met he asked if he could take some pictures of her. They would be nice to take with him when he went abroad. She was a bit reluctant at first but as her infatuation with him increased Emma allowed him to get close ups of her face. He arranged to meet her the following day and persuaded her to wear her bathing costume so that he could get full length pictures. All the while he moved closer and closer until she got used to the feel of him near her; the more he touched her the more relaxed she became. She felt so happy that when he asked her to drop the straps of the bathing costume from her shoulders and stretch full length on the sand so that he could get a close-up of her shapely arms and thighs; she let him have his way.

"You'll need a special suitcase to take all these pictures with you when you go away," she laughed.

"I'll never get bored," he said. "I can look at a different one every day."

They talked about their families; Jenkins spun Emma the same story that he used to lure other girls—he was an only child whose parents had migrated to Australia when he was eighteen leaving him to fend for himself. He had relatives, but he did not get on with them and decided to make a career in the Army.

"Being alone is not easy," he confided "but in the regiment I met lots of people my own age and made some very good friends.

"Now I'm not sure I did the right thing," he added. "There is talk of war with Germany, and if it comes I will be in the middle of it."

"Let's hope it's only talk," she said, "and there will no need for you to fight."

Emma was besotted by her soldier, so much so that only three days after they first met she sneaked away from her sisters in the hotel in the evening to meet him on the beach again. When he greeted her as she stepped off the tram he cupped her face in his hands and kissed her tenderly on the lips. She was taken by surprise by the way he held her close, but it felt so good that as they walked she did not resist when he paused several times in full view of passers-by on the promenade to kiss her lips and squeeze her. The more they kissed the more excited she became; her young body filled with strange feelings of emotion and pleasant longing in her stomach. She became so intoxicated by his breath and weak from the closeness of their bodies that she had to cling to him for support.

Strolling arm in arm as the Blackpool lights came on he told her what she wanted to hear—that he had never met anybody like her, so lovely, so warm-hearted. Her head was reeling from his long kisses and sweet talk and when it got dark she took his hand and led him onto the beach and they lay down together on the cold sand. He put his tunic around her shoulders to keep her warm.

"Emma, I never thought I could get to like a girl so much and so quickly," he said. "I found you by chance only three days ago, but I feel I have known you much longer. I would love to get to know you better but unfortunately I have to go overseas in a couple of weeks. Promise I can come and see you when I get back?"

Under his spell Emma Johnston gradually abandoned all the inbred inhibitions and social customs of her middle-class upbringing. First it was long, passionate kissing as they lay down on the sand together as pleasure slowly enveloped her body. When his fingers stroked the tender flesh between her knees and he whispered that he needed her Emma's heartbeat quickened and she found it hard to breathe. She was so overwhelmed by the passion within her that when he moved his body to lie on top of her she put her arms around him and pulled him closer.

She let her knees fall apart and the more he said he loved her and wanted her the tighter she clung to him, eager to show that she

57

loved him too and frantic to satisfy the hunger deep inside her.

He couldn't believe it was her first experience of lovemaking, that the girl he was lying with was a virgin. She gripped him tightly around the neck repeating over and over that she wanted him, needed him until their passion exploded on the wet sand of Blackpool beach. Afterwards they lay in each other's arms, whispering words of love until passion ebbed and the sand under her naked buttocks felt cold again.

When the time came to return to her family she could not bear to be parted from him. She wanted his loving to go on for ever.

"I don't want to go back to the hotel," she pleaded. "I don't want to leave you. Let me stay with you tonight."

"I want to be with you too, but I only have a small room in a guesthouse and girls are not allowed there," he whispered.

But she would not take no for an answer. "I'm not leaving you ever again," she insisted. "If I cannot go with you, then we will spend the night together here on the beach".

Jenkins closed the net. "It's too cold," he said. "We have to find a place. If we are going to spend the night together the best thing to do is collect our belongings and take the late train to Liverpool. I'll get a nice room in a hotel and we can be together there for as long as we want to."

She nodded enthusiastically, and they went arm in arm to his guest house to collect his belongings. He stood outside her hotel while she disappeared inside to gather some belongings. Her family were at dinner and she dared not delay in her room in case one of them suddenly appeared. She emerged from the foyer a couple of minutes later with a small bag into which she had hastily bundled a few clothes. They hurried to the railway station to catch the late train for Liverpool. When they came out of Lime Street Station he took her to a hotel and they signed the register as Lt. and Mrs Peter Morrison.

Thereafter followed days of unbridled passion as she and her lover lived in a twilight zone of sexual pleasure, emerging from long periods of feverish lovemaking and sleep only long enough to eat or vacate the room for the cleaning staff. He persuaded her to let him

58

take pictures of her nude body in various poses on the bed, pictures he would hold close to his heart, "something to look at when I am lonely in a foreign country, something to remind me of the beautiful woman I will someday claim as my own."

Between lovemaking they made plans for the future. She was so besotted that it was easy for him to expand the web of deceit he had already created. He said he would find a place to rent in London and she could stay there until his regiment came back to England. He would get a licence on his return and they would marry. If her parents objected they could take a train to Gretna Green in Scotland and get marry there. He told her exactly what he knew she wanted to hear; there was no end to the lies he was prepared to tell to keep her in his bed.

Emma believed fate had thrown her into his arms on the crowded Blackpool beach. She knew her family would be worried, anxious for her safety, but she made no attempt to contact them, for if they found out where she was, they would come for her and take her home, and she could not bear the thought of being parted from Peter.

She made up her mind she would not make contact with them until Peter returned to his regiment. Then she would go home and tell them everything, how she had met a soldier, fallen in love and they planned to get married when his regiment returned from abroad. That was the plan and her parents would have to accept it whether they liked it or not.

Emma's world of make-believe came to an abrupt end two days before her soldier was due to return to barracks. They were naked in bed when Colonel Johnston bribed a porter to open their door with a passkey. When the red-faced Colonel burst into the room, Emma pulled the bedclothes over her head and shouted hysterically at him to let them get dressed and talk. But the Colonel was having none of it. He grabbed his daughter and tried to get her out of bed. She clung to Peter, pleading with him not to let her go but he ignored her pleas, roughly pushing her away. He did not anticipate such a confrontation and needed to make a quick exit. While the Colonel wrested with his hysterical daughter her lover grabbed his trousers and made his escape into a corridor. He stumbled along clutching his clothes stopping now and again to try and find the unlocked door of a vacant room where he could hide long enough to get his trousers on.

Colonel Johnston wrapped his screaming daughter in a blanket and carried the wriggling bundle over his shoulder downstairs, through the crowded foyer to a waiting taxi; he shouted at hotel staff to search for the bounder who had abducted his daughter. When he had unceremoniously deposited Emma in the taxi he went back upstairs looking for Jenkins and discovered him in a linen closet still naked from the waist up. Two porters held him while the Colonel kicked him in the testicles until he screamed in agony.

The police were called, but by the time they arrived the Colonel and his daughter had gone and they found only Jenkins in a toilet at the end of a corridor, bathing his bruised private parts in cold water to try and ease the pain. In the bedside locker in their room police found a cheap camera and some pictures of a young woman in all sorts of lewd poses. When they looked for him again to confront him about the pictures he was nowhere to be found.

Jenkins, worried about facing a court martial for using a false name and being caught in a stolen officer's uniform, paid the hotel bill while the police were upstairs he quickly departed for the railway station to get away from Liverpool.

On his way home from the mill on the day that Emma Johnston travelled from England, Patrick Kennedy confirmed to Sir Kenneth Montgomery that she had arrived safely.

"And she received a very warm welcome from Lady Eleanor, Sir," he added.

Kenneth was surprised to hear it and wanted to get more information from Patrick but thought better of it. It didn't pay to be too inquisitive and anyhow he would find out soon enough.

He was surprised that his wife had even bothered to make an appearance to greet the girl for when he left for the office that morning and mentioned it was the day Miss Johnston was arriving from England, she never acknowledged that he had spoken. Considering her erratic behaviour of late, he expected no different. Still, he was glad to hear that she had made some effort to make the girl welcome.

BOOK II

A NEW BEGINNING

By the time he was 25 Valentino felt he desperately needed a change. Sensing his frustration, Jinny tried to find him a job to get him out among people his own age, but he couldn't do farm work and jobs in the mill were scarce, even for able-bodied men. To pass the time he spent a lot of time in his garden growing vegetables for himself and a few neighbours and looking after chickens.

He got a part-time job in a greengrocer's in the town and got on well. He was used to growing vegetables in his own garden and knew the produce he was selling. Customers liked him because he ruffled through boxes of fruit and vegetables to pick out the freshest items for them. And when it came to handling money he never made a mistake; he knew every note and coin by touch.

With his experience in the shop he thought about getting a little business of his own.

"I know about fruit and vegetables and I can sell for myself," he told his sister.

"Well it's worth trying if you think you can do it," she said.

Their house was well situated in the middle of a long street on the main road into Murrinbridge with a front room that they rarely used, a back room that served as a living room and kitchen, and two bedrooms upstairs. He also had an old storeroom at the rear where he repaired appliances for neighbours.

Jinny thought it a great idea, and they cleared out the front room to make space for a shop. At first, he sold potatoes and vegetables displayed on trestles at the front window and in boxes on the footpath outside. Later he built shelves and stacked them with pots of Jinny's homemade jam and fresh scones and homemade apple tarts. When he got more shelving, he took in supplies of fruit. He kept his takings in a makeshift till fashioned from an empty biscuit tin.

The shop did good trade almost from the day it opened, and he felt things had taken a turn for the better. For the first time in years something exciting was happening in his life. He now had his own little business and it was doing well.

The one thing he missed was the company of a girl. He sometimes convinced himself that he might be able to do something about his love life if he had his own business. Success and a bit of money might open a few doors, might overcome prejudice, especially where a girl from a poor family was concerned. It was at times like this that he thought about Minnie and how life might have been if she had not married Danny Boyle.

Spurred on by his desire to make a success of the shop, he learned the craft of basket-making. The League for the Blind supplied him with materials, and whatever baskets he could not sell in the shop were bought by them. By the end of his first year as a weaver he produced a range of fashionable shopping baskets.

This happy state of affairs continued until the League discovered Valentino had deceived them. He was running a mini-factory using boys to boost production of his baskets, boys he repaid by hiding them while they mitched from school and whom he rewarded with a poke of sweets or a few pence to go to the cinema. The League severed their connection with him.

Cut off from his supply of raw materials, he was determined to keep going in the basket business and figured out a way to use willow bushes and sally rods instead of cane. Soaked in warm water and cured, his new materials were slower to work with, but the finished article was in demand as much as ever. He harvested the rods from bushes growing wild about the countryside and they cost him nothing. And, best of all, he found a dealer in Belfast who took every basket he could make.

Customers, mostly women from the street where he lived, came daily to purchase the basic necessities of life—potatoes, vegetables and fruit. He knew them by their first names and they enjoyed his good-natured banter; they gave him the latest gossip and he passed on to them any bit of scandal he heard in the shop. He built up a great rapport, sharing jokes as he flirted with them. He liked touching the women's arms and shoulders as he handed over their purchases and took the money from their warm hands. Sometimes he held on to their hands and if they did not resist he put an arm around them, suggesting a kiss and a cuddle might earn them an extra apple or orange. When he felt more daring he pinched a few bottoms as they were leaving. And because he was blind nobody took offence; instead, they were flattered by the attentions of the good-humoured, good-looking Valentino McKelvie.

With the mothers he got bolder as time passed, and the more liberties he took, the more he got away with. Eventually he persuaded one of them, Sara Ferguson, to lie with him in the shed behind the shop, and afterwards she told him she had such a great time they should do it together more often. He made a regular arrangement to have sex with her when her husband was on the night shift in the mill and before long he persuaded other customers to let him have his way with them. As well as whatever pleasure they got from the affairs, he plied them with free fruit and vegetables.

Valentino was in the throes of passion in an alcove behind the shop as Rosemary Mooney urged him on. Lying on a makeshift bed of potato sacks with her thighs wrapped tightly around him she whispered over and over that he was the biggest man she had ever been with and she wanted him, all of him. Her gyrations got faster and faster and her groaning louder and louder until Valentino was out of his mind with passion.

Neither of them heard the knock at the front door but when the second knock came, louder and more urgent, he took one of his hands from her buttocks and put it over her mouth to muffle her moaning.

"Hold yer whist, woman," he whispered, "or we'll be found out."

At the third knock he managed to break free and ushered her through the back door into the potato store and told her to stay there until he gave the all clear. She went into the garden pulling her knickers up and clutching her dress to her bare breasts. She cursed as she scrambled along in her bare feet clutching clothing, thighs still throbbing from their lovemaking, frustrated at being interrupted at the height of her passion, forced to let go of Valentino when he was at his best.

67

"I'll be with ye the minute I lay my hands on my damned door key," Valentino shouted through the closed door. The knocking became more urgent.

"Take it easy for God's sake or ye'll waken the dead," he shouted.

When he had his shirt tucked in and the braces over his shoulders, he opened the door. It was the deliveryman.

"I'm in a bit of a hurry this morning," he apologised, "for my wee girl is making her First Communion and I have to get home and put on the good suit."

"To hell with you and your First Communion," Valentino muttered under his breath. "I thought the bloody shop was on fire!"

The van man apologised. He sang out a list of the vegetables he brought into the shop. Valentino, excited as he was, deftly ran his fingers over them to make sure he was not being short changed.

The deliveryman couldn't help noticing that Valentino's fly was open, and the tip of his willy peeped out. He looked at the dishevelled shopkeeper and shook his head. Who the hell was he poking at eight o'clock in the morning? The gossip in the street was that he was the darling of the ladies, and to prove it he had more kids running around than Queen Victoria! He was some operator.

When he left Valentino closed the door behind him and let Rosemary out of the shed. She put her arms around his neck to resume their tryst, but he had got such a fright with the deliveryman that he had no inclination to continue. He pulled away, gave her a bag of potatoes and carrots and ushered her towards the street.

"Button up your fly," she whispered before she went through the door.

He cursed the deliveryman over and over again. He had a special arrangement for Rosemary to visit him when her husband was in bed after working the night shift at the mill; her old man was back on day work the following week, so it would be a while before he could have another session with her.

Even though he had regular sessions with the women he bedded, the one he desired most of all was Minnie Boyle. She was back from England with her two little girls and living on his street in a rented house. She came into his shop a couple of times a week to buy vegetables. She was always short of money, asking the price of everything and sometimes she put things back because she did not have enough to pay for them.

Rumours were rife about her. People said Danny Boyle, who didn't come home with her, had joined the British Army, others that he went off with another woman. Valentino didn't care which story was true—it was Minnie he was interested in and wherever her husband was, he was far away from Murrinbridge.

He was genuinely fond of Minnie and saddened by the state of poverty she had been reduced to since her marriage. Her situation was so bad that on occasions she came into the shop and bought apples for a couple of pennies and then sneaked out with a cabbage or a turnip without paying. He never confronted her with the theft as he didn't want to embarrass her and was afraid that if he made a fuss, it might stop her coming altogether.

"Things must be bad," he said to his sister Jinny, "when she has to resort to stealing".

It was clear that the lovely Minnie, the girl who had filled his head with such wild romantic notions when he was a boy, had fallen on hard times. Jinny said marriage had robbed her of the glamour of her teenage years and since her return from England she walked around with her head down, ashamed of her poverty.

"She has lost all the bounce and style she used to have," said his sister sadly, "and her clothes have seen better days. It's hard to believe, when you think how glamorous she used to be and the way the boys chased after her at the dances."

Valentino couldn't see how she looked now, nor did he care. All he knew was when she came into the shop his old feelings returned. Even before she spoke he recognised the light rhythmic tap of her high heel shoes in the hallway; as far as he was concerned, she was still the same Minnie he had fallen in love with when they were growing up. When she came near him he wanted to reach out and touch her. But he was afraid to take liberties with her like with the other women for the last thing he wanted was to scare her off.

A STROKE OF LUCK

One morning there was a knock at the door and Minnie was there.

"Sorry I'm so early," she said "but I need a few apples for the children going to school. And some potatoes too if you don't mind."

Her voice was shaky. Valentino sensed something was wrong.

"You know you're welcome any time of the day, Minnie. Have a look around while I get some change for the till. See what you need."

She mumbled something about having no money but might be able to pay him something at the end of the week. The voice was still very unsteady.

"Would that be all right?" she asked.

"Of course," he said to put her at her ease. "You're a good customer."

He half-filled a brown paper bag with potatoes and didn't bother to weigh them. On top he put half a dozen apples.

"Anything else?" he inquired.

She didn't answer.

When he took her arm to give her the bag she was shaking.

"What's wrong Minnie?" he asked.

She started to cry.

"Aw, things can't be all that bad," he said to comfort her.

"It's worse than bad, it's hopeless," she said, her voice quivering. "I'm so ashamed."

He didn't know what to do, what to say. He took a piece of rag out of his pocket and offered it to her—he didn't know what else to do. Minnie was in a bad way and he felt sad for her, but helpless.

"Jesus Minnie, don't cry," he whispered, "or you'll have me in tears too".

"Just give me a minute and I'll be okay," she said. "I feel so embarrassed asking you for credit, but I can't stand seeing the children go to school without something to eat."

Valentino remembered his own distress that day on the bridge

70

when he discovered for the first time he was blind, and how relieved he was when he heard Minnie's familiar voice. She knew what to do that day. Now he wanted to repay her kindness, to give her a shoulder to cry on but his blindness made him feel inadequate.

"Never let that happen as long as I have the shop—never let the youngsters go hungry," he said, his voice shaking with emotion.

He had a sudden urge to put his arm around her to comfort her. He put his left hand on her bare arm and held out the brown paper bag of potatoes. But he was in such an emotional state himself that he bumped her clumsily and the bag dropped to the floor.

"Aw, Jesus," he mumbled as bent down to get it. "I'm sorry, Minnie." He felt such an awkward fool.

"It's okay, Valentino. Don't worry. Nothing is spilled out."

He got down on one knee, but she took him by the shoulders and made him stand up again. She turned around to face him and put her hands on his shoulders.

"It was my own fault," she said. "I let the bag fall."

Her face was close to him and he could smell her breath as she talked, the same sweet smell as the day she cupped his face in her hands and ran her fingers through his hair. He put his hands on her neck and let his fingers touch the soft skin. She was so close he could feel the warmth of her though her dress. He had a sudden urge to kiss her and touched her face with his fingers until they found her lips. He could feel tears streaming down her cheeks.

He stepped away and pushed the front door closed, and when the lock clicked he put his arms around her waist and held her close to him. He cupped her face in his hands as she had done to him when he was a boy and kissed her on the lips. He began to breathe heavily as excitement welled up inside him. He let his hand slide down the front of her neck to her dress and placed his palm over her warm breast. He squeezed, and she gasped.

"You're hurting me—you'll mark me!"

He took his hand from her breast and moved it down to her waist. He kissed her again and put his hands on her waist, lifted her up and moved her back against the wall. Minnie put her arms around him and let her lips touch his neck. The softness of her and heat of her

71

body made him light headed; he felt his manhood swell inside his trousers and tightened the grip on her buttocks with his fingers. The only sound in the hallway was their deep breathing.

"Do you want me that much," she whispered as his fingers dug further into the soft flesh, "really want me?"

"You're the only girl I ever wanted," he whispered.

He lifted her off her feet and pressed hard against her.

"Easy, don't force, just let it happen." She raised her knees to let him between her thighs and stroked his bare buttocks as they made love.

Minnie felt good with his lovemaking, feeling his strong hands on her body, in the arms of a man who wanted her so much, so affectionate as he whispered over and over how much he wanted her, desired her all those years since she used to come to his house. It was a long time since she had been wanted this much by anybody. And it made her feel a whole woman again.

"I'll need another paper bag—that one is busted," she said. He got a new one from the shop and together they filled her potatoes and apples into it.

"Are you all right?" he asked, embarrassed by her silence, still not sure what to do or say to her.

"I'm okay now, I'm just fixing myself before I go."

"No more tears, Minnie," he said.

"No more crying," she echoed. "I feel much better now. It's great to know somebody still wants me."

After she left, he stood in the hallway for a while with his back to the closed door, shaking with excitement. He knew he was awkward, but she knew what to do and helped him. His pals sometimes boasted about how fantastic it was to have intercourse with a woman, but with Minnie it was better than he ever imagined it could be. He had not felt so contented or so confident for a long time.

He washed his face, tidied his clothes and then opened the front door for business. He whistled as he checked what he needed to order from the wholesaler when he came with the daily deliveries. All day long he was preoccupied with thoughts of when he might get an opportunity to make love to Minnie again.

In the kitchen after she had sent the girls off to school, Minnie took the mirror from its shelf and carefully examined her neck and chest for any tell-tale marks. She dabbed powder on blotches where the stubble from his chin had chaffed her skin and thought about what had just happened.

Sex with Valentino was the thing farthest from her mind when she left the house that morning to try and get a few things on credit from him. She was upset, and that's why she did not resist when he first put his arms around her to comfort her. He was a strong passionate man and from the moment his hand touched her bare arm she felt warm inside and relaxed—that's how she dropped the bag of vegetables. When he put his hands on the back of her neck there was no going back; she could feel him wanting her and even though she realised what she was doing was wrong, even dangerous, she did not have the will to resist him.

Standing in front of the mirror, she still had that warm tingling feeling all over. She ran a brush through her hair in long slow strokes, trying to bring a shine back into it.

"If only I looked as good as I feel," she said aloud to her image in the mirror. "I look like an old woman, but I'm still only 29 and I want to look and feel like a 29-year-old. If Valentino had his sight and saw how much I've changed, maybe he might not be so keen on me."

After his success with Minnie, Valentino had no time for other women and when they came into the shop hoping to spend some time with him in the shed, he put them off with all sorts of excuses— his sister was home, there was no room at the shed, it was becoming too dangerous when husbands were unemployed and liable to come into the shop at the wrong time; some customers were asking why he closed the shop so much when they needed potatoes and vegetables. He managed to fend them off for a while but inevitably they found out that there was a new love in his life and that's why he was no longer interested in them.

It was Sara Ferguson who let the cat out of the bag. One morning after another bout of love-making, Minnie straightened her clothes, tidied her hair and left Valentino lying on his side on the storeroom floor to recover. When she got home she remembered that in her haste she had not pulled his front door closed. She left the house again to rectify the situation, but it was too late. The Ferguson woman was already inside and found him sitting on a blanket of empty potato sacks scratching his head, naked from the waist down.

"Come on," she laughed, "time to get up and tend the shop."

He ran his fingers through his hair and started to feel around for his trousers.

"Help me up, Minnie," he said, "I'm exhausted."

"Too late, Pokey, Minnie's gone home a happy woman. This is your other friendly customer, Sara. I was hoping to get something extra myself but by the cut of ye it'll be some time before ye're fit to serve another customer. I'm sure ye won't mind if I help myself to half a stone of spuds. Don't worry; I'll close the door on the way out." She was gone as quickly as she came.

Whatever pleasure Valentino had in his session with Minnie that morning quickly dissipated the moment he discovered he had been caught. It was the worst thing that could happen. Up to then he managed to keep his liaisons with Minnie secret. The Ferguson bitch now knew for sure that she wasn't the only one. She was such a bloody talker; everybody would know about him and Minnie. It was the last thing he wanted. And the wily bitch had the neck to take a stone bag of spuds without paying when she left!

The business with the Ferguson woman was bad. It was the first time he had been caught literally with his pants down. Other things had gone wrong recently too, and he was under a bit of pressure. Mary Hamilton was pregnant and before the year was out would produce a child fathered by him; he suspected that some of his other women were pregnant too. Sara Ferguson was a vindictive bitch and she would bring the whole thing out into the open; she was not the type to keep her mouth shut. If husbands copped on to the fact that he had been having sessions with their wives there would be hell to play.

True to form, Sara Ferguson blabbed to the other women and

soon the word got around that he was two-timing. The women didn't like being made fools of by blind Valentino and some challenged him about it in the shop and vowed never to cross his door again. It was also the first time any of them had confronted him about fathering their children. He suspected some of them were his, but they all had husbands and he never thought much about it. The only thing that might save him from being exposed was that the wives could not afford to let their husbands know what was going on; they would have to keep their mouths shut.

In the months that followed, a crop of "war babies" appeared on the street, some bearing a striking resemblance to the not-so-green grocer. Husbands who had suspected something up to then, now knew for sure what he was up to. He knew that they knew, and he had to be extra careful when he was out and about in case he ran into any of them.

Once the word was out, none of his regular women came near the shop, when a week passed without one of them appearing, he realised that he was being boycotted. Minnie also stayed away rather than risk the wrath of the other customers. His business suffered but the financial loss was nothing compared to the frustration in his love life. The healthy sexual appetite he had developed since the day the women first let him have his way with them turned to a gnawing hunger that made him more and more agitated as the days passed.

When he could put up with the situation no longer, he took himself off on the bus to Derry and went into a whorehouse. When the girls saw the man with the white stick come in they greeted him with howls of laughter and they were wary about entertaining him; when he asked the price, none of them would answer and eventually he had to negotiate with the boss woman to procure a girl, but she made him pay an extra half a crown for the service. He cursed the bitches under his breath for making fun of him, but paid his money, had his time on a creaky bed and got the bus home. That was the start of a weekly pilgrimage to the whorehouse. In time the girls got to know him, put aside their prejudice and argued over whose turn it was to get the blind man and the half-crown bonus.

COLD COMFORT

Emma was enthralled by her new home. In the days following her arrival she was in a constant state of excitement as she eagerly explored Mill Brae and its surroundings. She spent hours studying the proliferation of paintings adorning the walls, mesmerised by the way landscapes and portraits and still life had been placed to emphasise contrasting pastoral and modern styles.

Lady Eleanor was delighted with her young companion and particularly with her infectious enthusiasm for the house and gardens. She was flattered by Emma's comments on the decor and furnishings.

To the rear, between the house and the river, was a small orchard and vegetable garden enclosed by a high red-brick wall. This part of the garden was carefully laid out so that mature apple trees on the north provided shelter from the cold winter winds for berries and other soft fruit. It was also designed to produce quadrants of blossoms in spring.

When Emma first visited the garden a crop of sweet purple plums had already been harvested, leaving only a few immature stragglers still dangling precariously from branches. Early varieties of eating apples had also been harvested, but there were still firm winter pears and big rose-tinted cooking apples hanging heavy from trees that had begun to shed their foliage. Throughout the garden birds feasted on windfalls. The mellow smell of over-ripe fruit helped overcome the pong of a steaming compost heap.

On one side she discovered an iron gate covered in ivy. The green parasite had grown out of control, its ubiquitous tentacles weaving in and out through rusted iron rails. With nothing better to do, she cleared some of the creeper to see where it led and used a brick to force it back and open it sufficiently to let her squeeze through.

On the other side was a field, a wild place between house and river, almost impassable because of the dense growth of bushes. She forced her way through, pushing branches apart with her arms until she reached a pathway. She stumbled over some willowy rods on the ground tied in a bundle. She continued towards the river and eventually emerged at a gravel path on the river bank. Her bedroom was at the rear of the house and she could hear water tumbling over the rocky bed at night when her window was open. This was the first time she actually saw it, a wide stretch of lively water with steep grassy banks on either side. Upriver there was a weir over which the smooth water slid before it began its journey down the rocky river bed until it tumbled into a deep pool downstream.

There was a footbridge slung high over the noisy, gushing water, a wide path of wooden slats suspended in mid-air by two great steel cables anchored to metal pillars on either side. This was the Swinging Bridge, the only crossing point on the river for miles, built to give pedestrian access to mill workers who lived on the other side. It was also a favourite courting spot for boys and girls from the village, according to the housemaids. Whoever designed it had an eye for beauty, thought Emma, for it blended perfectly with the surroundings.

A man and a boy were standing on the footbridge looking down at the water. The man had a walking stick hooked over his shoulder. She nodded to them as she passed and bid them "Good Afternoon". The boy glanced furtively in her direction, whispered something to his companion and the pair moved away to the other side of the bridge. She recognised the man with the stick—it was the blind man with the head of red hair called Valentino whom Patrick Kennedy had pointed out to her on the street in Murrinbridge the day she arrived in Ireland, the day that war broke out. On her way back, they had gone.

It was a lovely day and the smell of clover and wild flowers amid the bushes in the field was pleasant as she slowly made her way back; she was in no hurry. On her way back, the pair had gone. She passed the spot where the rods had lain on the path half an hour before and they had gone.

She had to force her way through the dense growth of bushes to find her way back to the rusty gate. Long thin branches stroked her face and the leaves felt cool against her skin, but sometimes a branch slipped through her outstretched arms and she had to duck to prevent it striking her face. She was conscious as she walked of the racket the birds were making, annoyed that a stranger had intruded into their private domain. She closed the rusty gate behind her and re-entered the manicured grounds of Mill Brae House.

Mill Brae House was a peaceful retreat from a world in the throes of another war, but it became clear to Emma soon after she arrived there that Sir Kenneth and his wife were not happy together there.

Life was normal during the day. The women got on well together, walking and talking and making plans, but when Sir Kenneth came home in the evenings, the atmosphere changed. From the moment they sat down to dinner it was clear husband and wife only dined together out of duty; they hardly spoke to one another. When either of them did break the silence, the conversation was mainly directed towards Emma.

There was something terribly wrong with their relationship, and Emma felt her presence was an intrusion on their privacy, but Lady Eleanor insisted that she join them at the dinner table each evening. Emma did not enjoy the experience. What should have been the most pleasant time of the day left her with an uneasy, uncomfortable feeling.

At home in England the evening meal was the nicest part of the day, a time to chat about things that happened at school, plans for the days ahead, clothes and shopping and holidays. If the girls argued or teased one another their parents intervened to prevent things going too far, warning that it would end in tears.

"Remember where you are and who you are," her mother would say. "You are meant to enjoy the company as well as the food."

Not once did she see Kenneth and Eleanor Montgomery embrace or even touch one another or utter one word of endearment.

Lady Eleanor had gone out of her way to make sure that from the very first day she was welcome at Mill Brae; she treated Emma as if she were a sister. Emma, for her part, found her host an interesting woman who could be very funny when recounting the antics she got up to with family and friends growing up in County Antrim. She was still a striking woman, at times graceful and bright-eyed, bubbling with excitement. Then for no apparent reason the mood would change, her shoulders drooping, her head bowed, and she would disappear upstairs, not to appear again for hours.

Sir Kenneth was a tall good-looking man with a square face and strong jaw and stout shoulders; deep blue eyes and dark eyebrows gave him an air of authority. He reminded her of the cool clean hero used to advertise after-shave lotions. Emma spent most of her time with Lady Eleanor but occasionally found herself alone with him in the evenings when his wife left the dinner table and retired to her bedroom. He was pleasant company, and a couple of times she felt like broaching the subject of her sudden arrival at Sperrin; she wanted to let him know how grateful she was for allowing her to come to Ireland and to thank him especially for keeping the contents of her father's letter to himself, saving her a lot of grief. But she thought better of it; it would be embarrassing for her and might make him uncomfortable too.

Her parents were not the world's greatest lovers, but they were affectionate when they were alone, and if they had guests her father made a point of putting an arm around his wife and kissing her on the cheek to congratulate her on being such a fine hostess.

The maids said Lady Eleanor's dark moods were due to medication. Even though she and Emma spent long hours together working in the gardens or on walks or drives into the countryside and on shopping trips to Belfast and Dublin, Emma had no idea what the nature of Eleanor's illness was, and it was never discussed. When they were away from the house her spirits seemed to lift and their times together were happy. The changes in her mood only seemed to come within the confines of Mill Brae.

Apparently there had been frequent rowing between husband and wife. She overheard the maids gossiping about it in the kitchen, remarking that it was a much quieter place since Emma Johnston arrived—no tantrums at dinner, no banging of doors in the middle of the night. She was shocked when she overheard them refer to Lady Eleanor as "that Protestant witch" and her husband as "a philanderer who took advantage of young mill girls". They talked about one girl in particular, a secretary called "Katie Reilly" who was "doing a lot of overtime for the boss" and for her favours "brought home a big fat pay packet every week".

"If she isn't careful," laughed one of them "she'll be bringing home more than a big pay packet one of these Friday evenings, the way she's carrying on."

Emma was surprised at the viciousness of the gossip because since she arrived she never saw any of the house servants mistreated in any way, or even spoken to harshly by either the master or mistress.

When one of the maids left because she was asked to do some extra work to cover for the illness of another, Lady Eleanor was furious.

"No matter how well you treat them they never seem to be satisfied," she said. "And what's more," she warned Emma, "be careful what you say, for they are not to be trusted. Everything that happens in this house is talked about in the village.

"It's the same with the mill workers," she added. "The Montgomery family have provided work for hundreds of families for more than a century, yet since I came to Sperrin two attempts were made to destroy the mill. Once they set fire to it and caused extensive damage; the second time they tried to blow it up. It's all part of an anti-establishment, anti-British thing. I find it very difficult to understand."

When Sir Kenneth offered over dinner to get a replacement, Lady Eleanor suddenly stood up and shouted at him: "You will do no such thing," she said angrily, "I am not having you bring one of your mill girls into this house!"

He was embarrassed by her behaviour and showed it. After she left the table, he turned to Emma.

"My wife has these outbursts now and again," he said. "Her mind is affected by medication and she imagines all sorts of things."

WHEN LOVE GROWS COLDER

In November 1939 the war that English Chancellor Neville Chamberlain assured the English people would not happen started in earnest. The British sent 160,000 troops to France to help create a defensive barrier on the Continent to stop a westward advance by the Germans. The first bombs were dropped on the remote Shetland Islands north of Scotland, and thousands of miles away in South America the pride of the German navy, the battleship Graf Spee was scuttled by her captain in the River Plate rather than surrender to British warships that had trapped her in Rio de Janeiro. That first British success, however, was to be short lived. In the year that followed, the Expeditionary Force sent to help defend France was driven back to the sea at Dunkirk and decimated on the beaches. The bulk of the force was evacuated but tens of thousands were left behind dead or taken prisoner.

One setback after another followed, and the defiant mood of the British people suddenly changed to one of desperation; the situation was so bad that, instead of talk about winning the war, people began to question whether or not they had the resources to repel a German invasion that seemed a real possibility as Hitler's forces swept westwards.

Once they had consolidated their grip in France and the Low Countries, the Germans turned their full attention to Britain. The assault began with a bombing blitz of London similar to the one that razed Warsaw as a prelude to the invasion of Poland. From September 1940 the blitz continued relentlessly night after night, culminating in the worst attack of all in May 1941 when central London was almost completely destroyed in an incendiary firestorm. Hitler was determined to bring the old enemy to its knees before sending his invasion forces across the English Channel.

Autumn of the same year brought an early frost in Ireland and with it a noticeable drop in temperature that hastened the end of summer. Giant chestnut trees overhanging the gate lodge at Mill Brae began to shed their foliage, leaves rocking from side to side as they wafted downwards in their thousands in the evening breeze to form a deep amber carpet on the lawn below. Great oaks behind the house stood like giant pillars of brown and gold, sheltering the gardens from the worst of the frost and shading the flowerbeds from the sun dipping lower and lower in the sky as winter approached.

Emma loved the changing colours and, though the evenings had turned cold, she still spent a lot of time in the garden. She savoured the heavy scent of mature fruit mingling with odours of decaying vegetation and the pungent woody smoke from fires lit by gardeners to burn leaves. A few apples and pears still clung tenaciously to the moss-laden branches of trees exhausted by another season of bearing fruit.

Ever since she had come to Mill Brae Emma had spent most of her time working outdoors. Lady Eleanor's health showed no signs of improvement, and as the months passed she retreated into the house, relying more and more on sedatives to combat her volatile moods and depression. So Emma took over the running of the gardens, the management of the outdoor staff, overseeing the pruning and harvesting that followed the seasons. She planned and supervised the planting of the flower beds; organised the preservation of fruit from the walled garden; saw to the planting and rotation of vegetables for the kitchen; and made sure the wide expanse of lawn at the centre of it all was always in immaculate condition.

On her occasional sorties into the garden Lady Eleanor liked what she saw and praised her young companion for her hard work, expressing regret that she was not well enough to help. As the months slipped past with no improvement to her health, she gave up the trips they used to make into the countryside. The mistress had lost all interest in what was happening in the world outside and spent more and more time in her bedroom retreat. The seasons came and went outside, but inside Mill Brae time seemed to stand still.

In the winter of 1941, the atmosphere inside the house was just as cold as it was outside. The three of them still dined together every evening as usual, when Sir Kenneth and his wife both conversed freely with Emma but never spoke directly to one another. When dinner was over Lady Eleanor invariably excused herself and retired. After she left, the atmosphere warmed between Emma and Sir Kenneth, especially at weekends when they left the big dining room for the comfort of an open fireplace in the sitting room. They sat there reading until it was time to go to bed. This was the time of day when Sir Kenneth perused the daily newspapers to catch up on reports on the war.

Emma was awakened by a commotion outside her bedroom one night. She got out of bed, put the light on and opened her door a few inches to see what was going on. Sir Kenneth was on his knees outside his wife's bedroom threshing about wildly, pulling at the door handle with both hands; he appeared to be drunk, so drunk he could not stand up. His words were slurred, and she could not make out what he was saying. When he finally managed to get up off his knees he lost his balance and fell again, hitting his head on the door.

Muffled shouts came from within the room. "Go away! Go away! You can't come in here."

Emma wasn't sure what to do. She didn't want to get involved, but if she did nothing the servants would come, and the incident would be blown out of all proportion. She went outside and knelt down beside him and whispered to him to keep quiet. She helped him to his feet and when she got him upright he put his arm around her shoulder. She stumbled as his full weight bore down on her.

With great difficulty she walked him across the landing and into his own room and let him fall heavily on the bed.

Despite the state he was in, he knew it was Emma. While she was untying his shoes, he raised his head from the pillow. "You're the best thing that happened in this house for a long time, Emma Johnston," he said haltingly. By the time she had his shoes and stockings off, his head was back on the pillow and he was snoring. Although it was quiet after that, Emma lay awake for a while to make sure there was no further trouble. In the two years she had been at Mill Brae, it was the first time she witnessed a full-blown row between them.

At breakfast next morning, not a word was spoken about the events of the night before. He was so drunk, Emma thought, that he might not even remember what happened.

After he left for the mill Lady Eleanor asked Emma if she had been awakened during the night, apologising if her sleep had been disturbed. Emma feigned surprise and lied that she heard some noise on the landing but when she opened her bedroom door, there was nobody there.

"I heard your door closing after Kenneth went to bed," said Lady Eleanor, staring at Emma. Emma made no reply. For the first time since she arrived at Mill Brae she detected a tone of sarcasm, that she had been caught telling a lie.

After that incident Lady Eleanor's attitude to Emma changed. Gone were the cosy afternoon chats in the comfort of her favourite room. The older woman spent virtually all her time in her bedroom, leaving only to come downstairs for dinner. She became reclusive; the only people she had regular contact with were her personal maid and the cook who visited her every day to take instructions for the evening meal. Apart from ordering dinner she took no part in the running of the house and gardens or in management of the staff.

Emma mentioned the change in his wife to Sir Kenneth after dinner.

"I can't imagine what I have done to offend her," she said apologetically.

The more Emma thought about the incident outside Lady Eleanor's bedroom, the less sense it made to her. If Sir Kenneth was having his way with mill girls—with Kate Reilly—why did he try to force himself on his estranged wife at home?

THE PROPOSITION

Emma was thinking about Lady Eleanor and what was to become of her one evening when she walked out of the sunshine into shade and suddenly felt chill. As she pulled her shawl tightly about her shoulders and made her way back towards the house she became aware of somebody behind her, following her. She turned around and saw Sir Kenneth taking a shortcut across the lawn.

"It's a lovely evening for a walk," she said politely when he came near.

He nodded, and they strode side by side on the white path bordering the trees, the silence broken only by the crunch of their shoes on marble chippings. She paused to look at berries on the shrubbery, pointing to a particularly heavy crop on holly bushes.

"The gardeners say it's a sign of a harsh winter," she ventured.

He made no reply. He walked on, head bowed like a man with the weight of the world on his shoulders. A couple of times he paused and turned toward her as if about to say something, but no words came, and he moved on.

Emma sensed he wanted to talk but did not seem to know how to start. Was he worried by the incident outside his wife's bedroom? The silence was awkward.

"If you're embarrassed about the other night," she said nervously, "there is no need to be. You were very drunk and you fell down on the landing and I helped get you to your room and left you lying on the bed. That's all."

When he still kept his head down, she continued.

"If a man wants to have a row with his wife in the privacy of his own home he is perfectly entitled to do so." She was surprised how easily the words came. "That's the problem with having a stranger in your house—it interferes with your privacy."

Finally, he broke his silence: "Oh! It's not your fault," he said. "That's not why I joined you—I came to apologise."

Then: "I was hoping to have a talk with you too," he added, "about the way things are, about my wife's illness and the atmosphere in the house. Eleanor shows no sign of improvement."

He stopped and looked directly at her. "She has been like this for a couple of years she is getting gradually worse. I was able to cope for a while because she allowed me to help her and talk about how she felt. Lately, however, she has turned completely against me, wants to have nothing to do with me.

"I had hoped that our relationship would change for the better when you came to stay with us. She loves having you around but towards me she has become even more intolerant.

"Now it appears she has turned against you too, and that's my fault," he said. "That is going to make life even more difficult for her because she has nobody left to talk to. It's also going to make it more unpleasant for you to live here if you have no company all day while I am at the mill."

Emma was taken aback by the matter of fact way he discussed his personal problems with her. Why was he telling her all this? 'Is he going to ask me to leave?' she wondered.

Before he had a chance to continue she interrupted him. "Lady Eleanor has been a great friend to me and these past two years have been a very happy time of my life. Whatever about her illness your wife has never shown me anything but kindness and has encouraged me to think of her home as my home.

"I am old enough to understand that the relationship between you is not what it ought to be. I also hear the gossip of the maids. I am sorry for you both because you are such nice people; I would never dare say anything unkindly or uncomplimentary about Lady Eleanor. She is a lady and she has never behaved other than as a lady towards me.

"I know she is hostile to me at the moment. Maybe she feels that I am getting too close to you, that somehow or other I have betrayed her. But that is just her illness and maybe her mood will change again."

He stopped and turned to face her. "You are young, Emma," he said "but you have the good sense of an older woman. That's why

I feel I can talk frankly to you. I believe you are mature enough to understand what I am going through at this time."

Emma was not sure where his talk was leading but there was something she had wanted to say to him for some time and felt this was her opportunity.

"There is something I should have discussed with you before this," she interrupted. "I know my father told you why he sent me here, and I shall be forever grateful that you did not disclose the contents of his letter to anybody, not even to your wife. I love Mill Brae—I am very content here and it has made exile from home easier to bear. If people knew the real reason I came it would not be the same.

"I am not a child. I fell head over heels in love with a soldier and though the affair was short-lived because of circumstances beyond my control I shall never forget the pleasure I got from it, brief as it was. Even though the passion I felt then still burns within me I have not thought about another man since. It has taken two years to make me realise that my fairy tale romance could not endure. Nevertheless, I have no regrets. I enjoyed the affair while it lasted, and I will always have wonderful memories of that period of my life.

"You kept my secret and I will keep yours—you have my word that nobody outside Mill Brae will ever hear from my lips anything that happens in this house, anything that might hurt either you or your wife."

"You don't have to thank me for anything," he interrupted her. "You have been a breath of fresh air since you arrived. What's past is past, and you are young and bright enough to learn from your mistake. That's what life is about—experience and learning.

"Unfortunately, it's different for me. I feel life passing me by, the best years of my life being wasted and for all my wealth and experience I am powerless to do anything about it."

He took a deep breath of cool evening air and heaved a long nervous sigh as he exhaled.

"This senseless idea that Eleanor is childless because God is punishing her for sins persists and her psychiatrist is unable to help her overcome it. I accepted a long time ago that she was not going to have a baby—being childless is not a crime—and since then all I wanted was a normal relationship such as exists between any husband and wife. At this stage of our lives more than anything else we both need companionship."

"This wrath of God thing—it has changed her. She doesn't want me anywhere near her, not close to her, not in her bedroom, not even in the house if she had her way. She has a fixation that the sole purpose of marriage in God's eyes is procreation and since she is a barren woman it is lustful and sinful for us to make love just to satisfy animal instincts."

His voice faltered, and he stopped walking and turned to face her again; he was close to tears.

"If you don't want to hear any more," he said tersely, "tell me and I will leave you."

She was flustered and unsure of how she should respond: "It's good to talk...get things out into the open," she stammered, searching for the right words.

He stopped and looked directly at her.

"You are not comfortable listening to me," he said and before she had time to reply, he walked briskly away, towards the house.

She was so surprised by his sudden change of attitude that she was speechless. By the time she recovered her composure he had disappeared into the dusk.

She completed her walk around the lawn and climbed the granite steps to the house, anxious to get inside and to her room as quickly as possible to avoid meeting him again. She was shaken by the encounter and needed time to make some sense of it. She was angry at his abrupt departure but sorry for the disturbed state he was in. Here was a handsome man, still in the prime of his life, wealthy, with a beautiful home. He had everything to offer but lacked the most important thing of all—love and companionship. What did he want from her—somebody to talk to, someone to unburden himself to? If doctors could not help Lady Eleanor what could she do to solve his problems?

Emma was still wrestling with her confused thoughts when she opened the door to let herself into the dark hallway. Suddenly he stepped out of the shadows, startling her.

"I need to finish what I want to say to you," he said hastily. He walked toward his study and she followed, and he sat down behind his desk. He motioned to her to sit on the chair opposite.

He offered her a drink and when she shook her head, poured a glass of whiskey for himself and took a long sip.

"No doubt you have heard rumour and gossip about affairs I'm supposed to be having at the mill," he said looking directly at her. She felt uncomfortable again; she did not want to hear this. She shifted her body sideways to avoid having to look straight at him while he spoke.

"The truth is that there are no other women in my life. Since I lost the companionship of my wife I am frustrated and I am lonely and I am under great pressure at the mill and as a result of all this I drink far too much. I don't want to be an alcoholic or have a nervous breakdown; I'm just a man who needs a woman, somebody to show me a little affection.

"Do you understand?" he said to her. "Am I making sense to you?"

She wanted to tell him she had heard enough, but before she had a chance to get the words out, he was talking again. He took another sip from the whiskey glass.

"You are a very beautiful girl and I know you are young and you have had a bad experience with your first love but more important I know you are kind-hearted and affectionate and that's why I thought of nothing else this past week except finding the opportunity to talk frankly to you about my situation, about your situation, about the possibility of helping each other.

There was an awkward pause for a few moments. He waited until she looked directly at him.

"I even thought about asking you if you would be my girlfriend, lover, mistress—call it what you will?"

She was visibly shaken.

"Does it shock you to hear me say that, Emma?"

She stood up and without answering or even looking at him and walked quickly out of the room. She stumbled up the stairs, locked the door of her bedroom and lay down on the bed, shaking. She took deep breaths as she lay on her back with her eyes wide open staring into the blackness. She had just been propositioned by a man twice her age, to betray the trust of the woman who had taken her into her home and made her welcome when her own family had disowned her! There was no other way to express what had just happened!

She began to cry. She was 21 years old, living in a foreign country to which she had been exiled by her parents, with no clear idea of what the future held for her. What was she to do? What options did she have? Go back to Lancashire? She had already ruled out home as an option.

Emma wanted to stay in Ireland. But if she spurned Sir Kenneth, could she remain at Mill Brae? If she had to leave the big house there was no realistic prospect of finding any work locally. Apart from the Montgomerys she had no friends and since coming to the mill village she had no opportunity to socialise with anybody, no chance to meet people of her own age group.

If she had to find a job what could she do? She could not earn a living from painting or get work in an office. She might get a job as a governess but how many families in such a depressed area could afford one?

She knew Sir Kenneth was kind and gentle and if he took a mistress no doubt he would treat her with respect and take good care of her; she would want for nothing. But would his mistress ever be a married woman, a mother with a family to care for? Or would she remain a mistress and spend the rest of her life wishing Lady Eleanor dead?

What would it be like if she became his mistress as he suggested? She would have happiness of a kind but while she liked Kenneth Montgomery, she never considered that she would ever have a relationship with him. She might marry him for his wealth if the opportunity came but that could only happen if Eleanor died. She was sure he would never divorce his wife, and if he did, did she want to get involved with a divorced man? The last thing she wanted was a sordid affair with an older man in a clandestine relationship that had no future.

She was still trying to find her way through a maze of probabilities when fatigue forced her eyelids together in the early hours of the morning.

The clock in the hallway began to chime half past nine as he came through the front door next evening. The atmosphere in the dining room seemed even more tense than usual. Lady Eleanor conversed only with the servants and Emma and Sir Kenneth dined in silence.

In the living room after dinner when Eleanor had gone upstairs he sipped whiskey and smoked a cigar and would have been completely relaxed if it was not for the unfinished business with Emma. They listened to the radio for news of the war.

To try and cheer people up, there was a repeat of Workers' Playtime followed by another episode of "Dick Barton—Special Agent". Emma asked if he had been following the adventures of Dick Barton and when he shook his head she turned it off, lingering until the green light on the tuner faded and died.

"Isn't it ironic," she said, "that we get all our war news from a radio made by the enemy."

She turned towards him and looked directly at him.

"I want to talk to you about that matter you raised the other evening," she said.

Her voice changed the atmosphere immediately. He did not look directly at her but at his hands folded on the coffee table in front of him.

"I have given it a lot of thought" she began. "You must realise how difficult this is for me because Lady Eleanor and you are the only friends I have in this country. I have family in England but no desire to return to them at this time. So, the last thing I want is to be put in the position of having to leave Mill Brae."

He had been on her mind all day and she had spent a lot of time rehearsing exactly what she wanted to say. She paused for a few moments to gather her thoughts.

She looked directly at him: "First, I don't know how much my father told you about me before I came here, so I'll tell you the story myself.

"I ran away with a soldier and lived with him for eight wonderful days," she continued "even though it turned out he was married already and took advantage of my innocence, my naivety, I want to say here and now that I regret nothing."

"My parents put my escapade down to immaturity, to infatuation, to downright stupidity and while I never admitted that they were right I realise now that what I did was to say the least very foolish.

"But I want you to know that if I lost my youth, my innocence, in that affair I also gained a lot. In one hectic week I left girlhood behind and became a woman. I learned how to love and to accept the love of another in the physical as well as the emotional sense."

"Since then I have led a chaste existence, a very comfortable and protected life here at Mill Brae but all the time hoping that something would happen, or somebody would come along and reawaken the love I know is still within me, love that I am still capable of giving.

"You are in a different position. You are a wealthy man, hard-working, enthusiastic and distinguished. Even though you are twice my age, you are still a young man and not bad looking either," she smiled. "But you too are caught in a loveless trap. You have a wife who apparently no longer physically desires you.

"When you spoke so frankly to me in the garden I was frightened and confused but since then I have had plenty of time to think about what you said.

"Despite the difference in age we have much in common—I know I am capable of making a man happy but I have no man in my life; conversely you are a kind and loving man but have no woman to share your affection with."

She paused, staring into the coffee cup held tightly between her two hands. Was it his turn to say something? Should he tell her to forget what he had said and put an end to the awkwardness between them?

She lifted her head and turned to face him.

"You know how fond I am of your wife and the last thing I want to do is hurt her," she continued. "Neither do I want to hurt you, to make you feel rejected. But as my mother sometimes pointed out, you cannot make a cake without breaking eggs. In certain situations somebody has to be hurt."

His heart sank. He stared at the fire, avoiding her gaze as she continued.

She paused to catch her breath and when he put his head down dejectedly, she asked him to look at her for she had something very important to say to him.

"I hated my parents when they told me I was being exiled to Ireland to live in a strange place among strange people," she said. "I had no way of knowing that I was going to such a beautiful place and such a friendly welcome, a place so beautiful that I now don't want to leave.

"So in Ireland I am going to stay, one way or another. I have made my mind up on that and it will not be changed no matter what happens."

She deliberately took a long deep breath. He looked at her.

"Once I made that decision I found it easier to make up my mind about this other more important matter.

"If you are prepared to compromise your reputation and marriage by taking me as a mistress then I will be your mistress."

She was so direct; he found it hard to believe she said it. He choked on the coffee and when he recovered his breath sat back in the chair and stared at her. He stood up and came towards her, intending to embrace her, but she pushed him away.

"No. Please stay where you are until I finish.

"As a mistress I will do my best to please you. It's clear I will have to leave this house and that will make me unhappy; and when your wife finds out about this arrangement she will be very unhappy too. But that situation cannot be avoided if we are to be together.

"It will be your responsibility to find another place for me and care for me. I want that clearly understood."

She stopped him when he wanted to say something.

"One thing more—I want you to make provision for me should our relationship break up or should you tire of me and take another lover. I need this assurance in writing for I have nobody else to turn to once I commit myself to you."

Sir Kenneth felt a wave of excitement sweep through his body. She had said yes, to everything.

And he said yes in return to all her demands, demands that were of little consequence to a man with his wealth. This young girl, this lovely young woman who had come into his home purely by accident was about to change his life.

It was his turn to speak and she sat back on her chair to hear what he had to say.

"It's up to me, Emma, to ensure that you will never regret the decision you made. In a small community like this word will soon get around about our affair and we will have to live with it. My wife will hear about it soon enough too, but I doubt if it will have much effect on her other than temporary embarrassment for its clear there is no hope of reconciliation between us, no future in our marriage. No doubt she will despise us both, so the sooner I find another house, another place where we can be alone together, the better for all concerned.

"As to financial and other matters there will be no need for written guarantees," he assured her. "As soon as I can make an appointment with my solicitor I will have a sum of money set aside in a trust fund out of which you will be paid a generous monthly allowance."

He promised he would look for a suitable house right away to which she could move when she felt the time had come to leave Mill Brae. It would be purchased in her name, his first gift to her.

Sir Kenneth was so excited by the girl's response that he could not sleep. The prospect of having a beautiful young woman in his bed, a soft warm body to love, made him feel like a man again.

Then he heard his bedroom door open and lifted his head from the pillow to see a shadowy figure enter. The light went on and Emma stood with one hand on the switch, the other on her lips.

"If you want to talk some more," she said softly, "come to my room." The light went off, the door closed slowly again, and she was gone.

He got out of bed and tiptoed after her making sure there was nobody on the landing before entering her room. The light was on.

She was standing at the side of her bed, her back to him, nightgown hanging loose on her shoulders.

The sight of her silhouette in the flimsy nightdress with the light behind her took his breath away. He felt blood surge through his veins as his body became excited. It was a long time since he had been this close to a woman. She stretched out her arms inviting him to come closer. When he put out his hands to touch her she led him to her bedside.

Emma put her arms around his neck and pulled her body up until their lips met; she kissed him, darting her tongue in and out of his mouth, forcing him to react to her. His body burned at the touch of hot flesh as she pressed hard against him.

He lifted her onto the bed and lay on top of her. She pulled him closer, whispering to be gentle with her, but he was so eager to have her that he lurched against her until she gasped in pain.

He could not restrain himself, so great was his hunger' and despite her protests, he used the full weight of his body to thrust deeper and deeper inside her.

"I want you to love me," he moaned over and over as he released his pent-up passion.

That night with only a room between them and the marital bed in which his wife slept, marked Emma and Kenneth Montgomery started something that was to have far reaching effects on their lives and the lives of so many people in the Sperrin Mill community.

THE RAVAGES OF LOVE
AND WAR

Poland was terrorised by the military. For those who did not bow to the will of the jackboot severe punishment was meted out by soldiers who clearly had orders to subdue the population by whatever means necessary and deal firmly with anybody who did not conform. The most disturbing aspect of the occupation was frequent attacks on women. Sexual molestation, practically unheard of in Catholic Poland before the occupation, was now a daily occurrence; the prettier the women, the more they suffered at the hands of soldiers. Body searches on the pretence of checking for arms often ended in girls being dragged into the back of a truck and raped. The situation became so bad that women were afraid to leave their homes to go to work.

Poland was not the only place where women suffered because of the war. In the North of Ireland tens of thousands of British soldiers billeted in small towns awaiting orders to go overseas became romantically entangled with local girls, young women from impoverished backgrounds swept off their feet by the excitement and glamour of men in uniform. When the time came to part the soldiers left behind a lot of broken hearts and distraught young women, many of whom found themselves expecting babies for men they were unlikely to ever meet again—some would die in war, others return to the wives they had left behind in England.

While a deeply religious Irish society was still trying to come to terms with the prospect of being overwhelmed by thousands of single mothers who brought shame on themselves and their families by producing bastard children, British soldiers were replaced by American troops. These brash, smartly dressed young men, fresh from training camps in the United States, were even more popular than the British among the Irish girls. They had good looks, smart uniforms, film star accents, and above all brought with them an apparently inexhaustible supply of luxury items never seen on this side of the Atlantic. The girls happily accepted cartons of cigarettes, silk stockings, radios, chocolates, chewing gum and cheap jewellery that the Americans showered on them; inevitably thousands more girls got involved in romances that lasted until the Americans departed Ireland in 1944 for the landings in France. There followed more unwanted babies, more broken hearts, more shamed families.

The presence of Allied troops in such large numbers in Ireland did not go unnoticed by the Germans. During bombing missions on English provincial cities, some of the aircraft continued to the North of Ireland to attack Belfast.

From the beginning of the occupation, the German Army paid Stanislaw for his coal in marks and that suited him while the occupation lasted for the German currency was much more valuable than Polish money. He used the cash to buy gold, silver, jewellery and paintings from people in Warsaw who had fallen on hard times. The gold and precious stones he concealed in a cache in his garden; the paintings he carefully wrapped and stored in the attic of a vacant house in Lubiala. The pictures would provide for his retirement, and for his son's future.

Krzysztof's mother was part of a group of women who tried to have the excesses of the German soldiers curbed by their superiors, especially attacks on girls and young women going to work and school. They were taken into the back of army trucks on the pretence of being searched for arms and subjected to all kinds of sexual molestation to satisfy the lust of their captors. Young women arrested for not having proper papers or failing to co-operate with the soldiers were held in an army and forced to co-habit with soldiers on leave from the Eastern Front.

His mother led a deputation to the Camp Commandant to complain about the behaviour of the soldiers and seek the release of girls who were held in the camp. The Officer received the deputation gracefully but scorned the charge that the women were there against their will.

"In every occupation," he said, "young women are naturally attracted to men in uniform. Poland is no different from any other country. "Any women who find themselves in the company of soldiers are there because of romantic attachment, not because of coercion."

Thereafter girls and women going to school and to work and even to church had to organise themselves in groups for protection Partisans hit back at the soldiers with night attacks on patrols, but this only resulted in indiscriminate killings of men on the pretext that they were carrying arms or plotting the movement of patrols for the Partisans.

The excesses of the Germans in Poland became too much for the gentle Justyna Walenski. After her husband left for the mine one morning she went back to bed with a glass of water and a handful of sleeping pills; she swallowed them one by one until they were all gone. In the quiet of her bedroom with death and deprivation raging all around her, she closed her eyes, entwined a rosary through her folded hands and allowed herself to drift off into a deep sleep. Her husband found her cold body that evening when he came home from the mine.

After her funeral Stanislaw made a will, placed it in a sealed envelope with other private papers in the vault of his bank and informed his solicitor of its existence and where it was located. He made a copy which he also signed and had witnessed and paid the bank a fee to have it sent via Switzerland to Sir Kenneth Montgomery in Ireland as soon as the war ended.

In the village of Sperrin Sir Kenneth Montgomery was feeling the pressure of war too. The Ministry men were not satisfied with the rate at which parachutes were leaving the mill. The need for them had become more urgent; they made no secret of the fact that the day was fast approaching when the British and Americans would go back to France and take on the German Army again.

At meetings with War Department, the messages to Sir Kenneth were always the same—push and keep *pushing for more production*. Bonus payments were introduced as an incentive to the workforce, allowing women working long hours to double their normal weekly wage.

He co-operated with the new regime under threat of losing control of the mill for the duration of the war. He worked long days and went home tired in the evenings. No matter how exhausted he felt, however, most nights he ended up in Emma's arms, leaving the troubles of the mill behind. She looked forward to nights of lovemaking in her bed not because she felt anything special for the man beside her but for her own pleasure and as an outlet for long pent-up emotions. She took control in bed, forcing him to do what she wanted, dominating him.

There was no love in the relationship. He had no illusions about that because she had made it clear from the beginning it was purely an arrangement and how far she was prepared to allow it to develop and for how long, he didn't know. He was enjoying life to the full again after years of emotional starvation and wanted it to go on forever. But at the back of his mind, he was conscious of the fact that she was young and might tire of him either as a lover or because she saw no future in a relationship with a married man. They were both acutely aware that he still had a wife—a sick wife—whom he could not abandon.

He figured there was one circumstance that might help prolong their affair. What if she became pregnant? A child might force them to stay together, if only for the selfish reason that Emma had nowhere else to go and would be completely dependent on him to look after her and a baby. They never talked about it but neither of them discussed or used any form of contraception and secretly he hoped that the inevitable would happen. She was young, she was healthy, and she had no inhibitions during their lovemaking.

A baby would change everything—his life, her life, their future, and especially the future of the Montgomery family and the mill. He had thought a lot about it and decided that if he had a baby, boy or girl, that child would inherit the bulk of his wealth, including the mill and his name. Whatever the consequences to his marriage he had his mind firmly made up about that.

But he was also conscious of the fact that pregnancy would bring to an abrupt end the cozy relationship they enjoyed at Mill Brae house. As the months passed Sir Kenneth found it hard to believe that his wife did not suspect what was going on despite the fact that loose-tongued servants were well aware that the master of the house regularly visited the English girl's bedroom.

A year after the affair with Sir Kenneth began Lady Eleanor still gave no sign that she was aware of what was going on between Emma and her husband. The warm friendship that existed between the two women when she first came to Mill Brae had long gone, but when they met at dinner the older woman was still polite to her.

Without company the days seemed endless especially when the dark wet winter evenings came. The only person Emma had to talk to was Sir Kenneth when he came home from the mill, often very late. They still moved to the smoking room after dinner but with the servants hovering about they had to be very guarded in what they said to one another.

Whatever suspicions Lady Eleanor harboured about her husband having an affair with Kate Reilly had long been dispelled. Kate was in a steady relationship with the young Pole, Walenski, and Sir Kenneth knew from her demeanour in the office that she was happy with life. Sometimes as he drove home in the evening he saw them walk hand in hand through the village so that she could catch the last bus home. He was glad she had found someone she was happy with.

Kate wondered about Sir Kenneth, what had brought about the radical change his life. Pressure from the War Department was still there but it didn't seem to be as much of a burden as it was before. He was more relaxed, happier in his work, even though he was busier than ever. And when evening came, no matter what problems there were, he did not dally in the office. Patrick was always parked downstairs at six o'clock, waiting.

He stopped drinking and the secretary wondered what had brought about the sudden change. She found it hard to believe that life in the big house with Lady Eleanor could have improved in such a short time. Still, she was glad that something had happened to change his miserable existence. And she was glad for herself, too, because she no longer had to listen to taunts about "doing overtime" with the boss.

Kate was friendly with the chauffeur, Patrick Kennedy. She sometimes helped him get Sir Kenneth into the car when he was drinking heavily. When she got an opportunity, she mentioned to him that Sir Kenneth seemed to be in much better form of late and had stopped drinking in the office.

"Have you not heard the rumours?" Patrick smiled. "The maids say that he is having an affair with Emma Johnston."

Kate took a deep breath. She had not heard and if it came from anybody other than Patrick she would not have believed it. The boss and Emma Johnston sleeping together in Mill Brae house! If that shrew of a wife of his found out she would throw the girl out—and Kenneth with her!

Kate thought of nothing else on her way home on the bus. For a long time he had been so unhappy, so lonely; that's why he had resorted to drinking rather than go home in the evenings. On occasions he was so starved of affection that when he came up behind her as she sat at her desk she sensed he was on the brink of throwing caution to the wind and putting his arms around her. But he was a shy man where women were concerned and even with the whisky he could not pluck up the courage to reach out to her.

Clearly, he had plucked up enough courage to proposition Emma Johnston, if what Patrick said was right. Kate had never met the English girl but from what Krzysztof said she seemed to spend her days around the gardens in Lough Brae mooning over flowers and plants and birds and bees. By all accounts she was a pretty little thing, about the same age as herself. They lived in the same house, so they were in close contact daily and perhaps that's how the romance began. More important, however, was the fact that she came from the same social class, moved in the same circles. This made them more acceptable to one another. If he was looking for a woman, a mistress, she had the right pedigree.

"The difference between her and me is that no matter how close we are in the office," she thought sadly, "to him I am still a common mill girl."

In bed at night she wondered what she might have done if he had made a play for her. She had never made love, so she could only guess what it was like. The only time she had ever been alone with a man was when she helped Krzysztof unpack some of his things at his lodgings; they sat on the bed to test the mattress. She had courted a bit and a few times got excited, but she always made sure to push her boyfriend away when she felt things were getting out of hand. She was terrified of getting pregnant, of having a baby. In a small town, pregnancy spelled disaster for an unmarried girl.

She wondered what it would be like, doing it for the first time with an older man. If he made a play for her would she have let him have his way? Would she feel dirty afterwards giving herself to a man old enough to be her father? Once when she was taking notes and he was a bit tipsy, she looked up and found him staring at her breasts and he blushed. That was the one time she might have taken the initiative herself, when she felt like getting up from her desk and putting her arms around him. If she had it could have been a beginning and who knows where it might have ended. He was a wealthy and a powerful man and whatever about his age he might have been glad to have her, and she might have been happy to take on the role of mistress.

But that was water under the bridge. According to Patrick bold little Emma from Yorkshire—her with the swinging hips and garden tips—had him in her clutches. And from the way he hurried back to Mill Brae House in the evenings whatever she was doing for him was working like a tonic.

"Well good luck Emma Johnston", she said tongue in cheek, "you'll need it when Lady Eleanor Montgomery finds out what's going on under her nose!"

She consoled herself that she had a man of her own, the waif from Poland whose rich family had sent him to Ireland to sit out the war, safe in the arms of the Montgomerys; and he was a lot younger than Sir Kenneth. After that first outing to the mountains she knew he was keen on her and they began to spend more time together. But their courtship progressed slowly; Krzysztof was busy carving out a career for himself at the mill, and she was busy keeping up with the extra workload created by the presence of the people from the War Department.

They were seeing one another for nearly two years before Krzysztof broached the subject of marriage; she accepted his proposal, but they disagreed over when it should happen. He wanted to get married right away and bide their time until the war was over in Europe when they could return to his homeland. She thought they should wait until the war was over before thinking of marriage and in the meantime, she secretly hoped he would get to like Ireland enough to stay there. In the end she had her way and they agreed to wait until war ended for Krzysztof was not even sure his parents were alive or that he had a home to return to.

Their relationship never got beyond cuddling and kissing; sometimes when they lay in each other's arms by the deserted mountain lake she felt good, happy to be with him but that was as far as she let herself go, never let things get out of hand. Even though he told her over and over how much he loved her, she would not allow him to become intimate with her, so terrified was she of having a baby.

Apart from the risk of pregnancy, Kate had another worry. She did not feel entirely secure in the relationship. Krzysztof was a foreigner—"the polecat" they called him in the village—and he intended to return to Poland. She was reluctant to commit herself to going with him. If she got pregnant they would be forced to marry and then what? If he decided to live in Timbuktu she would *have* to go with him.

She was also conscious of the fact that wartime romances seldom worked out for women. She knew local girls who had babies with British soldiers when they were stationed in Ireland. They had to leave home and go to England and ended up living in a dingy flat. When men were killed, girlfriends and babies were left in an economic and social limbo, single mothers forced to bring up children alone in a strange country, unable to come home to Ireland because of the stigma attached to an unmarried mother.

Gossip about Kate and her boss ceased and the talk among the mill workers shifted to rumours about goings on at Mill Brae House, about an affair going on between Sir Kenneth Montgomery and the

English girl, Emma Johnston, right under his wife's nose.

Lady Eleanor still gave no sign that she was aware of the gossip, but Emma knew it was inevitable that she would learn the truth and she was not looking forward to the confrontation that would follow. She decided what was needed was a diversion; a bold move that would give the wagging tongues in the village something else to talk about. She devised a plan.

She had met the good looking young Polish manager, Krzysztof Walenski, when he came with others to Mill Brae for meetings with Sir Kenneth. He had shown some interest in the gardens and sometimes she took him for a tour of the flower beds and shrubbery.

Emma felt this might be the time to get to know him better, let people see them together and give the impression they were more than acquaintances. So she started to visit him at his lodgings in the village. The first time she went there on the pretence that she wanted to make sure he was comfortably settled in; then she called because she 'just happened to be passing' on her way to the library; soon she was calling regularly in the evenings to see him. They talked about the war and their families and Mill Brae House and the mill. She always went there in daylight, making sure people saw her walking through the village to his lodgings. Krzysztof loved Emma's visits but was apprehensive about Kate and what she would think when she found out.

Emma made light of his worry. "Don't be silly," she laughed, "I'm sure Kate knows there is nothing going on between us, just as you and I know there's nothing going on between her and Sir Kenneth. Kate and Sir Kenneth work together; you and I are good friends."

Sometimes he walked part of the way back to Mill Brae with her. She flirted a bit with him in public linking her arm through his and kissing him goodbye as they parted company at the Gate Lodge. She did it deliberately to stimulate gossip, knowing people were watching. He liked her warm moist lips and she liked the feel of his strong arms around her. It brought back memories of Peter; he had held her so tightly it took her breath away. But that was all by the way—the most important thing was that the sight of them kissing in public would divert attention from her and Sir Kenneth.

The last time she visited his rooms he put on his jacket to walk her back to Mill Brae as usual, but she shook her head and told him to stay where he was. She had to go to the library on her way home and intended to spend some time there.

"Ah," he sighed, "does that mean I don't get my goodnight kiss?"

She turned her face to him and he put his arms around her and pressed his lips against her cheek. When she made no move to part, he took her face between his hands and gently brushed his lips from side to side over her mouth. Emma placed her bag and umbrella on a chair and put her arms around him.

"I think you are getting fond of me," she said.

Krzysztof moved his hands down her back to her buttocks and pressed his body against her. She stiffened.

"That's enough Krzysztof," she whispered.

"I just want to hold you a little longer," he pleaded.

When she relaxed, he pressed his lips against her neck. She tightened her arms around him and he drew her body upwards until her feet left the floor. He moved backwards, and they overbalanced and tumbled onto the bed. She laughed nervously as she landed on top of him. They were quiet for a while except for their breathing. The feel of him under her excited Emma and when he put his hands inside her sweater and touched her bare flesh, she closed her eyes and let the flush of blood from her breasts surge downward to her thighs.

Krzysztof opened his mouth to say something, but she put her finger to his lips and knelt over him. She pulled her sweater over her head and reached behind to unhook her bra. Krzysztof stared at the naked breasts hovering over him and pulled her down on top of him.

She pressed her soft lips against his and sucked his breath; suddenly he couldn't breathe, and his excitement turned to panic. For a moment he imagined he was back in the Kubinska house with Maria on top of him, gasping for air. It had happened one evening while his father was upstairs with her mother. That was the day he first found out that his father and Barbara Kubinska were lovers, and that Maria was his half-sister.

He tried to push Emma off, but she had her thighs planted firmly against his sides and he could not move her. She sensed his distress and took her lips away from his. She pressed her breasts to his face and held him like a baby against the warm flesh until she felt his body relax.

When he calmed down, she rolled off and sat on the side of the bed and peeled off her nylon stockings; she removed her skirt and lay down beside him.

"Now it's your turn," she said. He undid his shirt and trousers and dropped them to the floor.

"Love me," ......she framed her mouth to whisper Peter but stopped just in time. "Show me how good a lover you are, how much you want me."

It was his first time to make love and he was clumsy, and he could not find his way into her and she had to help him. Their movements became more and more frantic until his body could take no more and he collapsed on top of her, exhausted; when she got her breath back she pushed him off. He rolled over and they lay side-by-side, using the bed sheet to dry their perspiring bodies.

She turned over on her side and pulled his head to her and kissed him tenderly. "That was good, Krzysztof," she whispered, stroking his damp hair. "Kate is a lucky girl to have a man like you."

His head was still spinning from their frantic love making. "Emma, you are the only girl I ever made love to," he said. "I felt so clumsy. I know I was clumsy."

She got off the bed before he had time to say anything more. He watched as she picked up her clothes, dressed and ran her fingers through her hair to tidy it. He was still lying on the bed naked when she moved to the door. She picked up her knickers from the floor and threw them back to him.

"A souvenir," she laughed, "to remind you of a kiss that went too far."

Krzysztof's brain was in total confusion and his body still in a state of excitement after what they had done together. She was a beautiful girl and she had given herself to him and all he could think of was that he wanted her again.

But when his head cleared, and he sat up in the bed he began to have feelings of remorse. He could not help thinking that he had betrayed Kate and it made him feel bad.

He lay down on the bed again and buried his face in the pillow.

Walking back to Mill Brae, Emma regretted what she had just done. An affair with the Pole was not part of her plan, so how did it happen, how did she let it happen? Was it to make another conquest, to satisfy some craving within her for sexual gratification?

She had Kenneth Montgomery in her bed every night but with him she never reached the dizzy heights of passion that she did with her first love or with Krzysztof. When he put his arms around her as she was leaving she just meant to kiss him goodbye. Then something clicked in her brain and she could not stop herself from wanting more.

With Kenneth it was different—she was conscious she had to please him, to satisfy his lust for her. Was this the difference between an affair and being in love?

As the war progressed the Germans suffered more and more setbacks and became more vulnerable and the partisans in Poland took full advantage of their weakness. Innocent civilians paid a heavy price for partisan activity; the Germans struck back every time with indiscriminate executions. Still the Partisans continued to harass convoys of troops moving to and from the Russian Front.

The army liaison officer at the mines served Stanislaw with an order confiscating his house. He had no opportunity to recover the jewellery buried in the garden but made careful observations to ensure that if the ground changed he would still be able to locate the hole where he had buried it. He moved his paintings and personal belongings to Barbara Kubinska's house in Lubiala and made himself as comfortable as he could there.

Stanislaw's fears about the threat posed by the Partisans were confirmed when there was a major explosion deep in the mine. He arrived in the middle of the night to find flames bursting from the lift shaft. One hundred miners—many of them prisoners of war doing forced labour—were either killed by the blast or burned to death by the flames that swept upward along the coal roads from the bowels of the earth; others were buried alive.

The explosion created a fireball that moved upwards from one level to the next until it reached the lift shaft. It blasted everything in its path straight up the vertical opening and erupted like a volcano into the night sky. Water from underground streams filled the vacuum. Gradually the great man-made hole in the earth filled with black water, dousing the flames and sending occasional bursts of steam hissing up into the cold night air. Stanislaw cried as he watched the death throes of a mine turned into a mass grave by his own daughter and her fanatical comrades.

The massacre of miners, whose only crime was that they had been taken prisoner when the Polish Army surrendered, fitted in with Maria's policy of retribution against Poles who "co-operated with the German war effort".

"The Resistance have a duty to execute any Polish citizen who collaborated with the German war effort," she said.

"Collaborators!" he said angrily. "They were Polish soldiers, prisoners of war forced by the Germans to work in the mines."

"They could have refused to work and taken their punishment," she said coldly. "They chose to dig coal for the Germans and die collaborators."

Stanislaw stood up and glared angrily at her. "They have brainwashed you," he said. "They have turned you into a Communist Zombie!" He turned around and walked away.

She was furious and shouted after him: "We don't forget that you used slave labour to produce coal for the enemy."

Stanislaw felt the hair on the back of his neck stand up. His own daughter was threatening him.

WHEN LOVE IS BLIND

Emma forced her way through dense brush one evening on her way to the river when she came upon him kneeling on the grass, hook in hand, trimming the leaves off rods he had just cut. He was naked from the waist up and beads of sweat ran down his face and arms. He was so preoccupied with his task that he did not hear her coming.

"You're a busy man," she said.

Valentino turned his head around sharply at the sound of her voice; he was so startled that he missed the rod he was trimming in his left hand and the razor-sharp hook struck his wrist instead. He quickly dropped the hook and got to his feet when he felt hot sticky blood run through his fingers. He clamped his right hand over the wound to try and stem the flow.

"Oh God, I'm so sorry. I've made you cut your hand," she gasped, seeing blood spurting from the wound.

"It's all right," he stammered holding his good hand tightly over the cut. "I'll go down and wash it in the river and make my way home and have it fixed up." He knew from the amount of blood running through his fingers that it was a bad cut. He bent down to the ground and felt around for his shirt intending to wrap it around the wound to stop the bleeding. When he couldn't find it she picked it up and put it in his good hand.

'How the hell did I not hear her coming?' he thought angrily. 'The bitch must have sneaked up on me.'

"It's a bad cut," she said anxiously. "Come up to the house and let me dress it."

He shook his head adamantly. That was the last thing he wanted.

"It'll be all right in a minute when the blood stops," he said, wrapping the shirt around his arm. "I'll go down to the river and wash it." He wanted to get away from her as quickly as possible.

"You need a bandage," she insisted. "It's bleeding badly."

"I'll just get my hook and rods," he insisted, "and be on my way."

But she would not hear of it. "Forget about the rods and come here and let me tie something around it," she insisted. "You should go to a doctor—the cut is deep and should be stitched."

He put out his left arm to let her bind it. The sooner she got her way the sooner he could be on his way.

He felt her soft hands on his skin as she wiped off the excess blood and wrapped a piece of material around it tightly, securing it with a clip from her hair.

"The moment you get home take off the neck tie and if you do not go to the doctor, have somebody wash the wound and put a proper bandage on," she said. "Otherwise it will become infected."

When she had secured the wrapping, he thanked her. "I'll be on my way Miss," he said. "I'll just get my hook and rods together." He got down on his knees and felt around for the hook. Emma knelt down beside him on the grass and helped him gather the rods and held them together while he got a piece of string from his pocket and she tied it around them. She felt bad about being the cause of him cutting his wrist.

She picked up the blood-stained shirt and handed it to him. "Better not put it on," she said. "There's a lot of blood on it. Do you need some help? Can you find your way home?" she asked, concerned for him.

"I'm grand, Miss," he said when he had the bundle on his shoulder.

He slowly made his way through the bushes towards the river. She watched him until he disappeared along the embankment.

"What an extraordinary fellow," she said to herself.

He was confused and scared by the encounter. That was the English girl who was living with the Montgomerys. She often came through the Sally Garden on her walks to the river, but he always made sure he was well out of the way. The last thing he wanted was to be caught trespassing in the grounds of Mill Brae House.

She seemed a nice girl. There was genuine concern in her voice for his bleeding arm. And when she cleaned the cut and wrapped the neck tie around it, her touch was gentle. There was a beautiful lavender scent from her. Even though the neck tie was bloodstained when he put his nose to it he could still smell her perfume.

He would have loved to be able to see her. He knew from his sister she was in her early twenties and coming from the big house no doubt she would be prettily dressed. But what did she look like? He had no way of knowing what anybody looked like unless he could touch the features of their face with his fingers. He thought about nothing else on the way home except the lavender girl he had met by chance in the garden.

Emma was sorry she had startled him, but she had no way of knowing he was there before she stumbled upon him and clearly he did not hear her coming. Blindness was something she associated with old people like her aunt in Scotland, not with people like Valentino McKelvie. He was such a fine young man, handsome in a rugged sort of way, with solid square chin and strong features. He was nearly six feet tall, well built; and he was strong—she felt the hard muscles in his arm when she was binding his wound and he had picked up the heavy bundle of rods effortlessly with his good hand before he left.

A week after the incident she came upon another bundle of freshly cut rods and sure enough when she got to the bridge, he was there, white stick in hand, bandage on his wrist. He was pulling on the steel support rope to try and swing the bridge. He had heard her coming through the rusty gate earlier and concealed his hook and got out of the garden before she reached him. He wasn't going to be caught a second time. As she came closer, he turned around to face in her direction.

"I'm Emma from Mill Brae. How is the cut on your wrist? Can I have a look at it?" she said.

He reached out his arm and she took it in her hands and moved the bandage with her fingers to examine the wound underneath. It seemed to be healing but the bandage was badly soiled.

"That dressing has to be changed," she said. "It' will cause infection."

She held onto his arm, admiring the blue veins running up and down and the muscles on his biceps. She traced one of the veins, lightly stroking it with the tip of her finger.

"You have to look after that wound," she said, "and make sure you do not get blood poisoning."

Her skin was cool against his bare arm and the touch of her fingers excited him. She was stroking him, caressing his arm.

"Oh!" she said suddenly. The nerves in her arms were tingling. She let go and stepped back.

"Are you okay?" he asked.

"That was the strangest thing..." she started.

Valentino wasn't sure what the hell she was up to, jumping about like that.

"Your wrist is healing well," she said when she got over her surprise, "but be sure and get that dressing changed."

As she turned to leave, she remembered the rods in the garden. "The rods in the garden—do you want to come back and get them?"

"I do," he said. "I need them. I left them when I heard you coming. I don't think the Montgomerys would be too happy if they found me cutting bushes on their property."

"You don't have to worry," she assured him. "Nobody from Mill Brae comes here except me."

When they found the rods, she said: "It's getting late. I'll help you gather them."

They knelt down on the grass and together they gathered the rods into a neat pile. He was excited by the closeness of her, the sweet scent of her breath. It made him awkward and several times he bumped into her and when their arms touched, he felt her flinch.

"Are you okay?" he said, concerned.

"I'm not sure," she laughed. She took a couple of deep breaths. There was something odd about him. She couldn't believe it—every time she touched him she felt the tingle in her arms.

He put his hand out to find where she was and pulled it back quickly when his fingers touched her bare arm.

"Are you frightened of me?" she said, laughing. "I know you cannot see me but I'm not a witch."

"I'm not afraid," he laughed, "but I have no way of knowing whether you are a witch or not unless I can feel your face."

"Do you want to touch my face?" she asked.

He nodded. Emma took his rough hand and placed it firmly against one of her cheeks. She slowly moved it around her face, along the smooth fresh contours of her nose and eyes and forehead and chin.

"Now what do you think I look like?" she asked.

"Certainly not a witch—you have a pretty face," he said.

He let his fingers trace her shapely neck and ears and when she did not object he moved them to her shoulders and down her arms and across her chest until they brushed the cleavage in her dress. She took a deep breath when they touched the bare flesh of her breast.

"Let me try it," she said. "Let me feel your features with my eyes closed."

As her fingers traced the lines of his cheeks and nose and lips, a shiver ran down her spine. It was not an unpleasant feeling, but it took her by surprise, made her feel faint.

Her touch excited him and he placed his hands over the mounds of her dress, feeling the shape of her breasts through her dress. When she did not object he slid his fingers through a gap in the buttons of her blouse to the brassiere inside. She leaned backwards holding onto him for support. The feel of her bare shoulders excited him so much that he had a sudden urge to have her there and then, to take her whether she wanted to or not.

When she lay back on the grass Valentino realized she wanted it to happen between them just as it happened with Minnie and the others. She made no effort to resist his advances, not even when he knelt down on top of her, pinning her beneath him.

As he traced her waist and hips with his hands, she opened his shirt. He put his hand under her dress and roughly forced her undergarment down her thighs. She made a feeble attempt to struggle but it was too late—she could not escape the muscular body bearing down on top of her. She closed her eyes, let her legs fall to the ground and succumbed to his passion.

As she clung to him her mother's face loomed in front of her, screaming at her to stop and she panicked for a moment, but the lovemaking went on. Her head was spinning and her body out of control and she did not want to lose the intense feeling of pleasure it gave her. The faster he moved against her the more tightly she clung to him. Even when his passion was spent, and he went still on top of her, Emma still clutched in her arms, not wanting it to end.

Afterwards they lay beside one another for a while, the silence broken only by their deep breathing and the noise of water tumbling over the weir in the distance.

When she heard the laughter of children on the bridge she stood up. "I have to go," she said, retrieving her underclothes and fixing her blouse. "It's getting dark." There was a rustle of leaves and she was gone before he had time to reply.

When Valentino heard the squeak of the rusty garden gate he pulled up his trousers, buttoned his shirt and set off for the river. He retrieved his hook and stick but left the neatly tied bundle of rod behind. He had more important things on his mind than baskets. He felt great. He had just tumbled the little beauty from Mill Brae. Minnie was good, but this little English one was a real conquest. Jesus, nobody would believe had sex with the society girl from Mill Brae.

He chuckled to himself as he tapped his way home thinking about all those stuck up little bitches at the dances that wouldn't let him touch them—little nobodies who said his blindness turned them off. Well it didn't turn Minnie or the others off, and it certainly didn't turn the lovely young thing from Mill Brae off—and she was a real lady.

By the time Emma reached the house her passion had cooled, and she felt embarrassed and ashamed and frightened at what she had just done. How had she got involved with that man, a complete stranger? She was sorry for him because she felt responsible for the wound but how did she end up having sex with him? It was sheer madness. It was the second stupid mistake she had made inside a week. After the foolish romp with Krzysztof she vowed she would never compromise herself again yet here she was a couple of days later having sex with a man she had literally bumped into while out walking. What was wrong with her? Was it something inside her, some flaw in her personality?

In Blackpool, she had a torrid affair with the Jenkins, a man she knew nothing about. He had taken her in completely and it had cost her dearly but had learned nothing from her mistake.

She got involved with Kenneth Montgomery, a man who was supposed to be her guardian, the husband of her companion and friend. She got into bed with him rather than face the prospect of leaving Ireland.

She had seduced the gullible Krzysztof Walenski and convinced herself it was only to divert attention from Kenneth.

Now she had got herself involved with a blind man whom she had allowed—even encouraged if she was to admit the truth—to make love to her.

Where did she acquire this flawed pedigree?

THE MISTAKE

As part of the war effort Lady Eleanor opened her gardens and house to visitors to help raise funds to provide food parcels for servicemen languishing in German prison camps. Emma had become such an authority on the flora and fauna at Mill Brae that she was given the job of tour guide. The guests loved her lively animated voice, expressive eyes and the natural movement of her arms and hands as she described the plants and flowers.

Sir Kenneth was impressed by her knowledge of the proliferation of flora and the way her actions seemed to bring everything alive to her audience.

Flowers produced heavy pollen that hung over the gardens, trapped in the still air by overhanging trees; she invited the visitors to stop several times and fill their lungs with the scented air.

"Pollen rejuvenates the body, and turns your thoughts to love," she quipped. "What you are experiencing is the stuff that sweet dreams are made of, the very same odours that stirred the senses of the great pastoral poets and painters."

Krzysztof was invited to pay half a crown and join the last of the tours in the late summer of 1942. He wasn't very interested in flowers and plants but felt he had an obligation to support his boss's fund raising; it was also an opportunity to meet Emma again for she had not visited his lodgings since the evening they made love.

When the tour ended there were handshakes and congratulations for Emma. After the tour the guests were invited to afternoon tea but as they moved off towards the house she lagged behind to where Krzysztof was walking alone. She put her arm through his and they strolled together.

"You were not paying attention while I was talking," she said, as if reprimanding a schoolboy. "In fact, you looked quite bored."

"I'm sorry," he said. "My mind was on other things."

She suggested he should forget about tea and walk down to the river to enjoy the last of the evening light.

"There's always a cool breeze there and it will wake you up," she said.

He nodded but he was not really in the mood for talking; he was preoccupied with thoughts of home and especially about how his parents were faring after nearly three years of German occupation. She led him through the orchard and they edged through the rusty gate into the Sally Garden. She walked ahead of him, forcing her way through the bushes. She was strangely quiet, hardly saying a word until they emerged on the bank of the river when she asked if this was not the most beautiful place he had ever seen. He said yes to please her.

In fact, he knew that part of the river well from his evening walks with Kate. It was only a short distance from the swinging bridge where they watched fishermen upriver and children playing on the rocky river bed, searching for minnow stranded in summer pools. He did not feel the same with Kate since his sexual encounter with Emma—guilt hung over their relationship like a dark cloud. Kate noticed a change in his mood when they were together but when she asked him about it he lied that he was preoccupied with worry about his family in Poland.

Did Emma still want him? Is that why she took him walking to the river? He hoped so. Now that he was close to her again he wanted to reach out and touch her. They stood for a while near the swinging bridge, taking in the view. As dusk fell the air turned chilly. Looking at her bare shoulders he asked if she was cold.

"Time to go back," she said. He was disappointed but went ahead to clear a path for her through the bushes and she followed close behind, hands on his shoulders, guiding him towards the gate. When he paused she stumbled into him and he was conscious of her closeness. He had a sudden urge to turn around and kiss her. When she stumbled a second time he turned quickly as if to catch her, put his arms around her and pulled her close.

He was excited by the feel of her and imagined when she leaned against him that she was excited too. He kissed her, and she responded by pressing against him, the tip of her tongue darting in and out of his mouth. He used the palms of his hands to slide the shiny material of her dress upwards over her knees until his fingers touched the smooth of her thighs.

Valentino was in a sweat. He had been cutting rods when he heard voices and the noise from the rusty garden gate. He was about to tie his rods and head off home when he heard somebody coming. The only person who used that walk was the English girl. The place was so overgrown that he knew from experience that once he stayed away from the main track the chances of meeting anybody or being seen by anybody were nil. Just in case, he crouched low and kept still. Whoever it was, they were not alone. There were two voices, a man and a woman. He waited until they had passed and picked up the bundle to go.

Then he heard them again on their way back. He put the rods down again and knelt on the grass, waiting for them to pass.

In the silence he could hear water gushing over rocks in the river. He strained his ears to try and pick up the voices. One of them was definitely the English girl. She was with a man, but he did not recognise the voice. It might be the mill boss for there was talk that he was bedding the young one. They were laughing as they moved through the Garden. The voices were very close. Then there was silence; had they seen him? He pushed the rods aside and waited for one of them to say something.

"You have been teasing me all evening." The man's voice seemed very close.

'Jesus Christ what's happening', Valentino said to himself. His heart was pounding so hard it drowned the sound of the river. His trousers were wet from the damp grass and his legs were numb from kneeling.

The pair were talking excitedly to one another and though not too far away he couldn't make out what was said.

Suddenly he heard the woman's voice: "Stop!" Then louder, more insistent: "That's enough! Leave me alone!"

Now he knew what they were at. Many a dress had to be hoisted waist high in his back kitchen before he got down to business with his women. The English girl was no different—he had personal experience of that. When her companion spoke, he had a funny accent. It had to be the Polecat his sister talked about, the one working at the mill. Curiosity got the better of him when he realised what they were up to. He surmised the girl was about to get another tumble—and maybe she didn't want to get her pretty dress wet on the damp grass!

"She'll get a hell of a shock when her bare ass hits the cold ground," he chuckled. He was getting horny just thinking about her lying on her back among the bushes so close to him.

Krzysztof was excited too, whispering over and over how beautiful she was and how much he loved her and wanted her and how he had thought of nothing else since that evening at his lodgings. The pair went quiet for a while. Then Valentino heard her say: "I don't want to. I don't want to. Don't bite my neck!"

But Krzysztof he did not want to stop. He tried to force her onto the ground and when she resisted pulled the top of her dress down over her shoulders so that she could not move her arms.

Emma was in a rage. "You hurt me, you bastard!" she railed at him.

Her anger made him hesitate and she managed to free her arms from the dress and push him away.

"That was a stupid thing you tried to do," she said angrily.

"Don't spoil it," he pleaded. "I want you and I know you want me."

"You tried to rape me!" She roughly pushed him away and moved off towards the rusty gate.

This was getting good. She was upset, crying. Valentino held his breath to hear as much as he could before they went out of earshot.

"You asked me to come with you," he said as he tried to console her. "I thought you wanted me like you did before."

"I may have good reason to regret that evening," she said angrily. She stopped walking and turned around to face him. "You fool! I think I am going to have a baby!"

Valentino took such a deep breath of cool evening air that he had to cover his mouth with his hand to stop himself from coughing.

'This is going to be good,' he thought. 'The little bitch is up the pole. Why did she sound so surprised? Everybody knew about her and Montgomery. But nobody knew about her and the Pole nor about the day he himself tumbled her in the Sally Garden. No wonder she was in trouble'.

"I think I'm pregnant," she sobbed.

All he could think was to ask if she was sure.

"Of course, I'm sure, you fool! I'm pregnant and what's more," she said bitterly, "you might be responsible."

"Me!" he said in astonishment.

"I had been with Sir Kenneth for nearly a year and nothing happened. One time with you and I'm pregnant! You don't have to be an engineer to work that out!" she said sarcastically.

He was hurt by her outburst. "Why are you so angry with me?" he asked. "Whatever happened that day happened because we both wanted it. You make it sound as if I forced you."

"Keep your voice down or somebody will hear you," she snapped.

They moved off, but Valentino could still hear her railing at him. Once they went through the rusty gate, he heard no more; they were too far away.

When he was sure they had gone he stood up, unbuttoned his fly and relieved himself. He gathered the rods, made sure the twine was secure, slung the bundle over his shoulder, hooked his walking stick on the pocket of his jacket and slowly forced his way through the dense brush until he reached the river path. He took the cane in his right hand and tapped his way along the river bank as quickly as he could.

Inside the orchard, Krzysztof tried to make peace with Emma. If it was his baby, he told her, he would face up to his responsibilities. They would move away, get married and he would find work until the war ended when they could return to Poland.

"Kate will be hurt; so will Sir Kenneth, but in time they will get over it," he said. "The most important thing is for us to get married so that our child will not be born a bastard."

She turned to face him and put her hands on his shoulders.

"Let me make something clear," she said coldly. "I've had a lot of time to think about this. I'm not going to marry you. I'm not going anywhere with you. The only reason I told you is because we need to have an understanding. If I have a baby nobody is to know what happened between us, ever! If I have a baby it will be Sir Kenneth's. That's the way I want it. I will not have you involved in any way. You get on with your own life, back in Poland or wherever you want to and forget about me. My future is with Sir Kenneth and I will not tolerate you compromising me or complicating my situation any more than you already have by trying to create a relationship between us that does not exist."

The finality of her words shocked him.

"Whatever happened between us ends here," she said finally. "If you ever breathe a word I will deny everything, and it will be the end of you in Sperrin Mills."

He was astonished by the vitriol in her voice.

Inside the house they rejoined the last of the guests lingering in the dining room. Sir Kenneth approached her.

"You look very pale," he said. "Is something the matter?"

"It was dark when we were by the river," she lied, "and I got a fright when I heard somebody or some animal coming through the bushes. It was probably just a dog or a fox".

Valentino knew he had got an earful. There was gossip in the mill already about the English girl having an affair with old Montgomery; now he had it from the horse's mouth—they had been carrying on for ages. And did he hear right when she told the Pole that she was pregnant, and the Pole and not old Montgomery might be to blame for getting her into trouble? The little beauty wasn't even sure.

'If she came on to other men as easy as she came on to me,' he chuckled, 'sure anybody could be the father'. He might even be in there with a chance himself. He made a mental note to check back to the day they had sex in the Sally Garden, the week after he cut his wrist. If she had a baby, he would do a nine month count back just for the hell of it. Whoever the father was, she was in a right predicament. If she had been sleeping with old Montgomery all that time it was more likely he made her pregnant; there would be hell to pay when his wife found out. But what if it was the Polecat's kid? From the way she badgered him and warned him not to breathe a word about their affair she clearly did not want anybody to find out that she had been carrying on with the Pole.

Montgomery would have no reason to doubt her if she told him she was going to have a baby and he was the father; he wouldn't be the first man to have a cuckoo in the nest. Hadn't he himself put women from the street in the family way and their husbands were no wiser when the babies arrived. The main thing was not to talk about it. That's the mistake the English girl made, letting the cat out of the bag when she thought there was nobody listening.

He felt good about the secret to which he was privy. What he had overheard was important, very important, a major scandal involving one of the wealthiest families in the country; but only if her secret got out. If he divulged what he had heard would set tongues wagging but if it was traced back to him, he could be in big trouble. He was blind, but he was no fool—the private lives of gentry were not to be meddled in by the likes of him.

"Keep your fucking mouth shut, McKelvie," he muttered as he tapped his way home, "or you could end up in the height of trouble. Them mill people are a dangerous crowd to tangle with."

He was so preoccupied with the English girl and the Pole and Montgomery and the possibility that he himself might have had a hand in getting her pregnant that he momentarily lost his footing on the river path and fell sideways down an embankment. With his sally rods, white stick and lurid thoughts he tumbled head over heels and landed in a clump of nettles.

"Jesus help me!" he cried out as the poison from the stinging leaves brushed his bare face and hands and he got an instant burning sensation. The more he struggled to extricate himself and get back on his feet the more the nettles stung his bare face, neck and arms. His flimsy shirt and light trousers gave the rest of his body little protection. By the time he clawed his way back up to the grassy bank he was hurting all over—hands, chest, arms, legs and face. Worst of all was the excruciating pain between his legs—he had forgotten to button his fly after relieving himself in the Sally Garden and the nettles found their way to his crotch.

He put down the rods and felt around for his stick but could not find it and the pain from the nettle stings got worse. The more he rubbed his face and arms the more he suffered and in the end he had to abandon the search. He made his way home with difficulty, stumbling several times when he lost his sense of direction. As he walked the pain intensified and his skin started to blister. He cursed the nettles and swore at Christ and His Blessed Mother and St. Patrick for the agony they were putting him through. Passers-by who saw him staggering about cursing in the darkness shook their heads in disgust.

"Is there anything more obscene," a woman passer-by said to her husband, "than a blind man with too much drink on him?"

Before he even reached his front door, he called out to his sister for help.

"I'm stung from head to toe," he cried out. "For Christ's sake get me something quick before I die in agony."

When Jinny saw the state he was in she stripped him naked and covered his body in thick cream skimmed from the top of the milk can, smearing it liberally over the clusters of white blisters that had appeared all over his body. The treatment eased the stinging and exhausted by his ordeal and the pain he fell asleep; he woke up several times during the night groaning.

The cream helped ease the pain in his arms and legs, but he was still in agony with the stinging in his crotch. Even in the state he was in he could not get the hot little English girl out of his mind.

It took several days and a lot of cream to get rid of the ache from ugly blisters that covered his body. When he went back to retrieve his stick and rods they were gone, scattered by youngsters who used them to whip the tops of the long grass. He cursed the little bastards for destroying the fruits of a difficult day in the Sally Garden. He would have to go back for more, but he had to be careful. With all the goings-on there it was a dangerous place to be.

Valentino was bursting to tell somebody about his romp with the English girl. He could have a field day bragging about how he had tumbled the pretty little thing on the grass among the bushes. She was a real conquest, but he was not sure that anybody would believe him. They would demand proof and he was in no position to provide it. So, he did the sensible thing and kept his mouth shut.

Now that he knew she was having a baby he was in the same predicament. Who the hell was going to believe him? He might be proven right in the end, but that would not be for a long time yet—six or seven months at least—and people had short memories.

The truth was that he was too scared to tell anybody. If he blabbed about what he overheard between Emma Johnston and the Polish man it might get back to the people in the Mill and he would have the wrath of the Montgomerys on his head. It could even cost Jinny her job in the mill.

EMMA AND MOTHERHOOD

Emma Johnston was just as troubled as Valentino. She had made a serious mistake telling Krzysztof she was pregnant. He didn't have to know; she just blurted it out in a fit of anger. She had not told another soul, not even Sir Kenneth, about the baby. Her main worry was he would find out, for she could not rely on the fool Krzysztof to keep his mouth shut. If he told Kate it would be common knowledge in the mill. She had to tell him before he found out from somebody else.

So she told him about a nauseous feeling she had and asked him to take her to Derry to see in case she was pregnant. He was overjoyed by the news. It was what he had been hoping for since their affair began, and he felt sure that it was going to happen sooner or later. Emma was a healthy young woman and there was no reason why she could not produce children. He became very emotional at the prospect of becoming a father. After the trauma on his marriage and the years of disappointment, Emma was going to give him a child? That night after they made love talked excitedly about the possibility of their future with a son or daughter to share their lives. Next day he took her to the doctor and she emerged from the clinic to announce that she was three months pregnant.

"He thinks me a very stupid woman," she told Kenneth, "being so far advanced without realizing what was happening to me."

"This is wonderful news, Emma" he said, "a child in the Montgomery family after all these years, when I had given up all hope."

"Let's go to Belfast for the day and celebrate! It's a long time since you have had a shopping day."

"A last fling, you mean," she laughed. "Two things I have to remember from now on—not to put on too much weight and not to buy tight clothing."

Emma arranged another tour of the gardens at Mill Brae to raise money for the Red Cross Prisoners and entertained the guests indoors afterwards.

Although small in stature she was perfectly proportioned and used expensive clothing to show off her figure to the best advantage. As she sang for her guests Krzysztof looked in vain for some signs of pregnancy. She knew he was looking at her—they were all looking at her—waiting for something to pop from her dress when she hit the higher notes.

"I think everybody was a bit disappointed that my brassiere did not snap when I was singing," she said to Krzysztof when they danced together. "Don't deny it—I saw you staring at me."

She asked about Kate and how he was getting on at the mill and had he any word from home? She never once mentioned the row they had in the Sally Garden or her pregnancy. Krzysztof thought she looked radiant, more beautiful than ever.

She seemed perfectly at ease afterwards as the evening progressed. She sat close to Sir Kenneth most of the time and gave instructions to the servants as if she was the mistress of the house. Krzysztof found it hard to believe the youthful, good looking Emma was the boss's mistress.

"Krzysztof Walenski," he heard her calling from a distance, "come back to us!"

"I'm sorry," he blustered. "I was thinking about my family in Poland."

She regretted causing him embarrassment and apologised. "That was a stupid girlish thing I did just now," she said when they were alone, "calling attention to you. I know how worried you must be about your family."

Krzysztof put his arms around her shoulders, but she quickly pushed him away.

Her mood changed. "Remember what I told you last time we met," she rebuked him.

After that party the attitude of Lady Eleanor to both Emma and Sir Kenneth changed dramatically. The older woman no longer dined with them; she had her meals served in her bedroom and re-

126

fused to acknowledge the presence of Emma in the house. When they met, Lady Eleanor passed by as if Emma did not exist. One of the maids had obviously told her what was going on between her husband and Emma. To avoid confrontation Emma spent as much time as she could outdoors.

Sir Kenneth had agreed that the moment any unpleasantness arose, Emma would move out of Mill Brae to a new home he had made ready for her. It was a two-storey period house overlooking a lovely river with panoramic views of the hills of County Donegal and blood red sunsets westwards over the Atlantic Ocean. The house was nothing on the scale of Mill Brae, but big enough to accommodate her and a maid companion and Sir Kenneth when he stayed there, and far enough away from Mill Brae to allow them some privacy.

Emma felt bad about leaving Sperrin Mill. No matter how unpleasant the situation, she owed it to Lady Eleanor to show her appreciation for the wonderful time they had together, and she was conscious of the fact that she had hurt her friend deeply.

Before she left the house for the last time she found Eleanor in the sitting room.

"I'm going now," she said. "I came to say goodbye."

Lady Eleanor got up from the chair and without either looking at her or saying a word made her way to the fireplace and adjusted the chiming clock. When she was satisfied that it had the right time she walked out of the room to the front door, opened it wide, then turned and went upstairs to her bedroom. Emma watched until she disappeared around the turn on the stairway before she beckoned to the maids that it was time to go and they picked up her belongings and brought them to the taxi. The lady of the house had given Patrick Kennedy instructions that she was not to have the use the family car.

Emma breathed a sigh of relief when the taxi pulled up outside her new home, situated a respectable three miles from Mill Brae House on the other side to the town of Murrinbridge. Sir Kenneth was there to greet her.

"The place is sparsely furnished," he said "but after the baby is born, you can decide what you want to keep and what you want to discard. Considering the previous owner had a young family the house is in remarkably good condition."

Emma thought it a very comfortable place with a warm lived-in feeling. The garden had fruit trees and a few flowerbeds that had been well tended; during the winter she would design a new garden and have it ready for spring planting. The front sloped down to the roadway, but it had the advantage of being bathed in sunshine in the evenings when the weather was fine. Bay windows overlooked the road and the river beyond which formed the border between the Irish Free State and the Six Counties of Northern Ireland.

Living away from the village in the countryside was a novelty. When she settled into the house she went for walks in the evening. There was hardly any movement on the roadway apart from farmers going to and from the town with milk for the dairy. Even though it was early winter there was still a proliferation of blackberries, holly berries, red haws on hawthorn hedges, hips on wild rose bushes and a profusion of wild apples. On her walks she saw rabbits, foxes, hares, stoats, badgers, even rats and mice, dodging in and out of hedgerows and ditches, hiding among piles of fallen leaves until she passed. This was a time of full and plenty for animals and they made the most of it, feasting on grain left behind in the fields after harvesting, gathering damaged fruit, hazelnuts and acorns for the winter ahead.

Mill Brae was beautiful, especially its well-ordered gardens, but apart from the birds and occasional hedgehogs in the orchard harvesting windfalls there was little animal life there. Everything was so carefully manicured, so perfect, that fauna were regarded as intruders.

From her new home, well-tended fields stretched in every direction with differing shades of green turning the landscape into a patchwork quilt. There were winter crops of dark leafed kale and turnip, stacks of hay and straw for winter fodder and new grasses peeping through stubble left after the grain harvest. Nearer the river fields were sheltered by high hawthorn hedges but on the hilly land behind the house the landscape was criss-crossed by long lines of granite stone walls that stretched up the hillsides as far as the eye could see. Cattle and high-spirited horses still grazed in the fields and where the land was poorer sheep cropped the short winter grass.

On cold mornings after heavy night dew, some fields were covered with hoarfrost, spread over the grass like a white net. A farmer explained that it was not frost at all but a giant shroud of spiders' web with dew clinging to it. How many millions of the tiny insects had it taken to complete such a mammoth task, she wondered? And where did the minions disappear to when the dew dried, and the morning sun stretched the silken strands to breaking point?

As her pregnancy progressed Emma became more and more excited at the prospect of having a child of her own. She did everything the doctor advised. She wanted a strong and healthy baby and most of all she wanted to be fit and healthy herself to look after it.

She ate carefully to make sure she did not gain too much weight, did the prescribed prenatal exercises, and continued with the daily walk even when the weather was not good. Time passed slowly but she was bursting with life.

It was lonely living in isolation in the countryside as the days got shorter. She missed the company of the big house—fussing maids, people who came every day with supplies, visitors from the mill in the evenings. To relieve the boredom, she made a couple of trips to the mill office and introduced herself to Kate Reilly about whom she had heard so much.

Kate avoided any reference to her obvious pregnancy. But Emma quizzed her about how she was getting on with Krzysztof and teased her about the sound of wedding bells in the air. Kate put her off saying wartime was not a good time to make plans.

Emma did not feel comfortable with Kate. The Secretary had very little to say and was not very forthcoming when Emma asked if she had been to Mill Brae House recently.

"Krzysztof Walenski goes there occasionally for meetings of management," she said, "but I have no business there."

Emma felt Kate was not all that enamoured with her visits. She always brought a tray with tea and biscuits but seemed reluctant to chat. She spent her time typing and filing and making short visits to Sir Kenneth's office to take dictation. Emma never went into the boss's office and when he emerged occasionally he had a polite conversation with her but did not dally because other people working near Kate could overhear anything said between them.

Emma wondered if Krzysztof had told Kate about her visits to his lodgings in the summer. Could that be the reason for her coolness; or was it possible Kate was jealous of her and Sir Kenneth?

There had been talk in the past about a liaison between Kate and Sir Kenneth, but Emma didn't believe it at the time. Was it possible they did have an affair, carried on during those evenings when she claimed she was doing overtime and he did not arrive home for dinner until a late hour? Certainly, Lady Eleanor believed that Kate was more than a secretary to her husband.

As the end of her pregnancy approached, Emma had a cook who came daily to prepare meals. Sir Kenneth visited two or three times a week in the evenings. Her doctor came once a fortnight. Apart from that she had no other company. When she could no longer hide the baby bump she had to stop the visits to the mill and curtail her walks. Then snow fell in the middle of December; Sir Kenneth was terrified that she might take a fall on the ice and harm herself or the baby, so she was forced to stay indoors altogether.

She spent hours pacing around the house, feeling the baby moving inside her or silently gazing through misty windows at the frost covered countryside stretching down to the river and upwards again on the other side to the Donegal Mountains. She never tired of looking at the sunsets with their fiery orange rays pouring through the front windows of the house. The warm brightness provided a welcome contrast to the blanket of winter whiteness that lay like a shroud over the countryside. If she closed her eyes she could still remember the fragrance that hung around the fields and country lanes when she first came to her new home in late autumn. She loved going out early in the mornings while dew was still heavy in the fields to pick big white mushrooms that sprouted from the earth during the night. But her favourite time was evening when the fragrance of wild fruits and damp grasses produced an odour so powerful that it dulled the senses. She called it "the Fermentation of the Fall".

A HARD WINTER

The winter of 1943 was a particularly harsh one in Europe. The Germans, under pressure on all fronts, fought fanatically to hold on to territory they had taken during the first heady years of conquest. Though the Russians had broken the two-year siege of Stalingrad and American marines had got a foothold in Italy it was clear to the Allies there was still a lot of fighting to be done before they could see an end to the war.

Raids by the Luftwaffe on London and other British cities eased and the British and Americans took advantage of the lull to retaliate with heavy bombing raids on German cities. Carpet bombing made life hell for German civilian populations already plagued by food and fuel shortages as the tide of war turned against them. The destruction of their cities wrought havoc on the shell-shocked German population and left 20 million homeless in the depths of winter.

In Ireland, where cold weather snaps normally lasted for only a couple of days before the rains came to wash snow and ice away, the early winter snowfall lingered because of uncharacteristic low temperatures. More heavy falls of snow came after Christmas causing deep drifts that made roads impassable. Schools and factories had to close and the movement of goods and people by road and rail came to a standstill. Communities isolated in the countryside were forced to live on what meagre supplies they already had, supplemented by what they could use from their own produce.

Emma took to writing letters to pass the time—to her mother, her sisters, even to Krzysztof.

She lied to her mother that she had left Mill Brae House because Lady Eleanor had regained good health and was now able to manage her own affairs. She had moved to a house nearby and was working there for Sir Kenneth Montgomery. She made no mention of the fact that she was his mistress, or of her pregnancy, for she knew it would only add to her mother's woes and confirm to her father what he already believed, that his daughter's morals were sadly lacking. Neither did she mention her true situation in letters to her sisters, for she couldn't trust them to keep a secret.

Krzysztof was not to be trusted either. Though she warned him never to mention their liaison to anybody, he might have told Kate in a fit of remorse. This would explain her coldness on her last visit to the Mill.

In the final month of her pregnancy Sir Kenneth came most days after work and stayed the night. The maid, Ethel, took advantage of his arrival to have evenings off so that she could meet her friends in Murrinbridge even though it meant a two-mile trudge through the snow to get there and back. Once when she came home earlier than usual, she found Emma asleep in Sir Kenneth's arms in front of the fire. She left them. They would wake soon enough when the fire died and freezing temperatures outside permeated the room.

Prolonged disruption of supplies caused by the harsh weather meant that people living in the countryside and in isolated villages had to make their way to town on foot once a week to fetch the necessities of life. Saturday was the day they went to stock up; Emma was fascinated by women passing along the roadway outside her house with prams laden with bags of coal and logs slung underneath. Some of the prams had babies in them with groceries piled on top. Men with handcarts ferried coal to those who were too old or too ill to make the journey to town.

In the stillness, she could hear the laughter of the women and children. Everybody seemed to be having a great time despite the hardship caused by the weather. Children made the most of the unexpected school holidays. The youngsters rode makeshift sleighs and squealed as they pelted each other with snow; even the dogs joined in, adding to the excitement with their hysterical barking.

She envied the women, surrounded by happy children, having such a good time. It made her think about her own baby, wondering whether it would be a boy or girl. Would it be like her? Friends would tell her it was the image of Sir Kenneth. That would be something! For she was not even sure he was the father.

Kenneth told her he had made an appointment to see his solicitors about a new will to provide for her and the baby. Boy or girl he assured her, the child would not want for anything. He hoped it would be a son to carry on the tradition at the mill but if it was a girl, he joked, there was nothing to stop Emma having a son for him in the future.

The waiting seemed endless as the time for the birth approached and the only thing she had to look forward to was Kenneth's arrival in the evenings when they cuddled together in front of the fire and made plans for the future. For the first time Emma felt her life beginning to take shape. She had a man who adored her and would take good care of her she had a home of her own and soon she would have a baby of her own. The only thing that stood in the way of complete happiness was the fact that her lover still had a wife. If there was no Lady Eleanor she would willingly marry him.

The mill boss went to Mill Brae at some stage every day to attend to the staff and deal with problems. He stayed a couple of nights a week when he was working very late. Even though their paths crossed occasionally and sometimes they had dinner in the big dining room and talked about problems arising from the severe weather, Eleanor never mentioned Emma or her pregnancy.

Just before Christmas Lady Eleanor had an unexpected visit from a young man from the Montgomery family solicitors. He apologised for not giving her more notice but a "delicate matter" had arisen affecting her property rights and the firm felt she should be informed about it immediately.

"Sir Kenneth recently made a new will which radically changed the terms of the one he made after his marriage," he informed her when they were seated in her husband's office.

"He made no mention to me of any change to his will," she replied.

"Nevertheless, major changes were made," said the young man as he fumbled in his briefcase for the relevant paper. He briefly outlined the changes and spelled out the provision of an income for a Miss Emma Johnston of Leyland House, Templemount, Murrinbridge, "and for any children she might have, whether legitimate or illegitimate, of which Sir Kenneth was the father". If Miss Johnston had male issue the eldest son would inherit the mill and the bulk of his estate; if there was only female issue, then the bulk of his estate would devise to the eldest daughter. Provision had been made for a substantial payment by way of lump sum to his wife together with an annual income for life and a life interest in Mill Brae House.

Lady Eleanor was taking such heavy doses of medication at that particular time that she found it hard to take it all in, and did not seem to react to the news, much to the relief of the young solicitor, who had been warned by his superiors to expect a scene. He left her a copy of the will to peruse at her leisure, wished her a Happy Christmas and gave a sigh of relief as he went through the door.

After he left, Eleanor made her way to her bedroom, placed the unopened envelope in the bureau with her personal papers and turned the key.

Snow and frost persisted through Christmas into the New Year. As Emma's time to give birth drew near, Kenneth engaged a midwife to visit daily. The nurse, Helen Flanagan, had lived all her life in the district and knew every family. She was a good-humoured woman in her mid-thirties, married young with two growing children.

She told Emma that the previous three years had been the busiest time of her nursing career. There were babies coming every day and she reckoned it was "God's way of replacing all the people who were being killed in the war." In Murrinbridge girls appeared to have thrown caution to the wind, carried on affairs with soldiers and ended up with babies they didn't want and couldn't care for. Every week infants were handed over to orphanages for adoption.

"Imagine giving away your own flesh and blood," said Helen, "just to keep parents and the local priest happy. To tell you the truth I think they'll rue that in the years to come when those kids grow up and start looking for their parents."

When Emma pointed out that she was not married Helen could have kicked herself. That's what she got for talking too much; she had put her foot in it and was embarrassed. Her husband had

134

warned her several times not to talk so much or she would end up in trouble. Helen found it hard to take his advice—she talked a lot because she loved to talk.

"But ...you won't be giving your baby away ...to some stranger," she said trying to paste over the blunder. Emma smiled. She was not offended.

The nurse babbled on about people she knew and babies she delivered and marriages and deaths and even ghosts that haunted houses. She was a great talker; she had to be careful not to put her foot in it again.

She decided to give Emma a laugh.

"There is a big scandal in Murrinbridge at the moment," she confided, "about a man who runs a green grocery. Apparently when women came in to make purchases he propositioned some of them to let him have his way with them. He has the reputation of being a bit of a Valentino."

"And would you believe it," she laughed, "after taking his pleasure he had the nerve to charge them for their potatoes and vegetables!"

Emma broke into such a fit of laughter that Helen had to warn her to ease up or the baby would come there and then.

"That's only the half of it," she went on. "Whatever he had, the women came back again and again—apparently they couldn't get enough of him and it now transpires that he has fathered several babies. The parish priest is fit to be tied over the scandal for if it reaches the ears of his bishop he will be the subject of a very quick transfer—to Africa or Australia or some other God forsaken country. Bishops are not happy with priests who cannot control their flocks."

Neither woman could contain their laughter.

"What's going to happen to Valentino?" Emma asked when she got her breath back.

"Not a thing, "Helen quipped. "He's going to get away with it—because he's blind!"

Helen was so busy talking she did not notice Emma's sharp intake of breath, or the pallor of her cheeks change at the mention of the blind man who had the green grocers in Murrinbridge. Emma had almost succeeded in erasing the memory of her tryst with him in the Sally Garden. Now at the mention of his name the spectre of that stupid liaison came back to haunt her.

When she recovered her composure, the Nurse was still talking, explaining how husbands of the women he compromised threatened to unceremoniously deprive him of his manhood but were afraid to go near him for if the police were called it could all end up in the courts with a trial and witnesses and the whole sordid story would be out in the open. So, what could cuckolded husbands do except swallow their pride and make sure their wives bought their vegetables somewhere else.

"Of course, the poor man's love life has suffered greatly," she said tongue in cheek, "and he's not the only one—from what I hear, some of the women are sorely missing their steamy sessions with him in a store behind the shop."

Emma smiled, but she did not feel like laughing any more. She sat back on the sofa and closed her eyes.

Helen noticed the change in her. "Are you all right?" she asked. "You look pale."

When she opened her eyes again, she said: "I'm fine, just the baby moving,"

After a brief silence, she spoke again. She wanted to be sure the nurse was talking about the same man. "You know, Nurse, I think I might have seen that blind man. He was pointed out to me on the very first day I arrived in Ireland. And I saw him a couple of times afterwards, by the bridge over the river behind Mill Brae House. Does he have red hair?"

"The very man," the nurse confirmed. "That's Valentino McKelvie. He goes up to the Sally Garden regularly to cut cane to make baskets.

"You had a lucky escape!" she laughed. "He is a terrible man for the ladies."

After the nurse had gone Emma put her face in her hands and rested her head on the kitchen table. She felt uneasy and it had nothing to do with the baby kicking her from within. The story about the blind man had her worried. According to the nurse he deceived several men by having affairs with their wives and got away with it. She deceived one man but if he ever found her out, if he learned of her liaison with Krzysztof or worse still with the blind Valentino she might not get off so easily. If Kenneth suspected for one minute that she had sex with either the Pole or the blind man around the time she became pregnant, she was finished.

Temperatures plummeted below freezing point over the Irish countryside. Inside Emma and Kenneth snuggled beside one another on a sofa drawn close to the big fireplace when she had her first contraction. She knew what to expect and started to breathe through the pains. When the second contraction came she cried out. She was frightened by the severity of it and panicked, clutching at Kenneth. He summoned Patrick Kennedy and sent him to Murrinbridge to fetch Helen.

Helen reassured Emma that there was nothing to be frightened of. With a first baby it could be hours after the first pains before the baby came. So together they did the breathing exercises. Patrick Kennedy went off again to fetch the doctor.

Emma's anxiety eased with Helen's arrival, but the contractions got much more frequent and the pain made her cry out. A panic-stricken Ethel watched anxiously as Helen stood in front of the sitting room mirror calmly gathering her long black hair into a pile on top of her head, talking all the time. She tucked it under a white nurse's cap and secured it neatly with pins extracted one by one from between her teeth. Even with the pins in her mouth she never stopped talking. She did everything so slowly and deliberately that Ethel felt like screaming at her to forget about her hair and help Emma.

When the last hairpin was securely in place she put her hands on her hips. "Now, girl," she said, "this baby might come quickly and give us a surprise. From the progress it has made so far, I don't think it's going to be a difficult birth and please God I'm right. So, we won't attempt to move you upstairs to that cold bedroom. Instead you're going to have your baby here on the rug in front of a warm fire. Ethel and I will ease you down off the sofa onto the floor as soon as we get a few sheets under you."

Emma gritted her teeth as the pain grew more intense and though she writhed in agony and groaned at the worst of her ordeal she never lost faith in the woman in the immaculate royal blue and white uniform at the end of her bed, encouraging her to bring her baby into the world.

By the time the doctor arrived Emma's baby was well on its way. Helen assured him there was nothing to worry about—everything was coming along nicely. The elderly man knew from long experience that when Helen Flanagan attended a birth he was more or less an observer, poured himself a drink and sat down and watched his patient's progress. He marvelled at the deftness of the nurse's hands as she massaged the young mother's body, coaxing the baby from the womb. She never stopped talking, telling Emma to take deep breaths, when to push, when to relax and in between commenting on the weather, the war, how she fell off her bicycle while cycling in the snow and scraped her knees...she hardly gave herself time to draw breath.

The doctor nodded off with the whiskey and had to be roused by Ethel when the baby slipped into the world. Helen had the new born in her hands holding it by its feet. The doctor knelt down beside the exhausted Emma and cut the umbilical cord; Helen took the baby away to wash it while the doctor attended to the new mother. When Helen returned with the little bundle wrapped cosily in a blanket the doctor had a quick look to make sure he was okay before the nurse placed him in Emma's arms.

"A perfect little boy," Helen told her, settling him snugly on a pillow beside his mother. Helen turned the bundle around so that Emma could get a good look at her son.

The nurse sponged Emma's body, cleansing it of the blood and sweat of childbirth. The doctor found Sir Kenneth in the kitchen anxiously waiting for news. Patrick had told him not to expect anything until he heard a baby crying so he was surprised when the doctor suddenly appeared.

"Congratulations," he said shaking hands, "You have a son, a fine healthy lad; he and his mother are both well."

Sir Kenneth could not conceal his joy as Helen lifted the little bundle from the bed and placed it in his arms.

"Now Ethel," she said to the maid, "Emma has done her job. You and I have work to do." She nodded to the maid and the pair left the room to allow the new parents time to admire their baby.

"I have waited a long time for this day—the most wonderful day of my life," he said when they were alone. Tears of joy welled up in his eyes. "I will remember this day for the rest of my life," he said proudly, "and I owe it all to you Emma."

"I'm so happy it's a boy," she said. "I know you wanted a son."

The doctor interrupted them briefly to say he was leaving, and Helen and Ethel took the opportunity to congratulate Sir Kenneth on his son. The new father insisted that they all join him to toast the occasion and when Ethel brought glasses he poured liberally from a whiskey bottle and they drank to the health of the boy who would carry forward the Montgomery family name.

"Have you thought about a name for him?" Helen asked Emma.

"He will be called Mark after his great grandfather," she said, "the founder of Sperrin Mill."

Emma had no well-wishers calling, nobody to socialise with and nobody to show off her son to except Kenneth, so she decided she would feed the baby herself. Helen thought it a great idea.

"But you will have to be patient," she said. "Mothers think it happens naturally and sometimes it does but more often baby has to be taught how to feed properly."

In the weeks that followed Helen spent a lot of time with the new mother to make sure she was comfortable with the baby and that he was getting enough milk. She stayed with her at night and left Templemount in the mornings to continue her work as district nurse and see to the needs of her own family. Emma knew the arrangement would not last forever, but she was determined to hang onto the genial nurse's company as long as she could.

The boy was christened Mark Anthony Montgomery. A rector friend of Sir Kenneth braved the snow and ice to perform the baptism privately at the house. One of the Ministry men at the mill was Godfather and since Emma had no family in Ireland she asked

Helen to be Godmother. They had a meal prepared by the cook and toasted the baby with champagne and when the company got a bit merry Helen regaled them with stories about the funny situations she found herself in as a midwife. The rector was so taken by her performance that he urged her to write the stories down for he felt they were the sort of thing that people wanted to read during these dreadful times, something to give them a laugh and raise their spirits.

Alone with the boy, especially at bath times, Emma gazed at the tiny smiling child, looking for some sign of recognition. The harder she looked the more confused she became. Sometimes she imagined he was like Sir Kenneth, blue eyes smiling back at her; but other times he had the darker, foreign look of Krzysztof about him. In the end she gave up—he was just too young to tell. Then she noticed that the little bit of hair that appeared to be brown; that frightened her. She did not want to entertain the possibility that red headed Valentino might be the father.

"Do you think he is going to have brown hair?" she asked Helen.

"It's hard to say," was the reply. "Babies' hair colour changes. Some are born with black hair and turn fair. Others start out fair and darken as they get older. Mark's colour will more likely change by the time he is a year old.

"Please God it doesn't stay red," she said after the nurse had gone.

THE THAW

The frost and snow stayed a long time. Fields were still white in March when buds should have been on trees and land tilled and ready for planting. Supplies of coal were scarce because of the war and even when other fuels like coke and turf became available there was no transport to move it. Heat was provided for houses in the town by the local gasworks which managed to operate for a couple of hours a day. An army of unemployed men were put to work felling trees and chopping firewood. Families were limited to a couple of sacks of wood a week which they augmented by scouring the countryside for trees brought down by storms. Turf hauled from mountain bogs on sleighs helped provide a little warmth in houses bombarded night and day by sub-zero temperatures.

The freeze that held the countryside in its grip did not affect the warmth and joy within the confines of Leyland House. Emma was so happy, and her time was so taken up looking after Mark that she hardly noticed what was happening outside. The Nurse came every day and brought news from the town and checked that the baby was progressing as he should. Kenneth came every night from the mill and insisted on spending time with the baby before Emma put him to bed. Helen remarked to friends that she was sorry they were not married for they were one of the most handsome and loving couples she had ever met.

Kenneth told Emma that he had drafted a new will which his solicitors were perusing and when they were satisfied everything was in order, he would call to them and sign it.

On the morning of St. Patrick's Day 1944 Emma was awakened by the crash of breaking glass and Ethel came into her room in her nightdress shouting that the roof was falling in. Emma grabbed the infant from his cot and slid under the big bed, shouting at the terrified girl to get in beside them. They heard creaking timbers followed by a scraping noise and then another crash of falling debris. Ethel was crying hysterically. Emma crouched over the baby holding him tightly under her shoulder and held her breath to see what would happen next. There was a long silence broken only by the sobbing of the terrified maid.

"Whatever it was," Emma said after a while, "I think it's over."

She left the boy under the bed and slid out. Everything in the room was intact.

Outside snow and ice was piled against the back of the house and the lean-to glass sunroof had collapsed under the weight of it. She understood what had happened. The thaw had finally begun and snow and ice that had accumulated on the roof of the main house since the storms had slipped off and crashed to the ground, wrecking the glass annex on the way down.

Outside she saw long icicles break off the eaves of outbuildings and clumps of snow tumble from the branches of trees and shrubs.

There had been no sign of a thaw the night before but now at first light pools of water from melting snow had already formed in the fields. The whiteness that had enveloped the countryside for so long suddenly changed to a grey slush.

Emma got back into bed, cuddled the baby and fed him before handing him to Ethel to change and dress. Though she got a fright from the crash of the snow from the roof she was glad that the thaw had come. In a few days when the land warmed, snowdrops and crocus and daffodils would appear as the countryside to catch up on a late spring.

She had been confined indoors for so long that she was anxious to be out and about with the baby and looked forward to resuming her walks as soon as the spring sunshine appeared. She had plans to go to Belfast to buy clothes for the boy, and a new wardrobe for herself. She felt good; she felt healthy; and Mark was getting bigger every day.

She still had one major personal problem to deal with—how to tell her family that she had become the mistress of Sir Kenneth Montgomery and had a baby. She could not put it off any longer. She sat down and wrote the letter she knew she should have written long before he was born. It would have to be straight and to the point—whatever the consequences.

Emma thought about the shock her mother would get when she read the letter. She opened the envelope again and read what she had written to see if she could change the words to soften the blow. But there was no easy way to tell her. At least now she would know they had a grandson. She resealed the envelope and left it on the mantelpiece for Ethel to post next time she went to town.

Once the thaw started, snow and ice melted quickly as the cold front that had hovered over Britain and Ireland for months finally retreated eastward to Europe, still in the throes of war. Temperatures moved upwards as mild air from the Atlantic brought warm misty rain to the Irish countryside. After two days, the only snow still remaining was piled behind hedges in fields, the remains of deep drifts that had built up during the storms. The snow was replaced by ribbons of water congregating in low lying areas before draining downhill through ditches and streams until they eventually tumbled into the river.

Melt water ran quickly off the higher mountains and hillsides, gouging deep channels in the soil until it formed torrents of heavy brown liquid that tore at the roots of trees and bushes as it rushed downward. The sheer volume of water brought rocks and trees and bushes with it. Sheep and goats and cattle in its path were swept away in the foaming mud.

Emma had fires lit throughout the house to get rid of the dampness. She could not venture outdoors for Leyland House was surrounded by water flowing downhill from the land behind. Through the bedroom window she could see great pools trapped in the surrounding fields waiting for stone ditches to give way and release them from their unnatural prison.

By evening the river in the valley below had swollen to the limit of its low banks and towards dusk she saw it overflow and spread out onto meadows on either side. When darkness came she saw farmers in the fields with lanterns, driving animals to higher ground.

That night Kenneth phoned and told her not to wait up for him. He had to stay at the mill to keep an eye on the level of water in the mill race. He was not sure what time he could get away; if he was very late, he would spend the night at Mill Brae; flooded roads made travel difficult, especially in the dark.

Next morning Emma awoke to find water flowing past the house on either side. Ethel was already downstairs and called up to her that all the rooms on the ground floor were flooded. From the window they kept vigil all day as the lovely, normally lazy meandering river in front of the house rose higher and higher until it was transformed into a raging torrent; the roar from the seething mass of water was so frightening Emma closed the windows to shut out the noise. Water swamped the fields on either side of the river and invaded low-lying houses and farmhouses.

The water was black and foreboding. Uprooted trees bobbed up and down like corks, and bales of hay and straw were swept along on the strong current. Bloated bodies of cattle and horses and sheep rolled over and over on waves of dark brown foam.

She handed the baby to Ethel and tried to ring the mill again, but the phone was still dead.

"All we can do is wait and hope that somebody will come to fetch us before dark," said Emma, as much to calm her own nerves as to console the frightened maid.

There was not enough dry wood to rekindle the bedroom fire, so Emma went back to bed with the baby to keep warm. The maid closed the window drapes to retain as much heat as possible; it also helped muffle the roar of the river. Emma sang nervously to the baby.

Ethel prayed a lot. Emma could hear her in the next room.

"Blessed Mother of God protect us and this innocent child from the flood!" "Mother of God intercede with your Son to save us!" "Saint Brigid save us from a watery grave!" "Saint Patrick ...." She didn't finish.

She came into Emma's room, terror in her eyes.

"Don't worry," Emma tried to reassure her, "help will come soon. When Sir Kenneth realises our phone is dead he will come to fetch us. He will come. You'll see."

The maid was on her knees, rocking backward and forward.

"The nuns told us at school that when the end of the world comes the earth will go up in flames," she whimpered. "But St. Patrick got a promise from God that Ireland will be saved from the flames. Ireland will be covered with water and we will all drown; for St. Patrick says death by drowning is far less painful than being swallowed by flames."

"There will be no need for St. Patrick to intervene," said Emma. "The master will be here soon."

Waves of water from melting snow tumbled from the Sperrin Mountains into the narrow valley drained by the River Murrin. When the normally docile river could no longer contain the volume within its watercourse it overflowed onto fields on either side. As it approached the town of Murrinbridge the floodplain disappeared, and the swirling mass of foaming water funnelled into a narrow gorge between man-made earthen embankments on either side. Trees and debris from upriver farms clogged the arches of the old bridge, threatening to demolish it; the town Council recruited an army of volunteers to fill thousands of sandbags to reinforce the town's flood defences. American troops from a nearby camp pitched in to transport the sandbags to the river and army engineers advised where to locate them along the most vulnerable stretches of the earthworks.

The river level continued to rise as the hours passed. The situation became so critical that police advised families living in low-lying streets to evacuate to higher ground until the emergency was over.

The earthworks had been breached twenty years before during a similar snow melt. Whole streets had been levelled on that occasion by a wall of water that swept through them and had it not been for a timely evacuation there would have been serious loss of life. In the intervening two decades the embankments had been raised and strengthened and the riverbed deepened but such was the volume of water now forcing its way through the town that people heeded the Council's warning and sought refuge with relatives or moved into church and school halls well away from the danger area.

Three miles upriver the rampant floodwater caused immense problems at Sperrin Mill and Krzysztof and Sir Kenneth spent an anxious night as it surged down the millrace, driving the giant millwheel faster and faster until it spun at twice its normal rate. Engineers did everything they could to slow it down but as the hours passed and the volume of water increased their task became impossible and they were forced to let it spin out of control and hope that it did not do too much damage.

Sir Kenneth stayed in his office all day getting reports on the situation. He kept awake by sipping from the whiskey bottle in the drawer of his desk. Several times as darkness fell he tried to phone Emma, but the line was dead. He knew she and Mark were in no danger from flooding because the house was on the side of a hill, high above the river. But he needed to make sure. When he could not make telephone contact he sent Patrick Kennedy in the car to tell her he might not be able to leave the mill that night.

At five o'clock in the evening the Chief Engineer reported that the wheel was out of control. The transformers could not handle the surges of power and if they did not shut down there was a danger of fire and explosion.

The mill boss gave instructions to close the lock gates on the mill-race to try and stem the surge of water. Engineers raised the mill wheel to its maximum height to get as much of it as possible out of the fast-flowing current.

Water flowing around Emma's house gradually subsided during the day and by late afternoon was reduced to a narrow rivulet. The flooding around her home was due to a blocked culvert under the roadway in front of the house which caused water to form a deep pool in the front garden. Council workmen arrived just before dusk and cleared the blockage and water rapidly disappeared from inside and outside the house. The men advised the two women to stay where they were because practically all the roads in the area were flooded and it could take days to clear them. It would be dangerous to venture out on foot to Murrinbridge or Sperrin. Emma asked if they could get a message to the mill and they said they would do their best but couldn't promise because very few phones were working.

Behind the house was a pile of debris where the greenhouse had stood. The red brick garden walls had toppled under the pressure of water and marble chippings had been swept away from the patio and pathways. Deep channels were cut into the soil around the house, exposing the foundations. Inside the ground floor was covered with a layer of brown mud left behind by the receding floodwater.

Even closed windows could not muffle the high-pitched roar of the river as it swirled and barged down the narrow valley below. The last time she had heard anything like it was on a visit to Blackpool when she was a child. She remembered how during a fierce summer storm she and her sisters spent hours at their hotel window watching twenty-foot-high waves and boiling surf pummel the famous promenade.

The women had no contact with the outside world after the workmen left. The only sign of life was a group of farmers keeping an anxious vigil on a hillside on the far side of the flooded river, measuring the level of the rising water.

Ethel tried to salvage food from the kitchen but there was such a stench downstairs Emma discarded almost all of it. All she could use were a few tins of fruit and two unopened bottles of milk on a high shelf. There was water in the taps, but they could not use it for fear it might be contaminated by the floodwater. She was glad she was feeding Mark herself; at least he would not go hungry.

Ethel brought coal and wet wood blocks upstairs and by using a lot of newspaper managed to get a fire going in the main bedroom. Occasionally Emma went to the front window to see if anybody was moving about on the surrounding farms. After dark the river rose higher and spread wider, illuminated by eerie bright moonlight. Downriver she saw farm houses surrounded by water with lights in the upstairs rooms; the occupants had been foolhardy enough to remain in their homes while the floodwater closed in around them and were now stranded.

She wasn't worried any more for their safety. Leyland House was so far above the river that they were in no danger. Ethel was not so sure. She kept an anxious vigil as the floodwater crept up the side of the valley below them.

"If the river reaches us," Emma joked to try and reassure her, "it surely will be the end of the world." But this only made the girl more apprehensive, and she prayed even harder that the promise of a watery grave from St. Patrick would not come true.

"Don't worry, Ethel, if by any chance the floodwater comes any closer to us, Mark and you and I will climb the hill behind the house. We will not drown—no matter what St. Patrick says!"

During the long hours of darkness, she wondered where Kenneth was and what he was doing. She guessed he was having problems at the mill or maybe the roads were blocked and that was why he could not reach her. He would come when he could. She had to be patient. She went to bed early, exhausted by an eventful, anxious day.

A convoy of American Army trucks, tractors, trailers, and handcarts loaned by farmers and merchants ferried more than two hundred families and their belongings out of the danger zone in Murrinbridge that day. A few stalwarts stayed behind—sceptics who maintained that they had been through it all before and would come to no harm.

After dusk an eerie stillness settled over the town. The moon came out, illuminating a small band of Council workers at the bridge still measuring the rising water. If the stone structure collapsed or the embankments were breached it was their job to set off the town siren to warn anybody remaining in the low-lying streets to run for their lives.

Valentino was convinced from what he heard earlier that day that the ramparts could not contain the deluge and sooner or later they would give way. It was a matter of much speculation as to which would crumble first. If it was the one on the town side it would destroy shops and offices together with all their goods and insurance companies would have to foot a hefty bill. If the embankment on his side burst it could wipe out a lot of homes, maybe even entire streets. The insurance companies would be happier about that for few householders could afford the luxury of home protection.

So, he prepared for the worst. Any furniture that would fit around the turn in the narrow stairs was stacked in the bedrooms together with sacks of potatoes and vegetables, weighing scales and brown paper bags full of produce from the shop. He moved everything. He gathered together what cash he had, intending to give it to his sister when she went to spend the night in the church hall but decided against it. There would be a lot of rogues spending the night there and they were not beyond stealing his money even in the sight of God. He put it in a tin box and hid it in a corner of the attic. After moving their belongings upstairs Jinny made a pot of tea and sandwiches and they sat down to eat what she thought might be their last meal in that house when Valentino suddenly remembered that he had twenty chickens ready for plucking in a shed in the garden. He had to find some way of saving them.

When they had done all they could in the house Jinny packed clothes into a bag and set out on foot for the parish hall; Valentino stayed back saying he had to leave out some food for the chickens for it might be a couple of days before he could return to the house.

He had no intention of leaving but he couldn't tell her. Even if the embankment was breached he felt the water would never reach the upstairs rooms and if it did there was always the attic. In any case he was not happy at the prospect of having to spend the night in the parish hall among bossy women and rowdy children; and there were husbands he could not afford to meet either, even in an emergency.

In the hen-house he felt around with his hands for the roosting chickens and placed them one by one into potato sacks until he was sure he had all twenty. He carried the bags upstairs and put them on the linoleum floor of his sister's bedroom—they would be safe there for a day or so and if the flood came he might wring their necks and start to pluck them when he had nothing else to do. He brushed feathers from his hair and neck and clothes, turned on the battery radio and lay down on the bed for the night. The last thing he heard before nodding off was a couple of drunks singing as they made their way from the pub to the safety of the parish hall where they would sleep soundly whatever the night brought.

149

DELUGE AND DEATH

Sir Kenneth paced about the mill office all afternoon, worried about Emma and the baby. He could not understand why he had heard nothing from his driver. There was a maze of country roads and lanes around Emma's house and surely some of them were passable. Even if he had to go on foot to reach her he was determined she would not spend another night alone in the countryside.

At dusk he heard the crunch of tyres on stone chippings outside his office. He put on his coat and bounced downstairs. Before Patrick had a chance to say anything Sir Kenneth let himself into the front passenger seat.

"Where the hell have you been?" he said angrily. "I have been waiting for hours for you."

Patrick Kennedy got a whiff of whiskey in the front of the car. The chauffeur was taken aback by his brusque attitude.

"I have travelled nearly a hundred miles around the countryside trying to find a way to get to Leyland House," he said. "The roads everywhere are flooded. It's only in the last half hour that I found one that's clear of water, Sir, but we will have to make a long detour down the other side of the river and through the town to get there."

"Doesn't matter how far we have to go," he snapped, "just get a move on."

Patrick was angry about the way he was treated. He wanted to explain that he had not been idle, that he had been going around in circles all day trying to find a way through, but the boss was in no mood for explanations; he did not even have a chance to see that his own wife and children were alright.

He drove slowly in the darkness along waterlogged roads. Everywhere there were police flood warning signs and red lanterns and several times they had to enlist the aid of local people to wade ahead of them through the water to mark the deepest parts. Sir Kenneth was angry at the slow progress and a few times ordered Patrick to take a chance and drive through the floodwater.

"If the engine stalls we are finished," warned Patrick.

"If the engine stalls we will just have to walk," he snapped.

Eventually they made their way along a narrow hillside road until they saw the lights of Murrinbridge below them. When breaks came in the clouds and the moon shone through, they had a panoramic view of a town under siege from the forces of nature. Upstream floodwater had spread out over hundreds of acres of low-lying farmland but when the deluge approached the town it was forced through a bottleneck between man-made earthen ramparts; white water rapids funnelled through the narrow gorge. Once it passed under the old bridge and left the town behind the floodwater spread out again to form a long expansive moonlit lake. Patrick thought the whole scene resembled an hourglass. It was a pretty sight in the bright moonlight, belying the terror it brought to so many people.

As they neared the old bridge a policeman waved a red torch and stopped them.

"Where do you think you're going?" he said to Patrick when he rolled down the window.

"We are trying to reach a friend's house on the other side of the valley," he said.

"The situation with the river is critical," explained the policeman, leaning against the car while he signalled another vehicle behind to stop. "I have orders from the Council only to let emergency services across the bridge. Sorry, gentlemen, you'll have to turn around."

Sir Kenneth got out of the car.

"My name is Kenneth Montgomery," he said. "This is an emergency. A young woman and her baby are stranded in a house at Templemount and they need help. We have supplies of food and milk for the baby," he lied.

"I have my orders, Sir," replied the policeman. Then he recognised the mill owner and tipped his cap. "Stay where you are, Sir, until I deal with this gentleman behind."

When the other car turned and drove off the way it came, the policeman came back.

"Go ahead if it's an emergency sir but my advice is to drive like the devil over that bridge and through the streets on the other side until you reach high ground. The situation is as bad as it can be. It's only a matter of time before the embankments give way."

Sir Kenneth thanked the policeman, and they drove up onto the bridge. As they crossed Patrick felt a succession of thumps caused by trees crashing into the arches. The car shuddered under them and the driver slowed down.

"Keep going! Keep going," shouted his passenger. "You heard what the bloody policeman said!"

The chauffeur accelerated over the bridge and through dark street beyond, his wheels sending waves of surface water through the open doorways of abandoned homes. The public gaslights were lit; although deserted, some of the houses still had lights on exposing vacant rooms and abandoned belongings.

"People remove windows and doors," Patrick explained, "to allow the water to flow through if the flood should come."

"Keep moving Patrick," said his passenger impatiently. He was not interested in what was happening to the townspeople. He wanted to see Emma and the baby.

Patrick had enough. He had neglected his own family all day and this was the thanks he got for it. Sir Kenneth was only concerned about his own situation; he didn't give a damn about anybody else. Anger welled up inside him, but he decided to say nothing and drove in silence. Suddenly there was a high-pitched wailing sound that got louder and louder until it drowned the noise of the car engine. Sir Kenneth looked around anxiously, wondering what it was.

"That's the siren!" Patrick shouted excitedly. "The embankment is broken, or the bridge has collapsed!"

He accelerated, spurred on by the wailing noise.

The car travelled less than a hundred yards when a wall of white water came out of the darkness.

"Aw Jesus Christ!" Patrick called out as it crashed down on top of them. The momentum of the car kept it going forward for a few yards through the water before it was lifted by the wave and hurtled against the houses on one side of the street and landed on its side.

The two men inside shouted and cursed as they frantically clawed at the doors and windows to get them open. Patrick pulled and kicked at the door, but it would not move because of the pressure from the water outside. He rolled down a window, but it jammed half way and he could not get through it. Sir Kenneth cursed him for letting the water in. Within seconds, it had filled the car, enveloping the frantic passengers. They struggled with the door handles to try and get them open but the pressure of the water and the fact that the car was wedged against the wall of a house would not allow either to budge. Now and again their flailing arms touched one another but they could see nothing in the murky darkness.

When he could hold his breath no longer and his starved lungs were forced to inhale the cold black water Patrick had not the strength to struggle anymore and resigned himself to his fate; he closed his eyes, let the cold numb his brain and lapsed into unconsciousness.

Sir Kenneth got into the back passenger seat and kicked the door with all his strength but it would not open. He managed to roll down the window but by the time it had opened sufficiently to allow him to get through he had expelled all the air from his tortured lungs and was forced to inhale freezing water. In desperation he grabbed his driver by the hair, shaking him and shouting at him to do something; but Patrick was beyond helping anybody. Sir Kenneth struggled feebly for another few seconds before he too lost consciousness and his limp body floated upwards until it became trapped against the side of the overturned car.

Valentino slept until the siren roused him. He sat bolt upright in the bed and rubbed his eyes. "Jesus, they'll wake the dead," he said aloud. One of two things had happened—either the bridge had collapsed or the embankment had been breached. He sat still on the bed, holding his breath, listening for sounds that would give him a clue.

Even with the noise of the wailing alarm his keen hearing picked up another sound, a low rumble at first, gradually getting louder and louder; the floodwater was on its way. He heard a crash as the white wave of foaming water reached the first street of houses. He held his breath until he felt a thud as it hit his own front wall and the bedroom floor shuddered. He heard the sound of breaking glass as the floodwater jumped up the front wall and smashed his windows.

He got off the bed and stepped into freezing cold water. Frightened and confused, he stumbled around the room, up to his knees in it, before he found the wooden ladder he had placed on the landing outside. He hauled himself up the steps out of the water into the attic, shivering from cold and fright. While he tried to get his breath back he felt the house shake again and again as wave after wave pummelled it.

He prayed, mumbled pleadings to God and his Holy Mother not to let him drown but if his time had come please forgive him for his sins and let him into heaven. He knew he had done a lot of bad things in his life but Christ was supposed to forgive everybody in the end and he knew there were others who had done a lot worse than him, even murdered people; the priest said God was all forgiving and even Judas might be in heaven; if Judas could get into heaven surely there was room for a blind man.

The house shook again and again as each wave struck. He started to say the Our Father but became confused and got lost in the middle; he couldn't remember the words of a prayer he had said thousands of times since he was a child. He tried again and when the words would not come changed to the Hail Mary. While he prayed he was thinking; could he get out onto the roof if the floodwater reached the attic?

Valentino spent the most anxious hour of his life in complete isolation, his backside numb from sitting on wooden joists. As the first waves passed his street the water level settled; he ventured down the ladder using one foot to find how much room he had between the landing ceiling and the water. He estimated it was about two feet high in the bedroom. He went back to the attic and waited another hour and when he went down the ladder again the bedroom floor was clear. His precious radio that he had brought upstairs and put on the dresser when he went to bed was still on and he could hear the late-night music programme on the BBC—Vera Lynn was singing We'll Meet Again.

"I hope we will, Vera" he said aloud. "For a while there I had my doubts." He inched across the wet bedroom floor on his hands and knees feeling ahead to make sure the floorboards were still there; everything in the room seemed to be intact but the swirling water had moved things around. He bumped into an overturned chair and felt blood coming from his shin.

By some miracle, the mattress on his bed was still dry, but next door in Jinny's bedroom the chickens all drowned in the sacks; he cursed himself for not putting them on top of one of the beds, or up in the attic.

The water was still noisy as it gushed through gaps in the street where houses had collapsed but he sensed the worst was over; his house was still standing, and he had to sit it out and hope for the best. Once the water level settled rescue boats would come and get him. There was nothing more he could do so he took the radio up to the attic. Uncomfortable as it was, he lay across the bare wooden joists and fell asleep.

It was the following evening before help came. By then the worst of the flooding was over and boatmen were able to make their way along waterlogged streets that looked more like Venice than an Irish country town. The boatmen pleaded with the Valentino to leave the house, but he refused saying he was comfortable enough where he was. He asked for hot food and they gave him a can of thick soup and potatoes and he took it up to the attic when they had gone and ate the lot.

The boatmen continued their search for other people who had been reported missing. As they pulled away from McKelvie's house they saw something shining in the water beneath the boat. They quickly returned to dry land to report that the blind Valentino was safe and well but there was a car lying on its side against the front wall of the house next door to him.

It was another day before the floodwater subsided sufficiently to allow divers to force open the doors of the battered Austin Princess. Inside they found the bodies of the two men.

The District Inspector of Police drove to Mill Brae House to tell

Lady Eleanor. When he gave her the tragic news she sat on a chair, her body rocking to and fro, and sobbed. She had no idea even that he had been missing; she assumed he had gone straight from the mill to the Johnston woman.

When the policemen had gone the maids helped her to her room and she lay down fully clothed on the bed trying to absorb the terrible news she had been given. Kenneth was dead and a horrible death it was too, trapped inside his car until he drowned.

Imagining him screaming for help, she was overcome by remorse. She felt guilty about the way she had behaved to him in the final years of their marriage, guilty about allowing their marriage to founder, about driving him into the arms of another woman. She hardly spoke to him since Emma Johnston left Mill Brae, but she had shut him out of her life long before that. Now he was gone from her and from the English girl.

She had justified shutting him out of her life by blaming him for the way he had treated her, the way he had humiliated her by carrying on with mill girls. She was not prepared to allow him to use her as a bed companion while he was carrying on with others behind her back.

When Emma first arrived, life seemed to change for the better and she thought that maybe in time with the help of her bright young companion she might recover from her illness and be reconciled with her husband. Then she discovered the affair between him and Emma, a girl young enough to be his daughter. How stupid she felt living for so long in the house so close to them not knowing what was going on behind her back. He had made a fool of her again. Emma was her friend, her companion, her confidant, somebody she felt she could trust, but she too had betrayed her.

She wondered whether it might have been better if the maid had not told her what was going on. Those months since Emma left Mill Brae had been the loneliest in her life, so lonely that she sometimes thought about taking all her pills to bed with her some night and hope she would not wake up in the morning. The only thing that held her back was the anger she felt for her husband. Why should she make it easy for him? Why should she conveniently take her own life and allow Kenneth and his mistress to live happily ever after?

When Kenneth did not arrive, Emma was worried. She had heard Murrinbridge was overwhelmed by floodwater the previous night and there was a lot of destruction. She hoped Helen and her family were okay. As the hours passed and she had no contact with Kenneth she began to wonder what could have happened to keep him away. Why did he not send Patrick Kennedy to let her know where he was? She clung to the belief that the flood had caused such problems at the mill that he could not get away. And she knew he had no way of contacting her because the phone was still dead.

Helen was aware from the morning after the flood that Sir Kenneth Montgomery and Patrick Kennedy were missing but nobody was sure whether they might still be marooned somewhere in the countryside amid the maze of impassable roads. She thought they might even have spent the night at Templemount. She tried to ring Emma in vain. It was not until boats found Valentino in his house and spotted the Austin Princess submerged nearby that people became worried. Then the policeman reported to his superiors that Montgomery's car passed over the bridge seconds before the embankment burst and it was possible they did not have time to get clear. That's when rescue boats visited the spot again and came back to report that the car in the water was the distinctive Princess and two bodies were still inside.

Helen moved quickly to get to Emma as soon as she got the news. She pedalled as hard as she could on her bicycle, stopping only to check that it was safe to pass through stretches of floodwater still blocking the road. She had to get to Emma before anybody else brought the bad news.

Emma heard a noise outside and when she looked out the window saw a pale faced Helen putting her bicycle against the wall. She was not expecting the nurse and had a sudden premonition that something was wrong. She took Mark in her arms and held him close and sat down at the kitchen table.

The Nurse let herself in and paused in the hallway, tears in her eyes, trying to compose herself for the ordeal ahead.

She came into the kitchen: "I have bad news for you, Emma," she said, unable to hold back the tears, "and I am very sorry to be the one to bring it."

Emma's face blanched. "Has something happened to Kenneth?" She stared wide-eyed at the sobbing nurse.

"They found the car a little while ago and Kenneth and Patrick were still inside."

"Kenneth is gone, isn't he?" Emma's face blanched. "Kenneth is gone. I knew something terrible had happened, but I didn't want to believe it."

Ethel came into the kitchen. "What's wrong, Nurse?"

"There's been a terrible accident, "said Helen. "Sir Kenneth and his driver have been drowned." The police say they were trying to make their way here when it happened."

"Kenneth dead? And Patrick too?" gasped Emma, tears streaming down her cheeks. "Ah Helen, is there no hope? Is there no hope at all?"

Helen shook her head. "The car turned over in the water and trapped them," she said.

Emma's body convulsed with sobbing and a cold shiver ran down her back at the thought of Kenneth and Patrick struggling inside the overturned car as it filled with water. The end of the world had come for him at that moment just as Ethel believed it would, but she was sure he did not have the easy death promised by St. Patrick.

She handed the boy to the nurse, put her face in her hands on the table, and wept uncontrollably.

Emma moved about in a daze as she tried to come to terms with the misfortune that had befallen her, the tragedy that had shattered her comfortable, happy life. She wanted to get away from it all, leave the nightmare behind. But she had a baby son to think about and there was nowhere to go. She heard words of comfort from Helen, but they did little to assuage her mental anguish. She refused the doctor's offer of sedatives to help her get through what she knew were going to be difficult times ahead. Instead, when she felt well enough she helped Ethel with the clean-up downstairs. Carpets and linoleum had to be rolled up and dragged outside to be dumped and blazing logs were piled on fires to dry the wet floorboards. In this way she kept herself busy.

She had nightmares about the two men inside the car as the water enveloped them; she imagined she could see Kenneth's face pressed against the window desperately clawing at the glass, screaming for help. Did he think of her and Mark in those final moments as water filled his starved lungs or were his last thoughts of his ailing wife, seeking forgiveness for abandoning her for an adulterous affair with a young girl?

She heard nothing from the mill or from Mill Brae House. Helen told her there was no word about funeral arrangements because of a post-mortem examination of the bodies ordered in preparation for an inquest.

Despite their estrangement Emma felt Eleanor would be just as shocked as herself by Kenneth's death; but would she also feel that the Wrath of God had now touched her husband too, punishing him for his adultery. Could she be that cold hearted? She had suffered a lot from illness and the breakdown of her marriage—Emma had no doubt about that. Perhaps in her confused state she might even feel that what had happened was all for the best, ending a situation that had become a source of scandal in the county and a great embarrassment to her personally. Maybe in her depressed, hurt state she would feel that God had taken revenge for Emma's betrayal.

In the absence of any contact or information from either Mill Brae or the solicitors Emma found it difficult to take stock of her own life or make plans for herself and the baby. But of one thing she was sure—her worst nightmare had come true. She and her son were alone in a strange country with nobody but Helen to turn to for support.

It was the one thing she had feared most—that she would agree to become Kenneth's mistress and then for one reason or another she might end up alone again. She sometimes worried that he might be reconciled with his wife or tire of her and turn to somebody like

Kate Reilly, who worked so closely with him in the mill. That's why she asked him from the very beginning of their affair to provide for her.

No matter how shocked and sad she was by his death she had to think about her own future now, her and Mark's. Kenneth promised he would make generous provision for her in his will but did he ever get around to doing it? He told her he intended to see the solicitors after Mark was born to finalise his new will, but did he ever do it? If he had she felt sure he would have mentioned it. They were so preoccupied and happy with the arrival of the boy that they had not talked about it since they moved into Leyland House. They had no reason to—there was no urgency about it; Kenneth was a healthy man with no thought of anything happening to him.

She wondered about the house she was living in? It was to be his first present to her after she agreed to be his mistress, but she never saw any papers or any documents, and he did not discuss it with her after they moved. Who did it belong to? Would the bailiffs come to evict her when the funeral was over, and Eleanor laid claim to his property?

All she had was a bundle of receipts for bills he had paid and an account in the bank for housekeeping in which she had a little over £2,000, enough to keep her going for a while. If he had made provision for herself and Mark as he promised, there was no need to worry; if not, she had already resigned herself to the fact that she would have to swallow her pride and ask her parents to take her and her son back into the family home.

Emma wondered how Krzysztof would react to the death of his boss. From what Kate had said he was the number two man at the mill and it was likely he would take over the management.

The last thing she wanted was Krzysztof making claims about Mark, now that Kenneth was gone. She was more worried about him than ever, worried that their affair might be discovered, casting doubts on whose son Mark was. She was also worried about the blind man. Would he now feel free to talk about their encounter in the Sally Garden?

A representative of the undertakers arrived five days after the drowning to tell Emma about the funeral arrangements. The young man was ill at ease from the moment he knocked on her door. He informed her that a lot of important people including a representative of His Majesty King George had signified their intention to attend the church service. She understood his discomfort when, as he was leaving, he told her that the main concern of Lady Eleanor Montgomery was that the funeral should not be a source of scandal to the family or embarrassment to the mourners.

"She feels that it would be inappropriate for you to attend either the church service or the interment," he said.

He waited for some reaction and when none came, swallowed hard and continued: "But of course this is a matter on which you will have to make up your own mind. If you do decide to attend, however, her Ladyship feels that under no circumstances should you bring your son."

She assured him that she had already considered the matter and had decided not to attend. She did not want either herself or her son to be held up to ridicule on such a public occasion.

The deaths of Kenneth Montgomery and Patrick Kennedy overshadowed the devastation caused by the flood. Homes had been demolished, families lost all their personal belongings; thousands of farm animals were drowned, and farm houses and bridges swept away in the torrent. Landslides and mud-slides on the mountainsides carved deep gorges in the landscape, eroding great chunks of earth to expose bare rock far below. But it was the tragic death of one of Northern Ireland's most successful businessmen and peers that grabbed the headlines in local and national newspapers.

Sir Kenneth was buried in a family plot at the rear of Mill Brae House; hundreds of people attended including representatives of the business community throughout Northern Ireland and a large gathering of Bishops and Clergy of all denominations. The British royal family was represented by an Irish peer and a Junior Secretary at the War Department represented the British Government.

Two days after the funeral the Ministry men re-opened the mill.

Assembly of parachutes had virtually ceased but the production line was kept going in case further orders came from the Army which was preparing for a major airborne assault on the Continent. On the advice of Ministry officials Lady Eleanor appointed the youthful Krzysztof Walenski to manage the business. She needed some breathing space to get her thoughts together about what she had to do now that Sir Kenneth was gone. Her thinking was muddled and the constant tiredness from medication made her lethargic; she realised the problems she faced but did not have will to confront them. Her maid urged her to cut down on the amount of medication she was taking.

"That stuff is killing you," she said. "Even a horse could not cope with the amount of tablets you are taking every day."

Eleanor decided it was time to give it a try. She gradually reduced her intake of tablets. Alone in the house when the dignitaries had dispersed after the interment, she felt well enough to go to her husband's study, unlock his bureau and take out the sealed envelope she had placed there two months before containing the new will he had made after the birth of the Johnston baby.

Although she had already been appraised of the general contents when it was delivered she never had any interest in reading it; this was the document that confirmed the betrayal by her husband and Emma Johnston.

Her eyes moved down the paragraphs containing the new provisions underlined in red for her by the solicitors. She was to receive a lump sum of £300,000 together with an income of £20,000 a year for the rest of her life and a life interest in Mill Brae house.

It provided £100,000 for Emma Johnston with an income of £10,000 a year and title to the residence Leyland at Templemount.

Eleanor was not surprised. He had a duty to the girl after the predicament he got her into. But she was dismayed and felt utterly dejected when she read further and found that the mill itself was to be put in trust for Emma's baby whom he officially acknowledged in the will as his son. Worse still Mill Brae would also pass to the boy on her death.

In her present state of health Eleanor didn't want the burden of the mill and if she had inherited it in the normal way almost certainly would have sold it but she bitterly resented the fact that her home would ultimately pass into the hands of an English family, the Johnstons, who had done nothing to earn it except provide a brood mare for her adulterous husband. She put the document back into the envelope and placed it in the bureau.

The solicitors wanted to have the beneficiaries together at Mill Brae House for a reading of the will, but Lady Eleanor wouldn't hear of it.

"This is my home and as long as I am alive neither Emma Johnston nor her bastard son will ever set foot in it," she told them. She wanted them to proceed to have the will probated by the Courts as soon as possible so that the whole unsavoury business could be got over and done with.

"Deal with the Johnston woman as you see fit," she told the lawyers. "I don't want to have anything to do with her, and I don't want her setting foot in my home."

Patrick Kennedy was buried in the local cemetery following Requiem Mass in the village church. So many people came to pay their respects that the congregation overflowed into the adjoining graveyard. Even though she knew the amiable Patrick had died trying to reach her that awful night Emma did not go to the church; instead she wrote a letter of condolence to his young widow.

Although overshadowed by the death of Sir Kenneth Montgomery, Valentino was in the news too but for other reasons. He was the blind man who against all odds survived the terrifying flood, trapped in the attic of his house. He regaled Reporters with stories of how he fled to the attic when the great wall of water swept through the streets; he lied that he spent the night in prayer. He added further drama by telling them that he heard the thud of a car being tossed against the front of his house when the first wave of water struck; he thought he heard shouting.

"I didn't know who was in the car at the time," he lied, "but there was nothing I could do anyway. I was up to my knees in water in my bedroom and had to scramble up a ladder to the attic to save my life."

The newsmen vied with one another to find words to adequately describe the bravery and resourcefulness of this remarkable blind man as he crouched in the attic of his home while the floodwater swirled around below.

Reading about Valentino some of the men whose wives had been romantically involved with him were sorry that the flood water did not reach the attic and wash the blind bastard out of their lives forever.

"Too much to hope for," scowled one of them," the fucking Devil looks after his own."

Emma received her copy of the will by registered post with a covering letter informing her that this was Sir Kenneth's Last Will and Testament and that on the instructions of his widow it was proposed to proceed immediately to have it admitted to probate, a process that would take three to four months. If she or the trustees nominated to act for her son, Mark Anthony Montgomery, wished to raise any matter pertaining to the will before it was admitted to probate they should engage the services of an independent firm of solicitors to act for them.

She found the legal phraseology in the will daunting but was elated when she saw that he had provided generously for her as he promised. She gasped in disbelief when she read that Mark was to inherit the mill when he came of age and that he would also inherit Mill Brae House when Lady Eleanor died. He had honoured his promise to her, and more. It was such a relief. She now had the means to live an independent life and one day her son would inherit Sperrin Mill and the wealth that went with it.

The remainder of his estate—stocks and shares, property in Ireland and England, together with substantial sums of money in various banks and financial institutions—were to be placed in Trust for the benefit of the boy. The Trustees were Kenneth's solicitors and herself. Among the properties listed were "300 cottages in the village of Sperrin".

Emma put the will down on her lap and sat back to try and take everything in. It was as if a cloud had been lifted from her. She did not have to worry any more about the future, about survival for herself and Mark. She felt very emotional about Kenneth's generosity; clearly, he loved her, and the boy far more than she ever thought. She regretted that she did not try harder to return the love he had for her; tears spilled from her eyes.

When she recovered from the shock of knowing that her infant son would ultimately own everything Emma dried the tears and read on.

He left Kate Reilly £500 and Krzysztof the title to a house in the village. There were other minor bequests to various servants, and £200 to the unfortunate Patrick Kennedy who had perished with him in the flood.

Since Emma had no solicitor Helen gave her the name of a reputable practitioner. She telephoned, and a young man came to see her a couple of days later, took a copy of the will and told her he would act for both her son and herself, but only in relation to the will. Sir Kenneth's solicitors, he explained, would continue to conduct the legal business of the mill and once the will had been probated they would also act for her son until he took his inheritance when his infancy ended on his twenty-first birthday, January 15, 1964.

Krzysztof came unannounced the following week to tell Emma he had been appointed Manager of the mill until Sir Kenneth's affairs had been sorted out. He was proud of the confidence Lady Eleanor had shown in him and delighted to learn from her that he had been given a fine house in the village. He intended to move in as soon as he got the keys.

Emma was taken aback by his visit and was quite cool to him. She made sure that Ethel was close by while he was there for she did not want him to approach her, to show any sign of affection either for herself or the boy. The last thing she wanted was gossip about Krzysztof while the will was going through the courts, for that could ruin everything. He tried to talk to her about Mark, asking how he was; he looked forward to seeing more of the boy.

She stared at him. "Mark has nothing to do with you or you with him," she said coldly when Ethel went to the kitchen. "Remember we are acquainted through our association with the Montgomery family and we remain nothing more than acquaintances. I would prefer—indeed I am telling you—I don't want you coming to visit us again."

When Ethel returned she told her to show Mr Walenski out. Krzysztof put on his coat and left, annoyed by her coldness, finding it hard to believe that this was the same woman who seduced him that evening at his lodgings.

BOOK III

AN ILL WIND

Valentino heard about the will from his sister, that virtually everything had gone to Emma Johnston and her son. All of a sudden it occurred to him that what he had heard that night in the Sally Gardens suddenly took on a new importance. He knew something that nobody else did but he was too scared to tell, and he was glad that up to now he had the good sense to keep his mouth shut.

He had information that nobody else had and there might be some way he could capitalise on it. There was a lot of money and property involved and he could throw a spanner in the works and cause mayhem if he let it be known that he overheard Emma Johnston telling the Polish mill manager that he might be the father of the baby she was expecting. Should he try and meet the Johnston woman, maybe tell her out straight what he had heard, and suggest that a bit of money would make sure he kept his mouth shut?

He was well aware that what he was thinking about was blackmail. And that was an ugly, dangerous business

'If she got on her high horse and called the police, I'd end up in jail,' he thought. 'There has to be another way.'

What if he divulged the information through somebody else? If there was trouble, he could always deny it.

On the other hand, he was sure the one person more than any other who would love to know what went on in the Sally Garden that night was Lady Eleanor Montgomery. All the talk was that she was fit to be tied because her husband had left everything to his bastard son.

"She would definitely pay good money for the information," he muttered as he filled potatoes into half stone paper bags.

So, Valentino allowed financial greed to overcome the danger he knew was involved in such a course of action and told his sister Jinny what happened the night he came home covered in nettle stings. He wanted her to pass on the information to somebody at the mill, somebody who would relay it to the widow Montgomery.

Jinny was terrified by what she heard but out of loyalty to the Montgomery family felt that if her brother's story was true Lady Eleanor had a right to know what had been going on. So the following evening she waited for Kate Reilly outside the mill office and asked if she could speak to her about a private matter concerning the Montgomerys. Kate knew Jinny well for sometimes on the way home from work she sat beside her on the bus. As they walked towards the terminus where the bus was waiting Jinny related to her what her brother told her, the conversation he overheard in the Sally Garden between Emma Johnston and the Polish mill manager.

"The Montgomerys have been very good to our family over the years and my brother feels that Lady Eleanor should be told what went on," she said. "I know that you go to Mill Brae to meet her sometimes and that's why I decided to tell you. My brother has not breathed a word about this to anybody else, only to me. Nobody else knows about it except you."

Kate was astonished by the story. She was aware that Valentino McKelvie was blind, for she had made arrangements for him to go to Dublin to see a specialist. She was also aware that he had the reputation in Murrinbridge of being a blackguard who molested women in his greengrocer shop. Kate found it hard to believe that the Jinny's unkempt brother, red hair matted on his forehead, vacant eyes staring into space, could have bedded all the women he was supposed to, but there was so much talk going on about it that there had to be some truth in the rumours.

She found the story about Emma and Krzysztof even harder to believe and upsetting. She and Krzysztof were engaged to be married. Since they first went out together he told her that he had never been with any other girl. For some reason McKelvie had come up with this wild story not realising the implications of it. Krzysztof did not tell her everything—she discovered that for herself. It was not until Emma Johnston moved out of Mill Brae that Kate learned she had visited him on occasions in his lodgings and though he swore there was nothing to it Kate often wondered what exactly the English girl was up to with her fiancé.

She warned Jinny not to say a word to anybody. "And if your brother has any sense," she added, "he will keep his mouth shut too or he will end up in serious trouble. These are terrible allegations to make against anybody."

But keeping secrets was not a strong point with Jinny especially when she knew something that nobody else did. She divulged the story to a close friend in the mill and within days everybody was talking about an affair between the new Manager and the English girl, the one who had the baby for Sir Kenneth Montgomery.

Valentino swore at his sister when told him about the meeting with Kate. She was the wrong one to tell, he railed, for she and the Pole had been courting for ages.

"You should have gone to the widow herself," he fumed, "not to some jumped up office girl. What sort of fucking idiot are ye?"

Krzysztof was busy with his job as Manager. Kate was his Secretary, so he saw her every day and most days they had lunch together in the office. Since the death of Sir Kenneth, Kate was briefed by Krzysztof and the Ministry men before going to Mill Brae once a week to report to Lady Eleanor.

The mill secretary was not happy about the visits. At Mill Brae she felt awkward, ill at ease, in the presence of Lady Eleanor. It was all so cold, so impersonal—Kate arrived, made a brief report, answered any questions she was asked and was shown out again through a side door by the maid. She didn't want to go to Mill Brae, but she had no choice—she had to put up with the situation until the will was finalised; after that Lady Eleanor would have no further say in the running of the mill.

The week after she met Jinny McKelvie, Kate went to Mill Brae to make her usual report. The older woman wanted to know if the Ministry men were happy with the way the mill was being managed. Did the Manager get on well with the Ministry men, with the departmental managers, with the staff? When she did not have ready answers to some of the questions she was told to make a note and bring the information the following week.

Kate was angry at the treatment she got from Lady Eleanor but had to swallow her pride and bear it. If she had another job to go to she would have left the mill altogether rather than deal with her but there was no other job unless she went abroad.

On her way out that day she decided on a whim to get back at her employer by relaying to her the scandalous story told by the blind McKelvie.

"That'll give the stuck-up bitch something to think about!"

As the maid was showing her out she hesitated and asked to see Lady Montgomery again. She had forgotten to tell her something.

Kate was told to wait in the cloakroom and Lady Eleanor came in.

"You wanted to speak to me about another matter?" she asked.

"There was one other thing I should have mentioned to you," Kate said boldly. "It might be just idle talk—of no importance—but I think you should be aware of it in any case."

"This sounds ominous," said Lady Eleanor, raising her eyebrows.

"One of the workers in the mill who is known to me approached me a few days ago with a story about her brother, a blind man, who was in the field behind Mill Brae one evening and overheard a conversation between two people. He insists one of them was Miss Johnston and the other Mr Walenski."

Lady Eleanor looked at her, puzzled. What had this to do with their business?

Kate repeated the story related to her by Jinny McKelvie.

Lady Eleanor was astonished.

"This is incredible," she said staring at Kate. "Do you believe this woman, the story she told you?"

"Yes," she replied. "I believe her, but I should warn you that her brother has a bad reputation in Murrinbridge. There have been stories about him messing around with neighbours, married women who came to his shop to buy fruit and vegetables. Men living on the street beside him do not trust him and don't allow their wives to go into his shop anymore."

"But what reason would he have to concoct such a story?" asked Lady Eleanor. "What does he have to gain from it?"

"I don't know," replied Kate. "He may be looking for money."

"If there is any truth in this story it could cause problems with the will," said Lady Eleanor. "So, for the moment, keep this information to yourself. It wouldn't do to have it spread about the village."

Kate's stomach churned as she made her way back to the office. She had not intended to tell her about McKelvie but had done it on a sudden impulse and already was beginning to regret what she had done. She should have challenged Krzysztof about the story before going to Lady Montgomery.

Once the rumour of what happened in the Sally Garden spread about the mill Kate could hear sniggering going on behind her back again. It was just as bad as the taunts about her and Sir Kenneth; this time they involved the man she was going to marry. She decided the time had come to ask her fiancé some questions about what the hell was going on and get straight answers.

She went to his flat and confronted him. "People are talking behind my back. They're saying that you had an affair with Emma Johnston and that you, not Sir Kenneth, are the father of her baby!"

At first, he was indignant, hurt that she should repeat such falsehoods.

"This outrageous story is nothing more than malicious rumour", he told her. "I am surprised you could even think there was any truth in it. There have been rumours before about you and Sir Kenneth and there was not a word of truth in them either. Why should you believe these rumours about me?"

Kate was angry that he had tried to turn the tables on her. "This has nothing to do with me, or what I think," she said coldly. "This is about you and Emma Johnston! And it's not just gossip. One of the women in the mill came to me a couple of days ago and told me her brother was in the garden behind Mill Brae one evening and heard you and Emma Johnston together. He heard everything you said, and he remembers it clearly! Do you want me to repeat what she told me? I didn't believe her at the time and I still don't want to believe it but I want you to swear that there is no truth in these rumours."

Krzysztof went silent for a while. He remembered well the night

Emma had the row with him on their way back from the river. Had somebody overheard them?

"Well," said Kate, "I'm waiting!" She stared at him.

"I need some time to think," he said. "I'm confused."

Kate was livid. "What is there to think about?" she shouted hysterically. "Either you had an affair with her or you didn't."

He still didn't answer. Kate's heart sank.

"Jesus! Is it possible this story is true? That you had an affair with her, that you are the father of her baby?" She stared, wide eyed, at him demanding an answer.

When he turned his head away and averted her gaze, she got so angry she caught him by the shoulders and pulled him around to face her.

"Look at me! Either you had an affair with her or you did not! Tell me the truth!"

When she still did not get an answer, she shouted all the louder.

"If you are the father of that boy Sir Kenneth was entitled to know; now the poor man is dead and will never know.

"But his wife is alive—she is entitled to know!"

"I am the girl you were supposed to marry, and I certainly am entitled to know!"

He stood up, white faced and paced up and down the bedroom. He was frightened by her outburst, unsure what to say. If somebody had overheard them what was the point in denying it?

He looked at her: "I'll tell you exactly what happened, and you can believe it or not," he said.

He told her about the evening Emma came to his lodgings and how they got carried away and made love.

"It only happened once—there was no affair going on between us. Months later after a tour of the gardens at Mill Brae I thought she wanted me again in the Sally Garden, but we had a fight and in a fit of anger she told me she was pregnant.

"Those were the only two times I was close to her—the first time in my lodgings she seduced me, the second time I wanted her, and she rejected me.

"Emma told me that night she had been trying to have a baby for

Sir Kenneth for some time and was pregnant," he lied.

He sat down, waiting for Kate to say something.

She stood up and stared at him, speechless, astonished that he had admitted his infidelity.

"And the baby?" she said coldly. "Did she say Sir Kenneth was the father or that you were the father?"

"She told me he was the father. She had no doubt about that."

"Well," Kate said coldly, "there are people who say different."

When he made no reply, she got up to go.

"This is the end for us," she said, lifting her coat and gloves from the bed. "It is also the end for me as far as working in the mill is concerned. I have had enough of people laughing and sniggering behind my back. Goodbye."

He pleaded with her not to go. She was the only girl he ever loved, and he wanted her as his wife. She must give him another chance; they could make a life together away from Sperrin altogether, a new start.

Kate ignored him and moved to the door, turning away so that he could not see the tears spilling down her cheeks.

"This is the last time I will be made a fool of by you or anybody else," she sobbed. She walked out of the room, out of his life.

In bed that night she lay awake thinking about what she should do. Where could she go to get away from the mess that had been made of her life? She would give up her job at the mill and look for another. A fresh start somewhere else was what she now needed, far away from Krzysztof and her sniggering friends and the mill and Murrinbridge—disappear and leave the wagging tongues behind.

The only person she really cared for was Sir Kenneth, and he was gone forever. As long as he was the boss, she knew she would have been looked after. She was loyal to him and she knew he was loyal to her.

While thinking about him, she suddenly remembered she had to deal with one matter before she left—something he had asked her to do when he first appointed her his personal secretary. She would do that last thing for him—after that she was free to go.

One evening when he had been drinking he asked her to stay

back after the others had left, and when they were alone he showed her a secret compartment in his heavy oak desk. He never opened the drawer but gave her a key and told her there was something hidden there—a package with money for use in an emergency. It could involve himself or his wife or somebody else. If such an emergency arose he would let her know in good time who the package should be given to. There was only one key and she had to keep it safe—nobody else knew about it. When she was alone in the office, Kate sometimes wondered about that package and what was in it but she never let curiosity get the better of her.

On the morning after the row with Krzysztof, she went early to the mill and let herself into the main office. She squeezed the key from the lining of her purse and opened the panel in the oak desk. Inside was a briefcase. She undid the clip and looked inside. It was stuffed with bundles of cash tied with elastic bands. She took the bundles out one by one, nine in all, and each had a handwritten bank slip wrapped around it marked "£10,000". She pushed the money to one side and rummaged through the leather case looking for an envelope or a piece of paper, a note of some kind. She used her letter opener to cut the lining and still found nothing. She searched the drawer; it was empty too. There was nothing to indicate what she had to do with the money.

Kate sat back on the chair and gazed at the pile of notes in front of her—£90,000. She took several deep breaths, inhaling and exhaling until she regained her composure. Then she calmly replaced the empty briefcase in the drawer and locked it again. She removed her lunch from its brown paper carrier bag, packed the bundles neatly at the bottom and put her sandwiches on top. She put the paper bag on its usual place on the shelf beside her desk. It looked a bit bulkier than usual but not enough to attract attention. She closed her eyes and relaxed for a while to calm her nerves before she went downstairs and unlocked the front door to let the staff in.

She thought of nothing else that day except the money in the brown paper bag and kept a sharp eye on it to make sure nobody got too close. When lunch time came she made tea and had her sandwiches at her desk.

What was she going to do with it? The emergency Sir Kenneth had provided for had arrived but obviously not in the way he envisaged it. What did he have the money for? Was it a nest egg in case the mill failed or was burned down? He had been drinking heavily in the office at that time, the time when the estrangement from his wife started. She had no idea what to do with the money but nobody else was aware of its existence and there was no point in leaving it in the desk for somebody else to find.

The money was one problem but so was the awful predicament she found herself in personally. Her boss was gone, her fiancé was gone and soon her job would be gone and then she herself would be gone. She had no future in Ireland and it was wartime and she still had no idea where else she might go.

As far as the money was concerned she would have to use her own initiative, make up her own mind and do what she thought best. Kate took the paper bag with her as she walked out of the mill that evening and casually placed it at her feet while she waited at the bus stop. It sat on her knee while she chatted to other workers on the journey home to Murrinbridge. After tea she hid it in the attic of her home among a pile of magazines. The magazines were part of her past; the brown paper bag was her future.

In bed that night she put all thoughts of her shattered romance, her work, Lady Eleanor and Emma Johnston out of her mind and concentrated on the bundles of cash in the attic. Apart from a few families like the Montgomerys she was probably the only person in the country who could put their hands on £90,000 at a moment's notice. It was a fortune—enough to buy the mill village, lock, stock and barrel!

She had already decided that her future lay elsewhere, far from her native town and that future did not include anybody from her present existence. She would make plans and when she was ready it was up, up and away like a bird. And thanks to an amazing stroke of good fortune wherever she landed she had the means to be an independent woman.

Krzysztof was worried and not just because of the end of his relationship with Kate. When he took over the mill after Sir Kenneth's death and got close to the Ministry men he had asked them to get information from the War Department about the situation in Poland especially the area south of Lubiala where the Walenski colliery was located.

Two weeks later he had a written communication from London informing him that the international Red Cross had news that partisans had wrecked the mine, his mother was dead, and his father had left the area. This came via the Polish underground, but nobody could vouch for the reliability of the reports for most of the country was now in the hands of the Russians.

Krzysztof was heartbroken by the news that the gentle Justyna, who had shielded him from the world for so long, might be dead. He wondered whether his father had gone to live over the café with Madame Kubinska. He doubted it for the woman was a Jew and information coming from occupied countries was that Jews had been segregated and forced to live in ghettos and labour camps. Newspapers were full of reports of concentration camps in which Jews and political prisoners had been murdered. For the first time names like Buchenwald, Belsen and Dachau began to appear in the headlines over stories so grotesque that readers found them hard to believe.

His position in the mill had taken a turn for the worse. He was under a lot of pressure. His personal life was in turmoil because he had lost the girl he intended to marry and his liaison with Emma Johnston was being talked about openly among the workers.

In desperation he rang Emma. She cut him short, telling him she did not want to talk to him.

"Somebody is spreading malicious gossip about me," she railed at him, "and when I find out who it is my solicitors will deal with the matter."

When he put down the phone he felt that she said what she did more for the ears of somebody listening on the line, than for his benefit. He became more isolated and anxious as the days passed.

VALENTINO'S DILEMMA

There was a knock at Valentino's door early one morning and he hurriedly slipped on his shirt and trousers and went downstairs in his bare feet. He did not have early women callers any more but thought it might be his lucky day; one of his women might have relented and was back looking for a tumble.

"Are you Valentino McKelvie?" a man's voice said when the door was open.

"I am. Who wants to know?" he asked anxiously.

"My name is Sergeant McParland," said the voice. "I'm here to take you to the police station for questioning about the theft of property at Mill Brae House. Put your shoes on and be quick about it."

"I didn't steal anything from Mill Brae," said Valentino, shocked to find it was the police. "I never stole anything from anybody in my life."

"We'll talk about it at the station," said the Sergeant. "Now go and put your shoes on."

Before he had a chance to tie them properly two officers took him by the arms and lifted him into the Black Mariah.

They left him in a cell in the police station for more than an hour before he was taken to an interview room. There he was asked about trespass at Mill Brae House, causing damage to boundary fences and the larceny of sally cane the property of the Montgomery family.

"Not guilty!" he said firmly. "I never stole anything."

They also accused him of invasion of privacy by concealing himself in the garden, besetting the Montgomerys and their friends, listening to private conversations and repeating them to people whose business they were not.

They also referred to complaints about sexual assaults on women who frequented his shop in Murrinbridge, serious offences perpetrated against vulnerable people.

"Not guilty!" he said, shocked by the charges they were making against him.

He denied everything.

They put him back in a cell for another two hours before he was taken home. Nosey neighbours gathered on the street outside his shop when the police van dropped him. They wanted to know why he had been arrested, what he had done. An angry Valentino told them to mind their own business.

"We'll be back McKelvie," said McParland, making sure the neighbours heard him.

He went through the door and banged it behind him. When he calmed down and had time to think he felt the police were bluffing—otherwise they would have charged him and kept him in the barracks. Even if one of the women's husbands had made a complaint they couldn't prove that he had forced himself on any of them. If he had why did they keep coming back for more? Some of the kids might be his but there was no way to prove it. No matter how aggrieved the husbands felt or how much pressure they put on their wives he was sure the women would never face the humiliation of going into open court to give evidence against him.

He figured this business with the police wasn't about the women or the sally rods at all. They were putting pressure on him to make a statement about what happened in the Sally Garden—that's what it was all about. He had heard that Lady Montgomery was disputing the will and they might need his evidence to help her. He was blind, but he was no fool. The police were chancing their arm—for a reason. The widow Montgomery was behind all this; he was sure of it.

He didn't like the police, but he was scared of them. They seemed to be able to do what they wanted with people and he had heard that in court the judge always believed their version of events. They were fishing for information for Lady Montgomery or for the solicitors acting for her. But why should he give them information to pass to her when it might worth money to him to give it to the widow himself? Once this business with the police died down he would talk to somebody from the mill. The widow might be persuaded to part with a bit of money if she wanted him to repeat in court what he had heard. In the meantime, he would have to tread carefully.

On the other hand, the Johnston woman and the Polecat had everything to gain if he kept his mouth shut. If the widow Montgomery was not prepared to part with some of her money, Emma Johnston might be persuaded to show her gratitude with a wad of crispy notes. A couple of thousand pounds wasn't a lot to her but it was a fortune to him. With that sort of money, he could buy two or three houses and live comfortably for the rest of his life off the rents.

Next morning when he opened the shop door, they were there again, waiting for him.

"You're wanted at the barracks for questioning about certain matters that were put to you yesterday and which you denied," said the Sergeant.

In the station he was warned about public mischief, making false statements and the dire consequences of committing perjury if he repeated those statements in court.

They put the same questions to him and he gave the same answers. He was certain they were on a fishing expedition, and if he admitted anything, he was finished. They advised him to get a solicitor, but he said he had nothing to hide and. in any case. he did not have the money to pay for one.

Then a statement made by a woman called Teresa Bowden was read to him. It was an account of one of his visits to the whorehouse in Derry when she said she had sex with him for which he paid "the sum of £1 plus a half crown bonus because he was blind." He never heard of Teresa Bowden, nor did he know the names of any of the women he slept with, but her description of his visit was accurate.

He asked to speak to his sister for he felt things were getting serious and he needed help. A distraught Jinny engaged the aging Corny Sheahan a solicitor who had acted for them when they bought their house years before; within an hour he was admitted to the cell and confronted by an angry McKelvie, demanding that he get him out of jail.

"Give me time to catch my breath, Mr McKelvie," said the rotund solicitor wiping the sweat from his forehead. He sat across the table from Valentino in the interview room, put on his spectacles and opened a folder.

"Now, Mr McKelvie, tell me what this is all about so that I can see what kind of trouble you're in, the reason for your incarceration."

"I'll save you a lot of time and trouble," interrupted Sgt McParland. "I have a full list of the charges here for you."

Sheahan read the list and whistled through his teeth.

"Whatever you've been up to," he said sternly when he finished reading the charge sheet, "they are throwing the book at you."

"It's a pack of lies," Valentino said his anger rising again, "trumped up charges to force me to make a statement about something else. They are harassing and bullying me because I'm blind and defenceless. I'm prepared to admit collecting sally rods for my basket making from the Montgomery property; but that's all. And further the young lady Johnston told me it was all right to take the rods. That stuff about forcing women to have sex with me is all lies."

Sheahan left the cell to talk to the Sergeant privately. When he came back he advised Valentino to co-operate with the police; otherwise they would charge him with the offences and from what the Sergeant said they could make some of them stick.

"You'll get no mercy from a judge," he warned. "The police will make you out to be a thoroughly bad character. And instead of getting sympathy in court because of your affliction they will depict you as some kind of a monster.

"Sergeant McParland says he needs information from you about this business involving the Johnston woman living in Templemount and if you co-operate with him the charges will not be pursued. It's up to you."

Valentino panicked and decided that if he was to get out of jail he would have to take the deal McParland was offering. Sheahan left the room and returned with the Sergeant.

"I believe you have something to say to me," said McParland. "I have to tell you that what you say will be taken down in writing by me personally and anything you say might be used in evidence in court but not against you. If you make a full statement about this other matter there will be no charges against you. Do you understand all that?"

182

"I do," muttered Valentino grudgingly, "but I want Mr Sheahan to be a witness to anything I say."

He then recounted the story that he told Jinny about what he overheard in the Sally Garden, a conversation between two people whom he believed were Emma Johnston whom he had met and talked to once or twice while walking along the river at Sperrin Mill and the Polish man whose name he did not know but recognised from his accent. McParland wrote down everything, interrupting occasionally to ask him how sure he was of the actual words.

When he had finished, and McParland read the statement back to him he got worried that he went too far and had second thoughts; he told the Sergeant it was so long ago he could not be completely sure whether he heard those things that night or from his sister afterwards. He refused to sign until he had time to think about it. McParland was furious but at least he had a statement, a full account from McKelvie of what went on in the Sally Garden and it sounded convincing.

When Lady Eleanor received a copy of the unsigned statement from her solicitors she was astonished by the contents and instructed them not to proceed with probate of the will. Instead, they were to start proceedings to have it set aside on the grounds that Sir Kenneth had no issue to take the property the subject of the trust set up in his will. Solicitors acting for Miss Emma Johnston and for the Trustees of her son, Mark Anthony Montgomery, were not to be told about the challenge until the proceedings were ready and the appropriate documents lodged in court.

Valentino lay on the bunk in his police cell and put his hands under his head to cushion it against the thin horsehair sack that passed for a mattress. The sharp corners of the slats underneath bit into his shoulder blades and buttocks and the wiry hairs sticking up through the flimsy material covering the mattress went right through his clothes and pricked his skin.

"It's like lying on a bed of nails," he grumbled, but he knew there was no point in complaining. "No need for comfort in this establishment—normally the occupants are too drunk to feel anything."

He felt isolated. It was at times like this he missed his sight. He would have given anything to be able to sit up at the little table beside the barred window and write down all the things that had happened so that he could weigh the pros and cons and maybe end up with some clear idea of what he should do. If he could write it all down and mull over it for a while he might be able to make up his mind.

Even with his handicap he was quite shrewd; he made very few mistakes. And though figuring in the dark was difficult it had its compensations—there were no distractions.

He sat up on the bunk facing the wall opposite the cell window and tried to put things into separate compartments at the back of his mind, using it like a blackboard. He often did that at home when he had a problem.

First there was the conversation he heard that night between the Englishwoman and the Pole—that was the most important thing because of the implications it had for the widow Montgomery and the future of the mill. It would have been just a juicy bit of gossip if Montgomery and his unfortunate driver had not come to such an untimely end but that was water under the bridge so to speak.

Secondly there was the little English woman and her son—whoever the father was. If she got away with it, she stood to scoop a bloody fortune, which could be to his advantage, especially if he changed his story.

He was doing okay until he got to the third item when the words on the first and second points slid sideways off the blackboard and he couldn't bring them back. He started from the beginning again, but the same thing happened, and he had to abandon the board and try and keep the facts in his head like memorising lines from a poem.

Thirdly he had made a fatal mistake, telling his sister what he knew. He should have kept his mouth shut until he saw the lie of the land.

Fourth was the widow Montgomery frothing at the mouth by all accounts since she discovered the Johnston baby was going to get the mill, house, the village, money—lock, stock and barrel.

Fifth was the blackmail by the police to try and force him to sign his statement and go into court and tell some Judge what he had heard. He was convinced they were in league with the widow; all those allegations against him but not even one charge after he made the statement.

Then there was his predicament. If he signed the statement and was prepared to testify in court about what he heard would there be anything in it for him? On the other hand, if he didn't sign, if he was not prepared to go into court, would there be a chance of getting money from the Johnston woman? After all if a challenge to the will failed she was going to fall in for everything.

He still had the police to think about. Would they go ahead and put the charges against him out of spite? The thing he was most worried about was the soliciting charge—a criminal offence for which he could do a stretch in Belfast Jail. They could make that stick because they had the prostitute to testify against him.

Then there was this business of his liaisons with the women in the shop.

"We know you have been demanding sex for spuds," McParland had whispered in his ear, "and we can prove it. Any judge worth his salt will put you away for a long time for that." Sheahan said this was the most serious allegation, one for which he could do a stretch, blind or not.

He still felt that none of the women would stand up in court and admit they had sex with him. But you could never be sure—the police might put pressure on some of them to testify just as they put pressure on the Bowden woman to make the statement.

On the other hand, if he was a philanderer who sold spuds for sex and frequented houses of ill repute what good would his evidence be to the Montgomery widow in court; or to anybody else? If he was such a disreputable and despicable character nobody would believe a word he said.

The more he thought about it the better he felt. That was his trump card. The police could not afford to bring any charges against him if they wanted him to testify in court and be believed. He would be their star witness. His evidence might decide where the Montgomery fortune would ultimately go. But he had to be believed and if they made him out to be a scoundrel, no judge would believe him.

If the widow succeeded everybody would be happy—the police, the lawyers and that wimp of a solicitor who was supposed to be acting for him; the loyal mill workers including his sister would be especially happy because they looked up to the Montgomerys as if they were royalty. And with all that money at stake surely there was something in it for him. Would the widow be willing to throw a couple of thousand pounds his way? The problem was that when it was all over, and she had her hands on a fortune, she might decide to keep it all for herself. The more money people had the harder they found it to part with any of it. Even though she might never be able to get her hands on her husband's wealth without his help she might just ignore him afterwards and there was nothing he could do about it.

Yet if he changed his story and Emma Johnston held on to the fortune, she might be more amenable to paying. The more he thought about it the more he felt the Johnston woman, rather than the Montgomery widow, might be more willing to pay out a few thousand pounds.

The thing that worried him most was that if he had to give evidence it might come out in court about the women he had sex with in the shop. The Sunday papers, especially the News of the World, would have a field day. He could see the banner headline "SEX FOR SPUDS" across the front page. He would be destroyed and so would his business and neither he nor his sister would be able to lift their heads in public again. There had to be some way of avoiding a scandal and still bring the business to a satisfactory conclusion.

The more he thought about it the less apprehensive he felt about his predicament. If he could take advantage of the situation this case could be an important turning point in his life, a new start. If he got money he might even pay for an operation to get his sight back. God, he would give anything to be able to focus those dead eyes again. What he wouldn't give to feast his eyes on the voluptuous Minnie.

He had to tread carefully for if he tried to get money out of either woman and the police found out he could end up on a blackmail charge on top of everything else.

Thinking about getting his sight back and Minnie naked got him excited. The swelling in his groin was still there when he heard the cell door being unlocked. He sat up quickly and covered the bulge with his cap.

"You are free to go home for the moment," a voice said. "But don't stray too far. We'll be back for you in the next couple of days."

He put on his jacket and was led through the cell door and along a damp passage to the outer wall of the police station. He knew he was outside when he felt a stiff breeze threatening to dislodge his cap. He was familiar with many of the streets in the town, but this was strange territory and he had little sense of direction. The sun on his face was no help because he didn't know what time of the day it was. He waited for somebody to come along to point him towards the bridge so that he could make his way home. When he heard boys kicking a ball he called to them and they gladly accepted a penny each to take him there. As he neared the shop neighbours inquired if he was okay. He knew they didn't care a damn about him but wanted to let him know that they had seen him being taken away in the police wagon earlier in the day.

He locked the front door and went upstairs and lay on the bed to resume his analysis of his situation. But whether he was too comfortable or too tired after his ordeal he could not regain his train of thought. He was sorry they had let him go just when he was getting the facts sorted out in his head.

'Trust the police,' he mused, 'they always come at the wrong time'. He turned over and went to sleep.

He woke when the clock on the mantelpiece in the living room began to chime. It was four in the afternoon, time to start boiling the spuds and heat the mince balls and onions for the dinner. Jinny would be finishing her shift at the mill, but she still had a three mile walk home so there was time to get everything ready.

When he told her the police had taken him to the barracks again she said it was terrible the way they were harassing him when he was just a citizen doing his honest duty.

"That's what you get for telling the truth," he said, feeling sorry for himself. "They wanted me to sign a statement that I couldn't even read. No way am I signing anything written by a policeman."

Helen Flanagan was shocked when she heard the rumour about an affair between her friend Emma Johnston and the Polish manager at the mill. It came from a good source—Sgt. McParland's wife—but with McKelvie involved she was reluctant to attach much credence to it. She recalled the great laugh she had with Emma the first time she met her and told her about his exploits with married women. It was just a funny story at the time for she had never had a hint from any of the women when she delivered their babies that they had a liaison with him or even that he had propositioned them.

This story he told the police about Emma Johnston and Krzysztof Walenski was malicious as far as she was concerned. Mark was the son of Sir Kenneth Montgomery. How could it be otherwise? If all the loose talk was not stopped, it could be the ruination of Emma—her reputation would be mud in a town like Murrinbridge. Could the people in Mill Brae be behind it? She would not put it past them for as far as she knew Lady Eleanor was fuming when she discovered that the boy was going to inherit everything; it would be very much in her interest to cast doubt on the boy's parentage.

Had Emma heard the gossip, she wondered? She might not for since the drowning she never left the house and the only people she had contact with were Ethel and herself. It might be a good time to pay a visit.

"I know I'm a bit early this week, but I happened to be passing and thought I might as well give my godson his check-up," she explained when Emma expressed surprise as she opened the door to her. She examined Mark and weighed him.

"He's coming on great," she said. "He is putting on weight."

It was a fine day and Helen suggested that Ethel should take Mark for a walk.

When they had gone Emma brought a tray and they sat down to have tea and scones.

Helen turned to face her. "There's talk going around about you and Krzysztof Walenski," she began. "Have you heard it?"

"I have heard the gossip. Ethel's sister works in the mill and she tells me what goes on there." She had her eyes fixed on her tea cup, avoiding Helen's stare. "I know some of what's being said and I don't know if I want to hear any more. It's very upsetting for me, especially at this time."

"Have you heard anything from your solicitors?"

"No, nothing."

"That's a good sign," said Helen. She took a few sips of tea. She looked directly at Emma. "It's really none of my business but I am your friend and Mark's godmother and there are certain things you might not be aware of, things that I feel you ought to know." Helen's tone was serious.

"Remember I once mentioned to you a blind man, a shopkeeper in the town, who was supposed to have carried on affairs with married women. This man, McKelvie, has apparently been questioned by the police and has told them a story about being in the garden behind Mill Brae one evening and overheard a conversation between you and the Polish mill manager Walenski."

Helen saw the colour drain from Emma's cheeks. Without a word she got up from the sofa and went to the window, keeping her back to Helen.

"He says he heard you tell him that you were going to have a baby and he might be the father."

Emma still had her back to her, but the nurse could see her shoulders were shaking. She paused a while to give her a chance to recover.

"The police managed to get him to make a statement about it but because he is blind and doesn't trust them he has refused to sign it. Nevertheless, he did make a statement and Eleanor Montgomery has been told all about it. Well, what do you think of all that?" She ended as abruptly as she began.

Helen looked at Emma, waiting for some response, but there was none. She still had her back to the nurse, but from the way she was shaking the nurse knew she was crying. There was an awkward silence in the room.

Helen stood up. "I'm going now, Emma. I know you are upset but

189

if the police are involved these rumours will not go away. I think you should have a talk with your solicitor about it."

She closed the front door behind her and walked towards her cycle leaning against the gable wall. As she passed the window she could see Emma still standing in front of the mantelpiece in the sitting room with her face buried in her hands.

Emma cried after the Nurse left. She always had a secret fear that the blind man might come back to haunt her someday, but not like this. Nobody would believe him if he claimed that he had a liaison with her in the Sally Garden, but they might believe that while hiding there, he had overheard the fight she had with Krzysztof. She had been so preoccupied with the possibility that she was pregnant and so angry with him for trying to rape her that she never even considered the possibility of anybody listening to them.

She was not aware before Helen came that it was the red headed blind man who had circulated the story about her. Nor did she know the police were involved. If that was so it wasn't just rumour anymore; it had gone beyond that. Helen said they had a statement; if Eleanor Montgomery's solicitors got their hands on it they might use it to try and upset the will.

Emma paid a visit to her solicitor and when she explained what she knew of the situation to him, he rang Lady Eleanor's solicitors.

"They are aware there is some trouble over the will," he said when he put down the phone, "but no formal proceedings have as yet been lodged in the Probate Court. I have a feeling, however, from talking to them that they are getting ready for some kind of court action."

He advised her not to do anything for the moment. Such challenges were very rare, he said, because there was a long-established principle in law that a will "spoke from the grave" as it were, and Lady Montgomery's solicitors would have a very difficult task if the widow tried to upset it. Courts were very reluctant to interfere so long as the will was clear as to its intentions, properly drafted, and duly signed and witnessed. In his opinion there was no ambiguity in the will of Sir Kenneth Montgomery. It had been drafted by a reputable firm of solicitors, properly signed by him and witnessed by two office employees.

Two days after the visit the solicitor rang to tell her that he had now been informed by Lady Eleanor's solicitors that documents for a challenge to the will had been lodged in the Crown Courts in Belfast and he would receive copies by registered post. As soon as he received them he would retain a good probate barrister to advise her on the best course of action to deal with any proceedings.

When she met her barrister for the first time Emma raised concerns about Lady Eleanor exerting undue influence on court proceedings. She was assured she need have no worry on that score, for the courts were impartial and decisions were based on the merits of the case and on the law. Neither should she worry about the cost of litigation because in virtually all probate cases costs were paid in full out of the estate of the Testator so long as the action was not frivolous or vexatious. She listened to what the barrister had to say but was still uneasy. She dreaded having to answer his questions knowing that she was going to tell him lies about her association with Krzysztof. She was terrified of contradicting herself, of being caught out in a lie.

She related accurately how Sir Kenneth had taken her to Ireland as a companion to his ailing wife but mainly as a favour to her father who wanted her out of England in case war started. Almost from the beginning, she knew there was something wrong between Sir Kenneth and Lady Eleanor. There was coldness between them; they hardly spoke to each other except in her presence. They were estranged, even though they lived in the same house. She learned that Lady Eleanor was on strong medication and Sir Kenneth was given to frequent bouts of drunkenness. She had personal experience of his drunkenness—he often came home drunk from the mill.

She paused to give the barrister time to write it all down. She had to be careful and get the story right in case she was quizzed about it later on.

"One night he stayed downstairs drinking after Lady Eleanor and I went to bed. Sometime later I woke to find him sitting on the side of my bed staring at me. He told me to be quiet or Lady Eleanor would hear us. He then put his hand over my mouth lay down beside me and forced himself on me.

"I was terrified during the ordeal but afterwards I said nothing about it to anybody—not even to my maid—because of the trouble I knew it would cause. That was the start of the affair between us. He treated me as a mistress and I had to accept the situation because there was nobody to turn to for help. I had nowhere else to go. The only other friend I had was Lady Eleanor, and I knew that if I told her what was going on it would only make things worse and she would probably order me to leave the house. I was told by one of the maids that Lady Eleanor had verbally attacked her husband's secretary on the telephone over rumours of an affair at the mill."

"He came into my bedroom twice or three times a week and that went on for nearly two years. I was always unhappy about it because as well as forcing himself on me he physically hurt me and when I protested he threatened to tell his wife that I had seduced him."

She looked at the barrister—he seemed to be convinced that she was telling him the truth.

"He bought a house at Templemount and urged me to move there but I refused to go. I didn't want to leave Mill Brae and kept hoping that he would tire of me or find a new lover at the mill—that something would happen to bring the affair to an end before Lady Eleanor found out what was going on.

"When I found out I was going to have his baby my first thought was that he would dump me for another woman and I would be left with nothing and nowhere to go so I made him promise that he would provide for me. But I need not have worried—he was so elated at the prospect of becoming a father that he promised that neither I nor my baby would ever want for anything, that he would give me a substantial sum of money and title to a house at Templemount.

"Nobody was more surprised than me to learn that he had actually made a new will before the accident. And when I was given a copy I was astonished to learn that as well as Leyland House he had left me a large sum of money, enough to keep me in comfort for the rest of my life. But when I read further and discovered he left the bulk of his estate to our son I was astonished. I also knew there would be trouble."

The lawyers took her through the affair from start to finish making copious notes. They asked lots of questions, especially about the seduction, the marital problems the Montgomerys were having at that time and how the affair came out into the open with her pregnancy.

They were much more cautious when it came to her friendship with the Polish mill manager. As soon as his name was mentioned she took the offensive.

"Somebody is putting about vile rumours about the manager and me," she said angrily. "Something will have to be done about that." She began to cry and had such fits of sobbing that the consultation had to be suspended while the office secretary plied her with tea and scones until she was in a fit state to resume.

"This is a distressing business for you," said the solicitor, "but once the barrister has all the facts he will remove the burden of this litigation from your young shoulders, and you will feel much better."

"Now," said the barrister, "tell us all about this ...Krzysztof Walenski. Start from the beginning, the very first time you set eyes on him."

She related events accurately. Like herself, he was sent by his parents to Ireland to escape the war, was given a job at the mill and she first met him when he came to Mill Brae House as Sir Kenneth's guest. She was introduced but did not speak to him on that occasion. Some months later, in the autumn, she met him again when he came to the house as a member of a group who paid for a tour of the gardens, a charity event. When the tour finished, and the others went into the house to have tea he wanted to see more of the gardens and she took him for an extended tour.

That night, she continued, Lady Montgomery went to bed early and Sir Kenneth got quite drunk and it was left to her to see the guests off after midnight. Mr Walenski left with the others. Emma deliberately made no mention of the visit to the Sally Garden.

The next time she saw Mr Walenski, she lied, was when he came to sympathise with her after Sir Kenneth's funeral. She was so distraught at the time that she could not remember what was said, but he stayed only a couple of minutes. He rang her on the phone some weeks later offering his services if she needed any help, but she assured him she was able to cope. The only other contact she had with him was a note delivered by hand to her home in which he apprised her of rumours circulating in the mill and asking what he should do about it. She was so disgusted by the vile stories that she tore up the note and put it into the fire.

"And that, gentlemen, is all I know about Mr Walenski," she concluded.

They asked her a few more questions about the meetings between them, brief as they were, and when she had finished the barrister advised her that they would put all the matters she had referred to into a sworn statement, framed in the form of a legal document known as an affidavit and she would be asked to sign it in the presence of her solicitor. This was an important document for the Court; it put her side of the story succinctly for the benefit of the presiding Judge. And all she had to do when the appointed day came was go into the witness box and repeat exactly what was in that document.

They were of opinion that she would be an excellent witness for she was sincere, had a good natural delivery of speech and was quick to get to the point when answering questions.

Though she had told blatant lies Emma was convinced the lawyers believed her. She knew it was risky, but this might be the time to have a chat with Krzysztof. She needed to make sure they told the same story of what happened the night of the tour at Mill Brae House. She went into town next day and called him from the Post Office and asked him to come to her home the following evening.

DISCOVERY AND RECOVERY

In the weeks that followed the death of her husband Lady Montgomery gradually emerged from the depression that had plagued her for years. She began to take an interest in the day to day affairs of the mill, and as that interest increased, so too did her appetite for life. She felt physically stronger, more mentally alert, well enough to reduce the dosage of medication prescribed by her doctor. Now that she had responsibility for the mill she felt she had to have her wits about her; apart from daily meetings with managers and Ministry men she also had regular contact with her solicitor and barristers about the will.

She had three visits from her lawyers before they were satisfied they had enough information to allow them to prepare pleadings for the High Court challenge to her late husband's will. Three months later a heavy sealed package arrived at Mill Brae by registered post. She carefully slit the envelope and inside was a copy of the barristers' brief, a 37-page document with language as daunting as its size.

The first ten pages were a mass of legal jargon setting out the authorities and the various statutes and instruments on which the challenge was grounded; and citing the jurisdiction of the Probate Court to adjudicate on them.

This was the Practice and Procedure of the High Court. It was impossible to make sense of the language, a cocktail of archaic phrases more appropriate to Shakespeare or Dickens. She turned over the pages until she found one that mentioned her by name.

THE HIGH COURT
Probate Division
In the matter of: Lady Eleanor Honora Montgomery
Petitioner
and

STATEMENT OF CLAIM

Thereafter followed a series of numbered paragraphs citing matters relating to the will, to Emma Johnston, to Mark Anthony Montgomery, the Polish Manager, Krzysztof Walenski, Seamus McKelvie, bachelor and greengrocer, of Murrinbridge in the County of Tyrone, and to herself.

It set out the grounds on which the Petitioner sought to have the will struck down, including fraud and she smiled as she read that "the said Emma Geraldine Johnston had exercised undue influence over Sir Kenneth Montgomery to change his will by fraudulently and wilfully representing that the Testator was the father of the illegitimate child she was about to bear".

She read and reread this document and marvelled at the way the lawyers had grasped all the important points she had provided for them. She liked the language: "and the said Emma Geraldine Johnston did so wilfully mislead the said Kenneth Montgomery by representing to him that her illegitimate child was his son, when she had already represented elsewhere that another was the father of the child she was expecting."

It concluded by asking the Court for a declaration that "the said Kenneth Montgomery died leaving a widow and no issue capable of making legal claim to property the subject of a Trust devised to the male who appeared in the Registry of Births as Mark Anthony Montgomery."

One paragraph she did not like:

> *Further and in the alternative if the boy known as Mark Anthony Montgomery is and is proven to be the illegitimate issue of the said Emma Geraldine Johnston and the said Kenneth Montgomery, the said Mark Anthony Montgomery is not entitled to the benefit of the Trust set out in the will for the following reasons, which shall be established as matters of fact in these proceedings.*

There followed a long treatise on the incompatibility of illegitimacy and inheritance, which did not sound convincing to her, for she was aware of several family disputes in Ireland and England where the courts decided that illegitimate children were capable of taking estate from their natural father and in some cases were placed almost on an equal footing with legitimate issue of the testator.

The shock of Emma's betrayal and the death of her husband so soon afterwards in such horrible circumstances forced Eleanor Montgomery to dwell less and less on her illness and think about what she was going to do in the future. Gradually the depression and headaches eased and she felt well enough to stop taking medication altogether. The more she involved herself in winding up her husband's affairs and running the mill the better she felt.

She closed her eyes to the gloomy vista outside, rested her head on the back of the chair and let her mind wander to the events that were leading her to a court case in Belfast, the uncertain outcome of which would decide her future.

Court case or not she had already made up her mind on one thing. Until this business was over, she would be Lady Eleanor Montgomery but thereafter she would revert to her maiden name, plain Eleanor Parker. After her husband's betrayal she had no intention of retaining the title that came with her marriage. As far as she was concerned the Montgomery name was dead and gone and she saw no point in subverting her own identity to the ghost of a dynasty that had run its course.

In the middle of all the gossip about Emma and Krzysztof Walenski, Kate Reilly disappeared, fuelling even more rumour. Nobody seemed to know why she left or where she went. The girls in the office assumed she had been sacked after the death of her boss but the truth was that one morning the staff could not get access to the offices because Kate did not show up with the key and she never came back to work again. Eleanor assumed the girl's disappearance had something to do with Krzysztof Walenski and the affair with Emma Johnston. When she confronted the Mill Manager about it he insisted he knew nothing of her whereabouts other than what he had been told by her mother—that she left home without a word and had not been seen or heard of since.

Eleanor knew that when the challenge to the will came to court it would cause a lot of unwanted publicity; there was no way of avoiding it. Even if Emma Johnston decided she did not want to go to court and sought some kind of a settlement, she would not agree. She was determined to have the will struck down and only a ruling by the court could rebut the legal presumption that her husband had a son and heir.

The whole business had other, more personal and far reaching implications for Eleanor. If it transpired that Walenski or somebody else was the father, did that suggest that Kenneth who had been bedding her for more than a year, was incapable of making the girl pregnant?

The more she thought about it the more she wondered whether her own inability to conceive might have had more to do with her husband than it did with her, as the doctors once suggested. She was the one who had gone for all the tests, who put up with mauling by specialists and surgeons. All had told her the same thing—there was no biological reason why she should not conceive.

She remembered how angry he became when she mentioned the possibility that he might have a problem; he had not talked to her for days afterwards and the subject was never mentioned again because she never seriously entertained the idea that there could be a problem on his part—until now.

On a wet afternoon, she decided to inquire further. She went to his library and searched through shelves of books for medical reference books to see what they had to say about male infertility.

She discovered that although rare, it was not entirely unknown; there were documented cases among populations all over the world particularly in countries affected by famine or diseases like leprosy, malaria or tuberculosis. Among these people, the birth rate was significantly lower than in more prosperous populations and the medical people ascribed it to low fertility among males. There was also some evidence that childhood illnesses such as measles and diphtheria sometimes affected male fertility. But even when all these causes were taken into consideration the number of cases was small compared to the problems that beset women. Female reproductive organs were far more delicate than men's and were affected by age, by genes, by malnutrition, even by changes in the environment.

The more she read the more intriguing she found the subject. Her research became interesting for another reason—in some of the books she found pages had been marked by turning down the corners. Who else other than her husband could have done that? It was just too much of a coincidence that she was now reading the same material he had already been though.

Eleanor was angry. It now appeared that while she was slowly losing her mind because she blamed herself for the failure to give her husband a baby, he obviously had doubts about his own ability to father a child; yet he never confided in her. If there was something wrong with him doctors might have been able to help.

'If he was so macho why was he so interested in the subject?' The more she thought about it the angrier she became; she was more determined than ever to find an answer.

With Kate Reilly gone Eleanor had another problem; she had no go-between for the blind shopkeeper. She was so obsessed with doubts raised about her husband's virility that more than ever she needed to know for certain if McKelvie was telling the truth about what he heard in the Sally Garden. Did he really hear the Johnston woman say that the Polish manager was the father? If those words were spoken by Emma Johnston they might go a long way to confirm what she was now discovering about Kenneth. Things she was finding out about begged the question: Whose fault was it that there were no children of the marriage?

If the court case established that Krzysztof Walenski was the father of Emma Johnston's baby where would it leave her and her life?

"Probably more depressed than ever," she thought sadly. "It means I have wasted the best years of my life and needlessly put myself through mental and physical anguish. But one way or another, I have to know. I have to know."

Eleanor had more or less made up her mind that if she managed to overturn the will she would throw herself completely into the management of the mill and as a woman of substance she might even take an interest in local affairs, maybe dabble in politics. She intended to discard everything identified with her late husband and his family except the wealth that went with it. If he had deceived her by hiding behind false masculinity all those years while she struggled to retain her sanity, she owed him nothing.

On the other hand, if the case went against her she would have little option but to leave Mill Brae and move to England and try and make a fresh start.

She went to Belfast to buy new clothes. She had taken to dressing and grooming herself for meetings at the mill and sessions with the legal advisors. Much of her bubbly personality returned—she was charming to the barristers and solicitors, got on well with the mill managers and took time after meetings to visit the spinning rooms and talk to the women. She felt that whatever the future held she had growing confidence in her ability to face it alone whether as the boss of Sperrin Mill or starting a new life in another country.

Valentino's fortunes showed no sign of improvement. He was still boycotted by his customers, forced to live as celibate as a Christian Brother and harassed by the police because he refused to sign the statement he had made to Sgt McParland about the Johnston woman. Every time they took him to the barracks for questioning they produced the same list of charges—stealing from the Montgomery lands, invasion of privacy of the Montgomerys and their guests, consorting with known prostitutes and having carnal knowledge of vulnerable women who came to his shop. Valentino knew he should never have trusted McParland when he promised that if he made a statement they would drop all charges.

The police clearly had a lot of influence over his solicitor for the old man pestered him to sign the statement, which he insisted he was "morally and legally bound to do". Valentino put him off using all sorts of excuses—harassment by the police, growing confusion in his own mind about what he actually heard, his blindness, the threat of prison hanging over his head and malicious rumours being circulated about him. He complained that he was treated like a criminal even though he had never been charged with any offence in his life. He was embarrassed, his sister was embarrassed, and he was getting a hard time from neighbours who believed that the police were after him for good reason. When pressure failed to get results Sheahan suddenly disappeared off the scene. McKelvie called to his offices several times only to be told that he was in court or at a consultation with a client and unavailable.

Nurse Flanagan got her children ready for school before setting off on her bicycle to make the daily rounds of mothers and babies. She was a well-respected and trusted figure in the largely rural community she served. Women confided in her, often looking for advice about family problems that had nothing to do with the health of their babies. The biggest problem most young mothers had was coping with pregnancies. Many were so financially and physically stretched trying to look after the children they had that the last thing they wanted was another mouth to feed; the problem was they had no sure way of preventing it. Helen counselled the women, the vast majority of whom were Catholics, on the natural method of birth control but in most cases, it didn't work. Husbands took their pleasure when they felt like it and if that coincided with their wife's fertile period it was just too bad, and his hard-pressed wife had to bear and cope with another baby.

The first concrete evidence Helen got about the sexual exploits of Valentino McKelvie was when Minnie Boyle came to her for help, thinking she was pregnant. She didn't want another baby especially when everybody knew she had a husband in England whom she hadn't seen for years. Minnie begged her for something to get rid of it; otherwise she would have to go to Derry and pay for a back-street abortion. In her anguish Minnie let slip to the Nurse that she had an affair with the blind shopkeeper.

"And the baby you're having now… is that McKelvie's?" asked the nurse.

"Yes," she said. "I have not been with anybody else. Danny Boyle's family will go mad if they hear about it. You have to do something for me."

She warned Minnie not to tell anybody that she was pregnant and especially not McKelvie.

Minnie came home from church one Sunday morning and found the police waiting for her. She sensed immediately it was bad news. Danny Boyle had died of a heart attack in England the previous day. Apparently, he had been living in a hostel for the homeless in London and was on his way back there from a football match when he collapsed and died before they got him to hospital.

Her brother stayed away from Danny Boyle's funeral in case his presence caused problems for Minnie. Jinny attended the Mass and burial out of respect for their neighbour.

Minnie had not entered the greengrocer's shop for months for fear of antagonising the men on the street who had organised the boycott. So, he could hardly believe his ears a week after the funeral when he heard her outside talking to the deliveryman. His heart started to thump at the sound of her voice and he felt himself getting excited. When the vanman departed she came inside and walked around looking at what was on offer.

When another customer left he sensed she was still there. "And what can I do for you, madam?" he asked sarcastically. "I haven't had the pleasure of your company for a long time."

"You never know what you might be able to do for me," she said. "Remember I'm a widow woman now."

Mini was teasing him but he didn't care. He was so excited he needed to take a leak.

When he returned from the privy she was sitting in the kitchen.

"Close the shop," she said. "I need to talk to you privately." Valentino was more than happy to oblige.

"I don't know where to start," she said when she sat down. "Danny left me nothing. I haven't a penny and I need to pay for his funeral.

"That's why I'm here," she said. "My parents have been helping me since I came home from England but there's no way they have the money to bury him. And I don't want it said to my girls at school that their father's funeral was paid for from the parish paupers' fund."

"Minnie's difficulty is my opportunity," he figured, mimicking Republicans who wanted to mount attacks in England when Churchill was up to its eyes in the war with the Germans.

"Well," he said. "I suppose there's no harm in having a chat." He moved across the kitchen and stood behind her, putting his hands on her shoulders. Then he slid them down the front of blouse until he had one breast in each hand. She jumped up suddenly from the chair and pushed him away.

"Don't be stupid. That's not why I'm here. I've just buried my husband and I came to you for help for I have nobody else to turn to. I need £30 to pay the undertaker."

He moved away from her, surprised by her directness and the way she reacted when he touched her. He scratched his head as if he was thinking it over. "£30 is a lot of spuds at half a crown a measure," he said.

Before he got a chance to say anything else, she said: "I'll pay you back the only way I can if you're still interested."

He couldn't lie. "There's nobody else," he confessed. "Minnie, I'm desperate! I need a woman so badly I would pay any money. I'll give you the £30 but I can't wait another minute. I need you today."

She pushed him away again. "No! Not now. No more in the shop. We have to find another place where we won't be seen together. And not until Danny's funeral has been paid for."

Before he had time to argue with her a customer knocked at the door and when he went back into the kitchen after he served the girl Minnie was gone.

"Bitch," he muttered. "When I get the knickers off you you'll be sorry for the torture you're putting me through."

When Minnie told Helen Flanagan that she was getting the funeral money from Valentino the nurse wanted to know how she was going to pay him back.

"I would prefer to sleep with him than go on my knees to the Parish Priest looking for charity," she said. She asked Helen if it would be possible to get her some contraceptives. "Knowing him," she said, "he will be looking for value for money. But I want no more babies. You helped me before when I thought I was pregnant, but I might not be so lucky the next time. I don't want to take any more chances."

"I'm glad you're getting a bit of sense, Minnie Boyle," said the nurse. "Whatever hope you have of holding your head up in the parish, you will have no chance if you produce a baby when your husband is dead."

"No more babies—definitely," said Minnie.

Minnie stepped onto the double-decker bus in the town square and sat in a seat near the back on the lower deck so that she could keep an eye on Valentino who was already seated near the front. The only other passengers were schoolboys running up and down the aisles playing a chasing game. She sat at the rear because she did not want to be seen with him until they were well clear of the town. Several times he turned around listening for some sound that would tell him she was there.

When the bus left the terminus, Minnie walked forward and slipped into the seat behind him. She whispered that he should follow her upstairs and they went to the top deck and sat on the bench seat at the rear.

"Jesus, woman," he said, "I thought you had left me in the lurch when the bus moved off and no sign of you. I was going to get off again at the next stop."

"I told you we have to be careful," she whispered.

From the moment he felt her warm body against his in the narrow seat, he began to get excited. He put a hand on her knee and when she left it there he moved it inside her thigh. Minnie got a shock when his fingers touched her bare flesh. She took a deep breath, grabbed his hand and held her knees tightly together.

"There are children running around," she pleaded. "You'll have to control yourself."

His heart was thumping in his chest. He put his hand on her knee and she quickly pushed it away again. The odd sensation from his touch was as bad as ever.

"No," she pleaded with him again. "You have to wait until we get to the hotel. Did you bring the money?"

From his hip pocket he took a small round bundle of notes tied with an elastic band. She squeezed his hand as she took it from him and counted it.

"I'm very grateful," she said. "You're the only one I could turn to."

He put his arm around her waist and squeezed her. She kept talking to try and take his mind off her. "We'll settle the bill with the undertaker, make our way to the hotel and book a room. It's a nice day so we might take a bit of a walk. We have time to spare. Maybe we'll go to Fosters restaurant and have something to eat.

"When all this business is behind us," she prattled on, "we can go back to the hotel and there will be nobody to interrupt us, no prying eyes to spy on us."

"Jesus, woman I'll never survive that long," he said pleading with her. He suggested they go to the hotel first, have a session, then go to the undertaker. "We can eat anytime. I need you more than I need food."

"You have to be patient," she whispered. "Pretend we're on our honeymoon. If you behave yourself until we get to the hotel I promise you the best time you ever had."

He was still pleading with her to change her mind when the bus reached Derry and it was time to get off.

THE GO-BETWEEN

Helen parked her bicycle beside the front porch at Leyland House and by the time she retrieved her bag from the carrier Emma was at the open doorway waiting to greet her. She looked anxious.

"You left in such a hurry the last time I thought you might not be back," she said.

From the moment she came through the door Helen thought Emma looked a worried woman. When Ethel took Mark upstairs the nurse broke the silence.

"Have you thought any more about this man McKelvie and the story he's putting about?" she asked. "More important have you decided what you are going to do about the court case?"

Emma shuddered: "My solicitor says that if McKelvie's evidence is believed things could go badly for me. He would dearly love to talk to him face to face but the barrister is adamant that any attempt to make contact with him would be disastrous if it came out in court. It's a very difficult situation."

The two women went silent for a while.

Helen looked at her. "I might be able to help there. I have a friend who is close to McKelvie and she owes me a favour. What if I used her as a sort of go between to find out what he's up to?"

"Oh, Helen if you could it would be such a help," she said eagerly. "But I don't want you to compromise yourself. Eleanor Montgomery is a very powerful woman and she could do you a lot of damage if she finds out that you are supporting me. You have to think about your own position."

"Don't worry," Helen assured her. "I will make sure to keep myself well out of it. But before I approach my friend I need to know something. Is there any substance in this story?"

Emma got up and walked to the window and stared into the garden. When she turned around again she looked straight at Helen and nodded her head. "I'll tell you the truth, Helen, because you are the only friend I have, and because I trust you."

"Yes," she admitted, "I am ashamed to say that I did have sex with Krzysztof—once. I went to his lodgings one night on an errand and things got out of hand. It was just one of those stupid things that happened in my life—a bad decision made on the spur of the moment. And I have to admit it was as much my fault as his. Yes. It is possible that I might have become pregnant that night but my affair with Sir Kenneth started a long time before that and it is far more likely, and I firmly believed, and I still believe," she lied, "that Kenneth is Mark's father."

Helen said: "It is important to try and remember dates accurately. If I had those dates I might be able to work out exactly when you became pregnant."

"I have already been over that with my doctor," said Emma. "I cannot say for sure the time I got pregnant, but it was around the time I had the encounter with Krzysztof."

"What about this story McKelvie is telling about you and Krzysztof Walenski in the Sally Garden, the night you told him you were pregnant?" Helen asked. "Did you tell him you were having his baby?"

"I was angry and upset that night because he tried to force himself on me; I honestly cannot recall my exact words," she said. "I know I told him I was pregnant and warned him not to come near me. I have thought about it so much recently that I am totally confused now as to what was actually said."

Helen didn't like what she heard but promised that as soon as an opportunity arose she would make it her business to try and get McKelvie's version—what he claimed he heard and just how sure he was. Ominously Emma had already confirmed at least part of the story circulating in the mill.

The day was endless for Valentino. He had to sit on a chair in the undertaker's waiting room for almost an hour while the stupid clerk prepared a detailed account for Minnie. There was a funny odour in the place that became more noticeable every time a door nearby opened. He recognised the smell of decay, of death, the same whiff he got when he went to a wake house where the body was laid out in an open coffin. He got the same smell when he opened a sack of potatoes that had a few rotten ones inside. He didn't like it.

Eventually Minnie came out of the office. She offered him the receipt, but he refused to take it. He wanted to get out of the place quickly and go to the hotel. The sun was shining outside, and she insisted they go for a walk along the river. When they turned back towards the hotel, she steered him into a restaurant and ordered a meal. It seemed a long time before the food came and there was further delay because she had to strip the fat from his steak and cut the lean meat into small pieces so that he could eat it with his fork. She insisted on dessert and a pot of tea afterwards and he became more and more frustrated with the delay. It cost a fortune—nearly three shillings each—and though he grumbled he paid up promptly so that they could get out of the place.

The grandfather clock in the hotel foyer chimed 8 o'clock as she picked up the room key from reception and the pair went upstairs. Minnie was amazed by the way he managed the steps, never faltering. When it came to the landings he took them in his stride using the handrail as a guide. He insisted on opening the door with the big key. Inside Minnie was impressed by the luxury of the place—a beautiful bed and lockers, polished rosewood table and mahogany chairs arranged beside a large bay window that overlooked the busy street below. He sat down on the bed and though it was still daylight she closed the heavy curtains.

She told him to undress and moved a chair beside the bed so that he could fold his clothes over the back of it. He heard her running water and flushing the toilet in the bathroom and got annoyed again. Was she going to take a bath? If she was he made up his mind, he would go in after her for he was not prepared to wait any longer.

He only managed to strip to his long johns when he heard her coming back from the bathroom and he got a whiff of strong perfume. He felt her hands on either side of his head and she kissed him. Minnie felt the tingling sensation again when he put his cold hands on her warm buttocks.

"We'll get into bed," she whispered, and he let her go. She went to the other side, drew back the covers and he heard the creak of the

208

mattress as she lay down. He peeled off the long johns and got in beside her. He felt her wince at his touch.

"What's wrong with you woman?" he said, annoyed that she moved away from him.

"You have to put something on," she whispered.

"But I just took everything off," he said angrily, sliding his hand down the front of her nightdress.

"I don't mean clothes, you idiot," she laughed as she pushed him away again. "On your willy! You don't want to make me pregnant, do you? Lie on your back and I'll put it on for you."

He did as he was told, and she knelt on top of him and he felt great when her fingers touched his flesh as she slipped on the contraceptive. He had heard about these things but never used one before. It felt very tight and when he complained she told him not to worry for it would not affect him.

"And with this on," she added, "we can have as much fun as we like without the risk of me producing a baby."

"God forbid!" he muttered.

When she was satisfied the sheath was in place exactly as the nurse had instructed she smoothed it gently with her fingers, lay down beside him and gave him a long kiss. His body shivered with excitement. She rolled over on her back and pulled the nightgown up around her waist. In an instant he was on top of her, forcing her legs apart.

"Bitch," he murmured. "You have been teasing me all day. I have been waiting a long time to get between your legs again."

He lay on top of her and felt the heat from her naked body. Her lips were pressing into his neck and he was in heaven. He moved against her and she responded by tightening her arms around his neck and her thighs around his buttocks.

Valentino's gyrations increased, and his breathing quickened, but little else seemed to be happening. He couldn't find his way inside. Minnie put one of her hands down between their sweating bodies to guide him, but it was no good; he had gone limp.

She felt the anger rise in him. "Woman," he gasped "now see what you've done with your teasing and your French letter. I can't even

209

get it up for you!"

She rolled him over on his back and knelt astride him again and tried to massage him back to life, but it was no good. He had gone so soft that the cover was slipping off and she had to keep pulling it up.

Eventually he pushed her off, disgusted that he could not make love to her.

"I'm impotent, impotent!" he said over and over. "I've been going crazy for a woman for ages and now I can't perform."

"It's only a temporary thing," she consoled him. "You're far too anxious. You'll be fine in the morning. It's just a thing that happens sometimes."

He was not a happy man but there was nothing he could do about it. He was so frustrated and angry that he turned away from her and pulled the covers of the bed up over his naked sweating torso. Then his anger turned to fear, the same fear he had experienced that day on the bridge as a boy when he discovered he was losing his sight.

'Jesus', he thought, 'blind and impotent. I might as well jump in the river.'

He pretended to be asleep so that he would not have to talk to her about it. She kept her lips against his neck and whispered to him that if he awoke during the night and felt up to it all he had to do was rouse her and they could make love for as long as he liked.

She awoke later, and he had turned around to face her. He was trying to lift one of her legs so that he could get closer. She pretended to be still asleep. Then she felt him moving against her. Valentino was back to his old form. He turned her on her side and pushed hard and she began to move with him as the love sickness welled up inside her. She remembered the sheath, but it was too late to do anything if it had slipped off.

When he had exhausted himself, he relaxed for a while but lay close and several times during the night she awoke to find him making love to her again. When she was in her teens, she imagined that lovemaking would be like this, but in her marriage it never was—with Danny it was usually a quick dart and it was all over.

Valentino was much more passionate than her husband. His lovemaking was like everything else, no half measures. Serving in the shop he was quick and efficient; making baskets his nimble fingers kept going even when he was talking; when he made love, he gave until he had nothing left to give. This was the lad she remembered from before her marriage, the lithe young man with tousled red hair and good looks. Lots of girls fancied him but sadly none were interested in having a boyfriend who was blind. They used to talk nonsense about marrying a blind man and running the risk of producing blind children.

When he got up during the night to go to the toilet she was relieved to see he was still wearing the sheath. She told him to get rid of it. When he got back into bed she took a fresh one from the pack and kept it beside her in case he wanted her again. She awoke at daylight to find him touching her. She rolled him over on his back, knelt on top of him to put the fresh sheath on.

"That bloody thing is going to revolutionise sex," he said. "If I could get my hands on some of them I could make a fortune."

In the morning while they got dressed for breakfast she said she wanted to talk to him.

"Do you realise there's something wrong with you," she said, not sure how to broach the subject.

"I'm fucking blind," he said, annoyed at her for bringing it up again. "Everybody knows that."

"There's something else, something odd that I've been meaning to talk to you about."

"Jesus, woman, am I going to die or something. Put me out of my agony," he said, mocking her.

"Do you not realise that when you touch a woman it makes her feel strange?"

"Aw Jesus, I'm not that ugly, Minnie. I'm not a monster, am I?"

"I don't mean anything like that," she said. "It's hard to explain. Sometimes when I touch your skin, it tingles, like an electric shock."

He scratched his head. "I think you're raving mad, woman," he said.

"No, I'm not; and I'm not the only one that felt it either. Remember when we used to go to the dances? I felt it then and some of the other girls had the same experience. That's why they were reluctant to dance with you. It made them tingle all over, uncomfortable."

He was astonished.

"Nonsense—they didn't want to dance with me because I was blind," he said. "Everybody knows that."

"No, they didn't want to dance with you because they felt funny when you touched them and they got frightened. Some of them thought it was because of your blindness, others because you had red hair or because you were always messing about with radios and batteries."

He couldn't believe what she was saying. "Are you saying every time you touch me I shock you?"

"No. Not every time. That's what puzzled me for a long time. But I figured it out. You only give a shock when you're exited. You know—when you want to have sex with me."

At breakfast he was quiet. He found it hard to believe that what she said was true, but he did recall that on a number of occasions, women acted strange when he touched them. He remembered that night with Minnie at the dance, the night he thought about doing himself in by jumping off the bridge. Is that what made her drop the paper bag in the shop that first day when they made love in the hallway? He remembered the English girl behaved very strangely when she was with him, when she put the handkerchief around his bleeding wrist. And when they had sex in the Sally Garden that evening, she definitely behaved oddly.

"It's not an unpleasant feeling," Minnie explained later when he asked her about it again. "In fact, after a while it makes me feel good, a bit like the feeling I get when you're making love to me."

"At least that's something," he said grudgingly. But her talk about the shocks left him uncomfortable, self-conscious.

During a brief hearing in the Probate Division of the High Court in Belfast affidavits were lodged, preliminary issues settled among the lawyers and the Judge fixed a date for the hearing of the case of *Montgomery v Johnston*. Leave was given to serve witness summonses on a number of people, including Valentino McKelvie.

The case had been a long time coming and he had been told that most court actions never actually went to a hearing because the lawyers often got together and worked out a compromise. He was sure this would happen in this case because the last thing these upper-class people wanted was to have their names dragged through the mud in a public scandal. Everybody knew if the case got into court the newspapers would have a field at the expense of Eleanor Montgomery and Emma Johnston. Sir Kenneth Montgomery's infidelity was one thing, but it was inevitable that Emma Johnston's affair with the Pole and the lack of certainty about who the father of the Johnston baby really was would make headlines for the duration of the trial.

Mixed in with all this was the evidence of a blind man who eavesdropped on Emma Johnston and the Polish mill manager the night she told him she was expecting a baby and you had all the ingredients for a story that would be perused word by word throughout the length and breadth of Ireland. And if that weren't enough it might also come out in court that the star witness, McKelvie, the blind man who lay alone in the attic of his home while raging floodwaters demolished houses all around him, the man whose courage was headlines in the papers, was in fact a scoundrel who demanded sexual favours from the wives of his impoverished neighbours in exchange for vegetables from his shop.

He had to find a way to extricate himself from the mess but at the same time felt that he had to get something out of it, something to compensate him for all the hassle he had from the police. There might be some profit in it for him but there were also risks for he had been warned that lawyers could make things very difficult when they got him in the witness box. And if the judge suspected he was telling lies he could go to jail.

Still, he decided it was a risk he had to take.

After her husband's death Valentino saw to it that Minnie and her children were financially better off than they had ever been in exchange for her favours. Just as important was the fact that she did not have the worry of an unwanted pregnancy thanks to the nurse who supplied her with contraceptives.

When the request for rubbers suddenly stopped, Helen got worried. Had Minnie got careless again?

"He has found somebody who can supply him on a regular basis," she divulged. "In fact, he has started selling them under the counter in the shop—to friends he knows will keep their mouth shut. He thinks there's good money to be made on them."

Helen shook her head. There was no limit to the rogue's enterprise. But at least it relieved her of the burden of procuring them. In future she would direct her customers to the vegetable shop. It would take the pressure off her.

The nurse decided this was a good time to raise the subject of the court case.

"I'm sure Valentino has more important things on his mind these days with this court case," she said.

"He's worried sick about it," said Minnie. "He is finding it hard to sleep at night."

"He's not the only one," said Helen. "Emma Johnston is very worried about it too and with good reason. Lady Montgomery has powerful friends; if things go against Emma she and her son will be destitute.

"You know Emma and I have been great friends since she asked me to be Mark's godmother and she wants me to be a witness for her, but I'm terrified of being called to give evidence in court. You never know what awkward questions they will ask you."

She confessed she liked Emma Johnston a lot and didn't want to say anything that might hurt her but at the same time she couldn't tell lies in court once she swore to tell the truth.

"Everybody says Valentino is going to be the most important witness," she said, "and it would be a big help to me if I knew the truth about what he heard that night in the Sally Garden.

"I'm convinced Kenneth Montgomery was the father of the boy and that's what I intend to say in court but if it turns out I am wrong the lawyers will make me look stupid."

"He is under so much pressure from the police that he doesn't talk to me about it," Minnie said. "He is sick of the whole business and sorry that he ever told anybody what he heard that night."

Helen persisted. She wanted to know if he was sure it was Emma Johnston and the Polish lad talking in the garden or could it have been somebody else? Could it have been Montgomery himself who was with her? What exactly did he hear?

"Minnie," she pleaded, "you would be my friend for life if you could talk to him about it and of course I would never repeat what you told me. All I want is information to stop me making a fool of myself in court."

The nurse got up to leave. "And remember Minnie when this case is over the English girl can afford to be generous if it turns out right for her."

"I'll do what I can," promised Minnie.

The next time they met Minnie had lots of information for Helen. On their last visit to the hotel Valentino talked at length to her about what happened in the Sally Garden. She told the nurse about the interrogation by the police and the statement they wanted him to sign for Lady Montgomery and the threats and intimidation they subjected him to when he refused. In one last desperate effort to get him to sign a policeman promised that if he co-operated in signing the statement and backed it up with evidence in court it could be very much to his personal advantage. He was told that Lady Montgomery was a wealthy woman and a gift of a couple of thousand pounds was of little consequence to her—she could afford to be generous to people who helped her.

"They tried to bribe him, but he still does not trust them," said Minnie. He told them he would think about it.

Helen went straight to Templemount to pass the information to Emma.

Kate Reilly's disappearance was still a mystery. Her distraught mother told Krzysztof that she and her husband had searched the house from top to bottom for some clue as to where she might have gone and found nothing except bundles of old payslips and some magazines and books in the attic. Wherever she went she had taken very few personal belongings with her. Most of her clothing was still hanging in her bedroom.

At the mill the demand for parachutes ceased altogether after D-Day and nobody was sure what would happen to the workforce. Nothing could be decided about the future until the outcome of the court case was known.

Krzysztof spent his days moping over the loss of Kate. Now that the war was nearly over they should have been making plans to get married and settle down together. That's what he wanted more than anything else—Kate to come home to Poland with him and become part of his family. It was only after she left he realised how much he loved her and what a fool he'd been to get involved with Emma Johnston.

He vowed he would not give up his search for her. And even if he did not find her he still had hopes that when she had time to get over the hurt he had caused her she would make contact with him. In the quiet of his room he took her picture from the bedside locker and stared at the pretty face framed in a mass of tight black curls, remembering how happy they were together as they toured the countryside on their bicycles and warm embraces by the mountain lake.

"Kate, my love, where are you?" he asked forlornly.

The girl in the picture smiled but kept her secret.

Valentino decided to make one more visit to the hotel with Minnie and stressed it would be their last. This time the purpose was not just to bed Minnie—he had another more important reason. Instead of undressing in the hotel room he produced a pen and a bottle of ink and paper from his overnight bag and told her he had a job for her. He wanted to write a statement to give to the police. She was to put write down exactly what he told her and when it was finished he wanted her to read it back to him and he would sign it and she would sign as a witness to the fact that it was his signature. Even though he knew exactly what he wanted to say he mulled over each sentence before he allowed her to write it down and it took more than an hour to say what he wanted to say; she read it back to him, made a few corrections and they both signed it.

He went to the police station next day and asked the Sergeant to send for his solicitor and when they were all together in a room he handed over the statement.

The Sergeant was delighted to get the signed statement especially when he read it and found it was not much different from the one he gave in the police station. Sgt McParland had almost given up hope of ever getting McKelvie to sign. Before Valentino left the barracks old Sheahan appeared from nowhere to congratulate him on the statement and on the fine handwriting and the clear way it was all set out.

"I could not have prepared a better statement myself," he said. "It will stand up in any court of law."

Duplicates were made, and Valentino was given his copy and sent home in a taxi. He gave it to Minnie for Helen Flanagan.

Emma Johnston became physically ill when she read the statement from the blind man for it confirmed her worst fears—he had heard every word she said to Krzysztof. It was uncanny how after all this time he remembered so accurately. Since this business of the court case started she tried to blot certain things from her mind as if they did not happen but now when she saw the statement in front of her she knew every word was true.

"I would do anything to prevent that statement being read out in court," she sobbed.

"Are you prepared to pay thousands of pounds?" asked Helen. "As far as I know, the only way to stop it is by paying McKelvie money—a lot of money."

"I said anything, Helen, anything, and I mean it!"

Helen went back to Minnie.

"I have good news for him this time," she said. "Tell him Emma Johnston is prepared to pay four thousand pounds in cash if he changes his story—enough to buy a house for you, Minnie, and still make him a wealthy man."

When Minnie heard the huge amount of money involved she worried that he was getting involved in something that was out of his depth, but she agreed to give him the message.

When she told him what the Nurse said he sent back word that he would not change his statement.

"He says he has something else in mind," said Minnie, "and if Emma Johnston trusts him he has something up his sleeve for the court case to make sure she wins. But in turn he wants a written guarantee from her that when the case is over, provided she wins, and the will is confirmed she will pay him a sum of £4,000 in cash."

"He wants a proper written agreement," added Minnie "witnessed by you and kept in your possession until the court case is over. He doesn't trust anybody else with it. And if the lawyers find out about the deal he says he will deny everything even if he has to tell lies in the witness box."

Helen joined Valentino and Minnie in the store behind his shop the following week and produced an agreement signed by Emma and witnessed by her. Minnie read it aloud and when Valentino was satisfied it was what he had asked for Helen carefully folded it and slid it inside the cup of her bra.

"You better find a safer place than that, nurse," he said when Minnie told him where Helen hid it. "For that husband of yours might discover our secret if he makes a grab for you. That piece of paper holds the future for Minnie and me."

"Is that a proposal of marriage I hear?" said Helen.

"Go along and mind your own business, woman," he said. "We have more important things on our mind. Pull the front door after you on your way out."

Before Helen left the store he already had his jacket off and his shirt unbuttoned. Minnie looked at Helen, raised her eyes to Heaven and shook her head.

"For God's sake it's three o'clock in the afternoon," she pleaded.

"Any time is a good time for a good time," he quipped.

DRAMA IN COURT

Valentino and Jinny were among the first to enter Court VII of the Crown Courts in Belfast where the case was to be heard. The sense of foreboding he had since he left home that morning was not helped by the dank odour of stale air that filled his nostrils as soon as he entered the courtroom. Anything to do with the police or the law was an ordeal for ordinary people and for him, with his affliction, even more so; the claustrophobic atmosphere increased his sense of anxiety. He had never been in court before not even in the district court in Murrinbridge. Now he had been summoned to appear as a witness in the High Court. This is where all the big trials were held—political, criminal, land disputes and the like. He wondered how many people had had been sentenced to death in that courtroom.

He was so nervous that his hands were twitching, and he had to sit on them to keep still. There was tightness in his chest as if his jacket was too small for him. He opened the buttons and tried to ease the tension by talking to Jinny, quizzing her about the shape of the place and where the judge and the lawyers and the witnesses sat in relation to one another. Jinny was never in a court before either, but he persisted with his questions until he was happy that he had a good mental picture of the layout; he began to breathe more easily again.

The room was rectangular. He was sitting on one side with other witnesses facing the public gallery opposite. The judge's bench was to his right and close to it the dreaded raised witness box from which he would have to give evidence. Between him and the public gallery were benches for the lawyers—Kings Counsel in front facing the judge, junior barristers in the two rows behind and further back, solicitors and clerks. Behind them were benches for the Press and at the rear sat uniformed policemen.

There was a large window behind him and he could hear cars passing; a train whistled and let off a burst of steam not too far away. He felt the heat of the sun on his back and imagined if he had his sight he would see beams of sunlight coming into the room through the window, illuminating dust particles floating upwards in the stuffy warm air. The room had a musty smell, as if the windows had never been opened.

Jinny kept him informed about various people coming and going and bickering going on in the crowded Press Box as reporters jostled with one another for seats at the front pew. The newspapers had been waiting patiently for the case to come to hearing since it was first listed. A member of the aristocracy, his wife, his mistress, her boyfriend, an illegitimate son, a dispute over a very valuable estate and a blind man as the star witness—it had all the makings of a great story!

Because they had arrived early he and Jinny had escaped the attentions of the battery of photographers outside but both Lady Montgomery and Emma Johnston were not so lucky—they were spotted immediately and had to run the gauntlet of the cameramen. Helen Flanagan kept her head down and followed close behind Emma. She was wary of the pressmen but at the same time secretly hoped that if Emma's picture appeared in the newspapers, she would be visible in the background. It would be nice to be able to tell her children that she was a witness in such an important case.

The courtroom filled to capacity as the time approached for the hearing and there was a lot of noise and movement in the public gallery until all the seats had been filled. An usher ordered the policeman at the door not to admit any more members of the public. The buzz inside continued until a door opened somewhere near the judge's bench and the hum of voices died quickly as a voice boomed out in the crowded room:

"This court is now in session! Be upstanding for His Honour Baron Wilfred Lowry!"

There was a noisy clatter of shoes and boots on the wooden floorboards between the benches as everybody got to their feet. He stood up with the others; he heard a light footfall along one side of the room, going up three steps, then the grate of the legs of a chair on floorboards. Another noisy shuffle of feet as everybody sat down.

A man's voice announced that the "High Court of Probate of Northern Ireland" was now in session.

He was uneasy and so was his sister and he sensed that most people around him felt the same for they fidgeted with newspapers and shifted their bums about on the seats, wiping damp hands and brows with handkerchiefs, conversing nervously in low whispers.

As soon as the case was called Counsel for Lady Montgomery got to his feet and a deadly silence descended on the courtroom. It reminded Valentino of the eerie stillness in Murrinbridge that night before the river burst its banks. He crossed his fingers and hoped he would survive this episode of his life as well as he had survived the flood. Although he had to face danger when the deluge came at least he was in familiar surroundings; this was a more hostile environment, a world he knew nothing about. He had the tightness in his chest again and to add to his discomfort he had cramps in his stomach and the only way he could get relief was by passing wind, much to the disgust of people sitting behind him.

He wiped the sweat off his forehead with the sleeve of his jacket.

"Milord..." Counsel for Lady Montgomery began a long address to the Judge in which he outlined the background to the challenge to the will of the late Sir Kenneth Montgomery. He quoted at length the various statutes governing testacy and the correct practice and procedure for probate actions. It meant nothing to Valentino and the longer he went on the more uneasy and fidgety the packed courtroom became.

Valentino listened intently when the barrister quoted from cases going back as far as the Eighteenth Century about paternity, illegitimacy and the rights of illegitimate children, about deceit and fraud and the state of mind of an accused person before he or she could be found guilty of wilful fraud.

Then it was the turn of Counsel for Emma Johnston; he was much more to the point, asking the Judge to strike out the action without a hearing, citing a variety of grounds that Valentino did not understand. There followed nearly an hour of claims and counter-claims and argument and counter-argument between the opposing barristers. When they had done it appeared it had all been a waste of breath—the Judge announced that the hearing should proceed. There was an audible sigh of relief from the Press Box—they were fearful that the judge's ruling on the legal argument might rob them of the chance to hear the salacious details of the case.

Counsel for Lady Montgomery gave a summary of the evidence it was intended to call "to prove to the court that blatant fraud had been perpetrated by the Respondent for the sole purpose of hood-winking the late Sir Kenneth Montgomery into believing that the illegitimate son she bore was his flesh and blood."

"I choose the word hoodwinked carefully," he explained, "for I intend to adduce evidence that will convince Your Lordship that Emma Johnston was well aware from the beginning of her pregnan-cy that Sir Kenneth Montgomery was not the father of her child, that another man with whom she had a casual affair had made her pregnant with the son she subsequently gave birth to."

Valentino knew the lawyer was referring to what was contained in the statement he had given to the police. He listened intently be-cause he would have to give evidence about that statement when his turn came, and he had been warned by Sgt McParland that giv-ing evidence under oath in a court of law could be a very confusing business. It was not just a matter of going into the witness box and saying your piece. You had to answer questions put by the barristers and sometimes they would not allow you to explain yourself—they would demand a simple answer, yes or no. Judges and lawyers were clever people and part of their job was to catch out uneducated peo-ple like him, making liars and fools of them in front of the public.

When he asked his solicitor Sheahan about this he was told not to worry for probate cases were different from criminal trials. "In this case nobody is accused of any criminal offence," he assured him, worried that McKelvie might get cold feet and refuse to testify. "Witnesses are there to help the court come to a decision and the judge would never allow them to be bullied by lawyers."

Still, he didn't trust those clever dicks nor the police bullies whom he knew were sitting not too far away from him. He didn't trust Sheahan and he didn't trust the barristers and he didn't trust the police. He didn't trust the Johnston woman either—that's why he insisted on the written agreement.

He pricked up his ears when the Judge asked a question.

"I expect Counsel that you have witnesses who will testify to these matters. So far I have heard nothing but hearsay."

"By a strange coincidence, My Lord," Counsel continued, anticipating the Judge's question, "there was another person in the Sally Garden that evening and he will describe in detail a conversation he overheard between Miss Johnston and a man called Krzysztof Walenski, a manager at the mill owned by the Montgomery family. I deliberately say overheard because that witness, a man called Shemmy, otherwise known as Valentino, McKelvie, has an unfortunate affliction. He is blind, Milord, totally blind, and he has been that way since he was thirteen years old.

"But when he gives evidence, I am confident Your Lordship will be satisfied that he can positively identify the two people who were in the garden that night, that he heard what he says he heard and what he heard goes to the very root of this challenge to the Last Will and Testament of the late Sir Kenneth Montgomery."

When his turn came Emma Johnston's Counsel painted a sad picture of a vulnerable girl sent to Ireland by her family to avoid the German bombing of her homeland and how she came to be under the protection and eventually under the spell of a much older man, Sir Kenneth Montgomery, the very man into whose care she had been entrusted by her worried parents.

Just a year after coming to Mill Brae this mill owner—a man twice her age—seduced the girl and made her his mistress against her will and inevitably she found she was expecting his baby. When the baby was born, Sir Kenneth did the honourable thing; he accepted full responsibility for his actions and promised to provide for the young mother and her newborn son. In the event he did more. He made a new will in which he settled a substantial sum of money and a house on Emma Johnston and because he had no children by his marriage to Lady Eleanor Montgomery, made the boy Mark Anthony Montgomery his heir.

"Emma Johnston knew nothing about that new will," he continued. "She was completely ignorant of both the will and its contents and would probably have remained so until this day had it not been for the untimely death of Sir Kenneth.

"Counsel for the Petitioner in his opening statement attempts to make the girl out to be a woman of loose morals who inveigled Sir Kenneth into an illicit affair and trapped him by misrepresenting to him that the baby she was carrying was his child. The facts of this case will show clearly that nothing could be further from the truth.

"The court will be satisfied that this is not about loose morals or womanly deceit. It is about money and power and who will control Sperrin Mill and the Montgomery family fortune in the future."

"Yes, Lady Montgomery felt betrayed when her husband left the marital bed for another woman, and embarrassed and hurt when she learned Emma Johnston was expecting a baby, but she was more devastated to learn that the family mill and the greater part of his wealth would pass to this boy, Mark, whose maternal family were not Montgomerys but an English family, the Johnstons. And that fact goes to the very heart of these proceedings."

He dismissed the doubts about the paternity of the boy as "nothing more than small town gossip about the local gentry and the goings-on at the big house".

This challenge to the Will, he went on, was largely based on the evidence of a blind man who had been in a field behind the Montgomery residence, Mill Brae House, one evening and claimed to have overheard an intimate encounter between Emma Johnston and a manager from the mill, a young Polish man whom Sir Kenneth had also taken under his wing.

"The field where this assignation is alleged to have taken place is known in the locality as the Sally Garden—a piece of land attached to the grounds of the Montgomery house. It had one regular visitor—a blind man who went there to harvest rods to make baskets.

"This man, McKelvie, is an unsavoury character and that is about the most charitable thing you could say about him. There is ample evidence from the police that he is a liar and a thief, and a womaniser of the worse kind and that he regularly visited a whorehouse and associated with prostitutes."

"Counsel," interrupted the Judge, "have I misunderstood what you have just said? Is it your intention to call evidence to prove that a material witness about to testify is not credible?"

"Indeed, it is, My Lord. There are police witnesses in Court summoned not by the Respondent, but by the Petitioner, who are available to give such evidence. In fact, on the very night on which he allegedly heard a conversation between Miss Johnston and the young Polish manager, Krzysztof Walenski, that witness was stealing from the Montgomery family."

Valentino could contain himself no longer. He was on his feet, shouting: "I have never been on a charge in my life! This is the first time I ever stood inside a courtroom! I am not a thief!"

There was noisy interruption from the public benches after the outburst, with people shouting, "Good on ye!" and policemen telling him to shut up and behave himself.

The court officials were on their feet. "Sit down, sit down, everybody calm down, or I'll clear the court!" boomed the rasping voice of the tipstaff. He had to repeat the threat several times before the crowd settled down again.

"Mr McKelvie," said the Judge when the noise abated, "you will get a chance to defend your good name when you come to give evidence. Difficult as it may seem to you and particularly because of your handicap I must ask you not to interrupt the proceedings again, otherwise I shall be obliged to impose a sanction."

He turned his attention to the barrister. "Counsel, where is all this taking us? This is a Probate Court. Witnesses are here to help, not to face accusations of criminal behaviour."

"I am entitled to question the credibility of the witness," said Counsel. "I am entitled to show the court that his evidence is not to be believed."

"I have heard enough," said the judge curtly. "It's time we went into evidence. I will decide whether he is to be believed or not."

Valentino was still in a rage but what the judge said helped calm him. He gripped the seat with his two hands, clenched his teeth and bowed his head knowing everybody was staring at him.

The Judge ordered the Petitioner to call his first witness, Lady Montgomery.

There was an audible gasp from the public gallery as the elegant lady in a cerise velvet suit was led to the witness box. She slowly peeled off her elbow length white gloves and placed them on the pew in front of her, put her right hand on the bible and repeated in a clear voice the words of the oath. She smoothed her calf length skirt under her with one hand before she sat down. She turned in her seat to face the Judge, but he politely advised her that it was more important to face Counsel, who would be taking her through her evidence.

In the hushed court Eleanor Montgomery looked more like the Eleanor Parker of twenty years before. Emma Johnston could not get over the change in her—she looked like she had just walked out of the portrait hanging on the stairway at Mill Brae. Her face was beautifully made up; the lines had gone from her forehead; her eyes sparkled through dark eye lashes, smiling moist red lips; she looked like a woman half her age.

"I never realised she was such a beauty," said Helen.

"That's the Eleanor Montgomery in the portrait I told you about, the one hanging on the landing at Mill Brae, painted in Rome during their honeymoon," whispered Emma. "She looks as if she has just stepped out of that picture."

Eleanor said what she had to say, calmly and clearly, without emotion. She gave a full and honest account of events following the arrival of Emma Johnston from England, how the girl and her husband had become lovers and a baby was born and although she was hurt and greatly embarrassed by the affair at the time she had no reason to doubt that her husband was the baby's father.

She was very plausible, addressing Counsel when he put questions to her, turning towards the Judge when she gave her answers; she was soft spoken and there was complete silence so that every word she said could be heard. Helen Flanagan could not help thinking that if there was a jury in that courtroom Lady Montgomery would have won them over completely.

"I had no idea that there was anything amiss until some weeks after my husband's funeral," she continued. "His secretary, Miss Kate Reilly, came to my house and related a strange story about a blind man hiding in the Sally Garden behind my home one evening who claimed to have heard a conversation between Miss Johnston and my mill manager, Krzysztof Walenski."

"At first I was very dubious about the story," she continued, "knowing the sort of gossip that goes on in small communities about people like us. I decided, in any case, to inform my solicitors as a matter of course, since the will had yet to be probated. Like me, they were far from convinced that the blind man was telling the truth.

"Then the solicitors procured a copy of a statement made to the police by the blind man. Apparently, it was made while he was in custody being questioned about other matters, criminal matters. This man told the police almost word for word the story told to me by Miss Reilly. At that point I had to take the matter seriously. I was determined, if the story proved to be true, that Emma Johnston should not benefit from her deceit."

Lady Eleanor said that even though she and her husband had become estranged during her illness she was still his wife and though he was dead she owed it to him to have the business investigated so that the truth would come out. That was the one and only reason she was challenging the will in these proceedings.

"There is no question of vindictiveness," she concluded. "It is not jealousy on my part or anger that Emma Johnston and her son would inherit the family business."

Counsel asked her about the relationship between herself and her husband after the arrival at Mill Brae of her companion, Emma Johnston.

"Was this girl the cause of the estrangement that developed between you and your husband?"

Eleanor shook her head emphatically. "No, my Lord," she said, "the trouble in our marriage started much earlier. It stemmed from the realisation that even though I loved my husband dearly and he loved me dearly we could not have any children.

"In the years prior to his death this failure preyed on my mind and I became depressed and difficult and I did not behave as a dutiful wife should behave. I realise now that at a time when my husband needed my love and companionship most I shut him out of my life."

There was feverish scribbling in the Press box. Reporters made sure to get ever word of what she said. There were angry mutterings by some as they jostled for elbow room.

"Quiet please," said the tipstaff.

When the disturbance in the Press Box died down, she continued: "When the opportunity arose it was no great surprise that he sought solace in the arms of another, the vulnerable Johnston girl. And though we never discussed it I saw a great change in him when he learned that Emma Johnston was pregnant, and they moved out of Mill Brae. The birth of that baby served to underline further my failure as a woman and a wife and until Kenneth's tragic and untimely death I wallowed in self-pity, blaming everybody else for what happened and depending on large doses of medication for my very existence."

Lady Montgomery paused for a few moments as tears filled her eyes and she took several deep breaths. She opened her handbag, took out a handkerchief and dabbed them until they were dry again. Her distress brought tears to the eyes of people in the public gallery and some could be heard sobbing.

"Perhaps your ladyship would like a short recess to allow you to regain your composure," said the judge sympathetically. "I understand that it is painful to recall such an unhappy period of your life."

"I would prefer to continue," she said, "and finish what I want to say. I feel better now."

She put her handkerchief in her bag and lifted her head to face Counsel again.

"Then," said Counsel, leading the witness, "came the tragic and sudden death of your husband?"

"Yes, it was a terrible shock. I did not even know he was missing that night. He was such a careful person I could not understand what he and his driver were doing in such a dangerous place at such a dangerous time. The police had evacuated everyone from that part of the town and he must have known that. Poor Kenneth—he took a risk at the wrong time and it cost him and his driver their lives."

She fumbled for her handkerchief again and Counsel paused to give her time to compose herself.

"It's horrible to lose someone so close," she said, "but the loss is even greater when it happens suddenly, and you don't get a chance to say goodbye. Kenneth and I had our differences, but I never wished him any ill will, and I know he had no animosity towards me. My illness contributed a lot to the disagreements we had but he was always my husband and I know he always regarded me as his wife."

"When I got over the initial shock of his death I began to think about the mill and all those workers who depended on it for their livelihood and I resolved to do what I could to keep it going, to take a more active part in running the business.

"Miraculously this activity helped me regain my confidence, bring me back to my senses and think less about my illness," she continued. "For the first time in nearly six years the depression that poisoned my mind lifted and I was able to see things in a clear light again.

"This change enabled me to resume a normal life, take control of the running of Mill Brae house and meet with the people whose job it was to manage the mill.

"And, of course, when doubts arose about the paternity of the Johnston boy I felt I owed it to my husband to have the matter thoroughly investigated."

There was a lull for a few moments until everybody was sure she had finished what she had to say. Then loud clapping broke out in the public gallery.

Helen Flanagan was so moved by the witness that she would have joined in the applause had she not been sitting beside Emma.

The rasping voice of the tipstaff again demanded order in court.

Emma Johnston's Counsel tried to cross examine Lady Eleanor about her relationship with her husband prior to his death and about her bitterness towards Emma Johnston when she found out her husband was having an affair and particularly when she became pregnant, but the judge interrupted.

"You must confine yourself to the witness testimony in cross examination, Counsel," he said firmly. "You may probe the veracity of that evidence but even when animosity is alleged by one party against another, may I remind you again that this is not a criminal court. The witness is not to be badgered."

Counsel continued by probing the nature of her illness, when it began and how it had miraculously disappeared once her husband was dead but when he tried to quiz her again about the bitter relationship that developed between her and Miss Johnston the Judge said he would not allow that line of questioning to continue.

"The witness has been very frank about the relationship between her husband and herself and between Emma Thompson and herself. I cannot understand the need to pursue those relationships further. In any case I think you are losing sight of our goal—we are here to talk about the probity of a will, about the validity of the terms of that will. What people close to the Testator thought about each other is hardly relevant."

Counsel asked Lady Eleanor if she or her solicitors had had any contact with the witness McKelvie. Did she or anybody on her behalf offer any incentive to the blind man to make the statement?

"No," she said firmly "I first learned about the statement from my solicitors. I never met or had any contact either directly or indirectly with either the police or Mr McKelvie".

Counsel produced a copy of the first statement and pointed out to the Judge that since it was unsigned it should not be admitted in evidence.

"I have no intention of admitting the original unsigned statement from the police," said the Judge, "but there is another signed statement available to the court. That is admissible, but only if the witness who made and signed that statement is prepared to go into the witness box and be cross examined on it.

"More important, Counsel, is that this signed statement made by Mr McKelvie will only be admitted if I am satisfied that he is a competent witness and I fear that might give rise to certain difficulties. This is a unique case in many ways. Remember identification evidence is difficult at the best of times but with a blind witness involved it's going to be even more difficult for the court. Before I even consider Mr McKelvie's evidence I will have to be satisfied that his powers of hearing and voice identification are so good that his evidence is to be believed.

"I am grateful to Your Lordship for his guidance on the matter," said Counsel.

Before he had a chance to ask any further questions the Judge turned to the witness box: "No further questions, Lady Montgomery. You may step down."

All eyes were on Eleanor as she slowly made her way back to her seat. She went through the same motion of smoothing her skirt under her bottom and putting on her gloves before she sat down.

When Valentino's turn came, Jinny guided him to the witness box. She sat down beside him but was told brusquely by the Registrar to return to her seat.

Even though he could not see them Valentino felt intimidated by the hundreds of faces he knew were ranged in front of him. The moment he sat down in the witness box he could feel the sun on his left cheek, so he knew that he was facing across the room, his back to the wall, the judge to his right. His tie felt far too tight and his chest seemed to be bursting inside his shirt, but he made no attempt to loosen either.

The Court Registrar took his right hand and placed it on a book and he was asked to take an oath and swear to tell the truth, the whole truth and nothing but the truth.

He found it hard to concentrate as the words were read out to him and he was glad when he finished.

"So help me God," he said and retrieved his sweaty hand.

"There is a glass of water near you," said the Judge. "If you need to drink, ask the bailiff and he will hand it to you."

He let his fingers slide along the desk until he found the glass, picked it up and drank from it and put it back in the same place, out of reach in case he accidentally knocked it over. The bailiff watched the operation nervously and was glad when the witness put the glass down again without spilling a drop. Just because he was blind did not mean he was helpless.

Lady Montgomery's counsel led the witness through his story about what he overheard in the Sally Garden and the circumstances in which he later told his sister about it and how he was questioned by the police and his decision to make a sworn statement about the affair. He insisted that he was not mistaken when he said he had heard Emma Johnston and the Polish mill manager in the Sally Garden that night.

"It was them and nobody else," he said. "I knew Miss Johnston because I had met her walking along the river several times before that night."

Emma cringed in her seat and bowed her head, hoping McKelvie would not go into any more detail.

"I knew Walenski because of his foreign accent. I didn't hear everything they said but I heard most of it."

He said he did not make the statement to the police voluntarily but to get them off his back because they were hounding him night and day about other things. He thought that if he gave them a statement they would not bother him again.

He was pleased that he got an opportunity to have a go at the police and though he could not see them, knew they would be squirming in their seats with embarrassment. He decided to put the boot into them.

"I was told by one of the people who interviewed me in the police station that if I made the statement and was prepared to give evidence in court Lady Montgomery would not forget me when the case was over."

He knew from the reaction in the court as soon as he said it that he had dropped a bombshell. There were frantic whispers in the lawyers' benches and he could hear the buzz from the public gallery.

When order was restored Counsel asked if he was alleging that Lady Montgomery or somebody on her behalf offered him a bribe to make the statement.

"No," he said. "I made the statement because the police were hounding me. They came to my home on five different occasions and took me to the police station and accused me of all sorts of things, but they never made one charge against me. It was all intimidation and harassment."

"Mr McKelvie," interrupted the Judge. "Just answer the question for Counsel. There is no need to elaborate. If Counsel wants more information, he will ask you another question."

He turned to Counsel; "The witness has made an allegation that a bribe was offered to him in the police station on behalf of Lady Montgomery. That is a serious allegation. I want to hear more about that."

"The last time I was in the police station," said Valentino "one of the men talking to me said that something might be coming from Lady Montgomery if I made a full statement of what I heard that night and signed it."

"You have already testified that the local police questioned you on several occasions," asked the Judge. "Did you know the policemen you were talking to?"

"I know some of the policemen who questioned me, but I don't know who that person was," replied Valentino.

"How convenient," commented Lady Montgomery's Counsel, fuming over the allegation about the bribe. This was the first he had heard of it and he knew it could damage his case considerably. And McKelvie was supposed to be his witness.

Counsel said he had a difficulty and asked if he might approach the Bench; the two barristers then carried on a whispered conversation with the Judge.

Counsel for the Petitioner wanted to have McKelvie, his most important independent witness, treated as hostile because of the allegation he made about the bribe.

"He has changed his story, Milord, and I would like to have an opportunity to cross examine him on why he did so," said Counsel.

Counsel for Emma Johnston smiled and said he had no objection. He knew McKelvie had put Lady Montgomery's barrister in difficulty.

"I think you are over reacting," said the Judge. "We don't have a jury in the courtroom; if there was a jury I would have to abort the trial because of this bribe allegation. It is my intention to ignore it unless your learned colleague has proof of such a bribe. I repeat— this is not a criminal trial. I don't want to hear any more about this alleged bribe unless somebody can produce corroborative evidence that a bribe was offered."

Valentino knew they were talking about him and God knows what plot they were hatching with the Judge. Had he gone too far? He would have to think carefully before he answered any more questions.

When Counsel returned to the benches the Judge the witness he could leave the witness box.

He was taken aback but delighted that his ordeal was over, and his sister came to take him back to his seat. His hands were shaking and a couple of times he stumbled as he made his way between the benches.

Two police witnesses followed and gave evidence of taking McKelvie to the station on a number of occasions to question him about criminal matters, including complaints about trespass at the Montgomery home and larceny of sally rods from the grounds of Mill Brae House. The judge shook his head in disbelief. He pulled his wig forward until it covered his eyes, then pushed it back again and stared at the Counsel.

"There is not a whit of evidence before this court of these allegations and even if there was, what has it to do with the issue before this court?" He asked. "These are matters for a criminal court."

Before Counsel had a chance to reply he ordered the police witness to leave the witness box. People in the Public Gallery applauded.

A very nervous Sgt McParland then took the stand. He described the circumstances in which McKelvie volunteered a statement about the business in the Sally Garden, which he said was completely unsolicited. Neither he nor any other policeman at the interviews offered any deal to McKelvie to get him to make a statement and when he eventually did, they were naturally annoyed that he refused to sign it. Then at a later stage he arrived at the station one day with a signed and witnessed statement, the one that was now before the court.

The Judge asked if any charges had resulted from the interviews in the police station and when he was told no charge had been preferred he asked Counsel what the relevance of the evidence was. The lawyer pondered for a minute, then replied that it was to show that McKelvie had voluntarily given to the police a statement which he now alleged was made only after intimidation and a promise of a bribe.

"He is your witness," said the Judge. "Do you want the Court to accept his evidence, or reject it?"

"I want the Court to accept the voluntary statement he gave to the police, Milord, a statement on which the Petitioner relied heavily when initiating these proceedings. The police were not present when this statement was written and signed yet he now claims it was made under duress, that he was being harassed by the police at the time."

The only noise in the room during the exchange between the Bench and Counsel was the scratch of reporters' pens and pencils on notebooks.

"I take your point," said the Judge, "but this conflicting evidence is not much help to the Court."

The final witness gave his name as Alex McDonald who said he was a former policeman and had done some security work for Sir Kenneth Montgomery at the mill following his retirement. Coincidently he was in the police station on one occasion when McKelvie was being questioned about criminal matters including trespass and larceny.

"While I was present there was no threat or coercion from any officer," he said, "and when the statement came from McKelvie about what he overheard in the Sally Garden it was a surprise because I had been informed that he had refused on previous occasions to sign any statement, even when his solicitor had advised otherwise."

Valentino recognised the voice and stood up. "That's the voice!" he called out. "That's the man who told me Lady Montgomery would look after me if I signed the statement!"

There was bedlam in the court. The barristers were on their feet shouting at one another; reporters clambered over desks to get back into their seats. People in the public gallery stamped their feet and shouted at the witness; police at the back of the court tried to restore order, ordering people to sit down and be quiet. The tipstaff called repeatedly for order, trying to make himself heard above the racket.

The commotion was such that the Judge thought the situation was getting out of hand and left the bench and disappeared through a side door to the safety of his chambers.

Fights broke out when the police tried to clear the public gallery; people stood on their seats and refused to budge. Eventually when about half the gallery had been forcefully removed, order was restored. The red-faced tipstaff issued a stern warning that if there was any more trouble the court would be cleared completely.

The Judge returned when the Registrar was satisfied the trouble was over. He gave McKelvie a final warning—"Keep quiet or you will be charged with contempt of court and find yourself in the cells," he said angrily.

Lady Eleanor's Counsel grovelled to the Judge and apologised profusely to all present for the trouble caused by his witness and promised there would be no further outburst.

McDonald concluded his evidence by denying emphatically that he had offered any bribe or incentive either on his own behalf or on behalf of Lady Montgomery to encourage McKelvie to make a statement. He had no authority from Lady Montgomery or from her solicitors to act either as an intermediary or on their behalf.

Before he left the witness box, the Judge asked him about his presence in the police station when McKelvie was being questioned.

"As a former police officer, Mr McDonald," he said, "it might be in order for you to call into the police station for a chat with former colleagues, but how did you come to be involved in the questioning of a suspect? You are a civilian now like any other member of the public and had no direct interest in the matters under investigation."

McDonald was taken aback by the questions and looked to Lady Eleanor's Counsel for help. When it was not forthcoming he became flustered and his face reddened with embarrassment.

"The witness is free to go," snapped the judge brusquely.

The Judge then asked counsel to join him in his chambers so that certain legal matters could be clarified. Neither the public nor the reporters were happy at this development and showed their displeasure by more shuffling of feet on the dusty floorboards, but they had to put up with it. The Pressmen suspected some secret deal was being done behind closed doors—it was always the same where gentry were involved.

One of the policemen who had given evidence came to where Valentino was sitting and leaned over him.

"They are in there deciding whether to send you to jail or make you pay a hefty fine," he laughed.

"I wouldn't be the first innocent man to go to jail and I won't be the last. You did your worst, but I still caught you out—you and comrade McDonald."

The policeman withdrew quickly, his face red with anger.

The judge and barristers returned a few minutes later and to his surprise, he was called was called back to the witness box. "Mr McKelvie," he said, "first of all I want to remind you that you are still under oath. You understand that?"

"Yes," he replied. They were up to something. Maybe the policeman was right. Was he going to be sent to jail?

"Mr McKelvie, I want you to listen carefully to what I have to say. The most important thing in life is that a man is free to live the life he wants to live and in a democracy such as ours that freedom is accorded to him. But when a man dies he loses all the rights he had in this life except one; if he has made a will he has the right to expect that his Executors will implement the terms of that will. If Executors fail in any way in this regard, then the courts will step in and force them to do their duty. Only when you come to make a will yourself will you realise the importance of what I am saying.

"In this case, the will of the late Sir Kenneth Montgomery would have been implemented in full by his executors, a reputable firm of solicitors, had it not been challenged by his widow. And that will would never have been challenged by Lady Montgomery had it not been for the story you told your sister about a conversation you overheard between two people. You claim you are able to identify these people, despite the fact that you are blind. You said in evi-

237

dence that you may have spoken to one of them casually but never met the other one at all.

"Do you understand what I am saying?"

Sitting a couple of seats behind Valentino, Emma's heart skipped a few beats and she took a deep breath. If he was put under pressure and wanted to divert attention away from himself again, would he tell the Judge that he knew her well and they had been together in the Sally Garden? She took a deep breath and used her handkerchief to wipe the perspiration from her hands.

Valentino paused for a few moments. He nodded.

"Don't nod your head, man" said the tipstaff abruptly. "Answer yes or no to His Lordship."

"Right," he said.

The Judge continued: "Subsequently you were confident enough to make a statement identifying those two people and today you have given sworn evidence in this court about an alleged conversation between them.

"But even if you were in the Sally Garden that night and overheard the conversation set out in your statement, it still leaves the court with a major problem.

"The problem is this. If you were blessed with your sight and you came into this court and testified that on the evening in question you saw Miss Johnston and Mr Walenski together in the Sally Garden I would have to discard your evidence; and I'll tell you why.

"First it was dusk, and you said in your statement that these two people were some distance away. There are volumes of precedents in our law, in official court reports, where visual identification in poor light is notoriously unreliable and generally should not be accepted as evidence on which to convict an accused.

"This case is different. You come to this court with evidence that relies not on what you saw in poor visibility that evening because you saw nothing but on hearing and powers of perception which you say are so good that you could positively identify two people from their voices."

He paused while he leaned forward to consult some notes in front of him. "This gives rise to a question as to how good your hearing is and how good your powers of perception really are and how much reliance the court should place on what you say you heard," he continued. "To help the court resolve those difficulties, I want to conduct an experiment."

"I need your co-operation on an important matter, Mr McKelvie, so listen carefully," he said. "Six people will speak to you one at a time from the rear of the court. If you recognise the voice, give the name of the person you think it is. If you do not know the voice, say so. Don't guess Mr McKelvie. It doesn't matter if you do not recognise the voice or if you are not sure. Just say so. Do you understand?"

"I do," he answered, meekly. Was this the catch? He wiped beads of perspiration from his forehead with the cuff of his jacket.

The Judge did not have to ask for silence in the court. There wasn't a sound. He called on number one to begin.

"When the dreary prison bell woke me on Christmas morning and I realised where I was and the day that had come, I confess that I really felt depressed and unhappy. Visions of a wild stampede of little ones in long white nightdresses to find out what Santa had placed in their stockings, of the walk out to first Mass at Glen…"

"Sergeant McParland," said the witness.

Next was a woman's voice reading the same passage. She was a complete stranger.

"I don't know that woman," he said almost as soon as she started.

Another woman. It was easy this time. He heard an audible gasp from the body of the court when she stood up and started to read the passage.

"The English woman from Templemount," he said quickly.

A man this time. "Constable McAllister."

Another man, whom he did not recognise, but the next male voice was easy because he had difficulty reading the passage, and Valentino knew immediately it was the Pole.

"That's enough," said the Judge. "You are excused, Mr McKelvie."

He was sure he had got them all right, apart from the woman whom he did not recognise and one man. What's more he knew the book they were reading. It was about Christmas Day in Derry Jail and the writer was one of the prisoners, Louis J. Walsh, who subsequently became a Judge himself across the border in County Donegal. When he still had his sight, he had read it several times. He remembered the book had a strange name: "On My Keeping and In Theirs".

And there was something else—all the people who spoke had their backs turned to him! They thought that would catch him out.

Jinny took his arm and led him back to his seat in the body of the court. People clapped him on the back as he pushed past them and some of them whispered "Well done, McKelvie."

The raspy voice again called for order in the court. The next witness was Emma Johnston.

Emma fully intended to testify when she arrived at the court that morning and her barrister was confident that her testimony would be accepted. Unknown to him she had made an agreement with Krzysztof that if he said in court that he was not in the Sally Garden that evening with her, but might have been there with his fiancée, Kate Reilly, she would allow him to come and visit Mark at Templemount from time to time. Krzysztof was convinced that what she had told him that night when she lost her temper—that he might be the boy's father—was true and he wanted to be able to visit him.

But after seeing how McKelvie was treated in the court, she became terrified at the prospect of having to face questions from the lawyers and the Judge in that crowded, oppressive room. She felt she would be pilloried when she contradicted McKelvie and denied that she was in the Sally Garden that evening with Krzysztof Walenski or anybody else. If they tripped her up just once she would go to pieces in the witness box. Her lawyers told her simply to follow the statement she had made for the Affidavit but in her confused state she was not even sure she could do that. Worse still was the prospect of being found out for telling lies.

She leaned forward in her seat and whispered to her solicitor that she did not want to give evidence. He panicked and when he told Counsel, he asked for a brief adjournment, pleading that he had to consult the Respondent about a new development in the proceedings. After a brief discussion with Emma during which she refused to change her mind Counsel decided that if Emma Johnston was not going to testify there was no point in calling the other two witnesses—Helen Flanagan and Krzysztof Walenski—for the sole purpose of putting them into the witness box was to corroborate Emma Johnston's testimony.

When the hearing resumed Counsel announced that he did not intend to call any witnesses because it was his contention that there was not a shred of evidence from the Petitioner to prove that the boy Mark Anthony Montgomery was not the son of the late Sir Kenneth Montgomery and consequently the challenge to the will should fall.

There was a buzz of disappointment in the public gallery. People did not understand what had happened. The Reporters were dumbfounded. Some tossed their pencils in the air to vent their frustration at the turn of events; others buried their faces in their hands in despair. This was the one witness they wanted to hear more than anybody else, the scarlet woman at the centre of the whole plot. There was another shuffling of feet and more whispering: "The Johnston woman got cold feet—she is not going to testify."

There was no excitement after that. The lawyers made boring final submissions; each side tried to persuade the Judge there was ample evidence to make a finding in their favour.

Even more disappointment when the Judge announced that he would reserve his decision until a later date. He needed time to consider matters raised by Counsel in chambers.

Eleanor Montgomery felt cheated when Counsel informed the court that Emma Johnston was not going to testify. It was the one time she nearly lost her composure. She wanted to stand up in Court and vent her anger. But she held her peace. She did not expect Emma to admit in the witness box that Kenneth was not the father of her son, but she might have admitted her liaison with the Polish mill manager at the time she became pregnant.

LIFE AFTER DEATH

Early in 1945 the German army was forced to release its grip on Poland. It had lost Romania to the Russians and was cut off from the giant oil fields that had been its lifeline since the war began. Although they still fought ferociously to halt the Russian advance it was to no avail and the remnants of Hitler's defeated army were ordered to retreat westward and make a stand to protect the Fatherland.

Stanislaw packed the most valuable and least bulky of his hoard of possessions into two leather suitcases, ready for a quick exit from Lubiala. Timing was important—he had to be ready to follow the Germans quickly and make sure he did not get caught by the advancing Russians or by Polish Communists poised to take control.

His main concern was to get his hands on the gold and jewellery buried in the garden, for he regarded these as his passport to a new life in England. It would be pointless trying to make his way to the West without the means of re-establishing himself when he got there. He could not take with him the bulky paintings stored in the attic of the restaurant, but at least they were safe for the moment and he might be able to retrieve them at a future date when the political situation stabilised.

Stanislaw went to the mine and found his house a smouldering ruin. The Germans had left the day before and he suspected the burning was the work of Maria's friends. She might even have had a hand in it herself.

He used an old fork handle to probe the ground around the tree where he had buried the valuables and recovered the leather pouches still intact. He did not even open them to check the contents but put them into the lining of his overcoat and went back to Lubiala. The time had come to make his escape from Poland.

Comrade Maria Walenski departed Warsaw while the Germans were still shelling the remains of the Home Army in the Old City. She drove to the Ukrainian border and made contact with an advance guard of the Red Army. She was introduced to the political section and after establishing her bona fides, began an intensive period of indoctrination.

Ambiguity about ownership of the mill pending the outcome of the court battle between Lady Montgomery and the English woman meant that no plans could be made for its future. In any case the raw material for linen—flax—was in very short supply and a new synthetic fabric called nylon discovered during the war was rapidly replacing natural fibres.

The protagonists in the highly publicised court case had to wait almost six months for a decision. When it came in October 1945, the written judgement was just eight paragraphs long, typed on two pages of paper and Valentino could not understand how it took so long to produce it. His statement for the police had been put together in one hour in the hotel bedroom in Derry and it was just as long as the document from the court.

The judgement summarised the Petitioner's case in three paragraphs, paid tribute to the honesty and integrity of Lady Montgomery and devoted one paragraph to the blind witness McKelvie.

"I find that Mr McKelvie, despite his affliction, was a capable and competent witness, even though he relied on hearing rather than sight recognition and any court would have to give careful consideration to his testimony in a case of this nature. I say in a case of this nature because different considerations arise when giving evidence in a criminal case where a much higher standard of proof is necessary. If such evidence were tendered in a criminal trial there would be other considerations before a decision was taken about what weight, if any, should be given to it."

The fifth paragraph, however, drew attention to the fact that the time of the Court had been largely wasted because many of the matters raised were extraneous to what the Judge described as "a straightforward testamentary declaration".

"A man made a will," concluded the judgement, "and as with all wills, the testator devised his worldly goods to people he loved or to whom he was beholden in some way when he was alive. In this case the main beneficiaries were his wife, Lady Eleanor Montgomery, his mistress Miss Emma Johnston and her son, Mark Anthony Montgomery. The words the Testator used to make these devises are the mandatory words required by law. None of these devises give rise to any cause for doubt.

"Neither do I find any ambiguity in the words the Testator used for the disposal of the residue of his estate, which he clearly devised 'to Mark Anthony Montgomery, my son'. A great deal of evidence was adduced to convince me either that the said Mark Anthony Montgomery was or alternatively was not the son of the Testator. This is a matter, in my opinion, on which the Court thankfully does not have to make a decision, and for this reason:

"It is clear that the beneficiary of the residue of the Testator's estate is not the person referred to as 'my son' but the person clearly identified by name as 'Mark Anthony Montgomery' the same as is identified on a birth certificate produced in court and marked 'Exhibit C'.

"Therefore, it is the finding of this Court that the will the subject of these proceedings is the Last Will and Testament of the late Sir Kenneth Montgomery, and that it is free of ambiguity. I make no finding as to whether Mark Anthony Montgomery is or is not the son of the Testator, for probate law does not oblige me to do so."

The first Valentino heard of the court decision was from the nurse, who arrived at Minnie's house with a bottle of brandy to celebrate.

"Never mind the brandy," he chuckled, "can I grab that piece of paper you have been keeping warm inside your brassiere?"

"You'll do no such thing," she said. "The only paper you'll be getting is a sack of large five-pound notes as soon as the Emma Johnston gets her affairs straightened out."

He would have been happier if she had given the agreement to him but after a couple of glasses of the spirit he felt randy and wanted to celebrate right away with a session between the sheets with Minnie. The thought of the paper nestling between Helen's ample breasts had made him horny.

Eleanor Montgomery was disappointed at the outcome of the case but accepted the verdict and was glad at least that the Judge had vindicated her. It came as a relief in the end because it helped her to make a decision that she was unable to make before. Since her husband's death she had cleared her mind of the demons that had tortured her for so long and with the return of her confidence and good health she felt ready for a new challenge. She decided to sell her interest in Mill Brae and start a new life elsewhere.

The court case had settled the will, but it did not answer the most important question as far as she was concerned. Who was Mark's father? She needed an answer to that question before she could move on with her life. It preyed on her mind so much that she decided to swallow her pride, go to see Emma Johnston and confront her about it. And if she was not woman enough to tell the truth she would go and see Krzysztof Walenski. If he admitted that Emma told him he was the father that would be enough.

It had nothing to do with the will any more or Mill Brae or even Kenneth's wealth. That had already been decided and it was over and done with as far as she was concerned. Now it was a question of whether or not her failure to have a child was due to her inability to conceive or to her husband's inability to make her pregnant.

A week after the judgement she summoned the courage to call on Emma. If ever she was to get at the truth, it would only come in one of two ways—either the girl would relent and tell her that her husband was not the father, or Krzysztof Walenski would admit that Emma Johnston told him Mark was his son. She did not relish the prospect of meeting Emma Thompson again but felt she had no option.

At eight o'clock in the morning she knocked at the door of Leyland House and it was answered by the nursemaid, still in her dressing gown.

Ethel was embarrassed when she saw who it was and apologised for not being dressed to receive visitors.

"I am Eleanor Montgomery and I wish to speak to Emma Johnston," she said. "I would be obliged if you would let her know I am here."

The girl disappeared without saying a word leaving her standing at the doorway. Emma, taken completely unawares and still in her dressing gown, apologised for not being more presentable. Eleanor Montgomery was the last person she expected to see at her door.

She invited her guest into the drawing room. "I was just about to have breakfast," she said. "Will you join me in a cup of tea and some hot toast?"

"Thank you," said her visitor, "but this is not a social visit. I'm sorry to call so early and I know you think that I am taking a liberty by coming here unannounced, but there is something I have to tell you which I know will please you, and in return there is something I need to ask you about."

Emma was taken aback by her directness and fussed with the cups and saucers on the low table between them, waiting for Ethel to come with the tea and toast.

"Let the maid settle breakfast," said Emma. She felt that whatever was about to be said was best said well out of earshot of Ethel. The hot toast arrived, butter melting on golden brown bread.

"Will I pour the tea Madam?" she asked.

"Yes, we'll have it now," said Emma. "And would you be good enough to go upstairs and bathe and dress Mark."

When Emma heard Ethel's footsteps on the stairs, she closed the door of the drawing room and sat down facing the older woman.

"Now we can talk," she said quietly.

"First of all," Lady Eleanor started "I want to make it clear that I harbour no resentment towards you over the outcome of the court case," she said. "As far as I am concerned that is over and done with— no further proceedings, no appeal, nothing like that. My health has been much better these past months and for that I am grateful. For the first time in years I feel fit and well and able to take control of my own affairs. So I have decided to leave all that business of the will behind and get on with my life.

"I made up my mind some time ago that if the court case ended in my favour I would take over the running of my late husband's business and grow old gracefully in Ireland. If it went against me I decided the best thing to do was bow out gracefully and that is one of the reasons why I am here this morning. I am vacating the house and I intend to inform the solicitors that I will sell my life interest in Mill Brae to you and your son for a sum of £20,000, a sum which I am advised is quite reasonable.

"Irrespective of whether you take that option or not, however, within a month I will be on my way to America. I have already booked passage for myself and arranged shipment of my personal belongings."

"I am sorry that you are leaving your home," said Emma. "I feel bad about that. I never intended any of this to happen. I hope you understand that I am a victim of this unfortunate affair too. I came to Ireland after a very bad personal experience, and here I am, still in my early twenties, with a baby, and no husband..."

Eleanor cut her short: "I didn't come to talk about the past. All that is behind us now. You have to get on with your life and I with mine. There is no point in apportioning blame for what happened. I don't condone what you did, especially the betrayal of our friend-ship, but I know you are young and impressionable and you pro-vided companionship for my husband at a time when I shut him out of my life. As I said, I don't blame you for the affair—but I do blame you if you knowingly misled Kenneth."

She paused, waiting for Emma to say something, but there was silence. She gave no sign that she either agreed or disagreed with what Eleanor said.

"The only reason why I came here today is to ask you a question. One question—and I need an answer, a truthful answer. Before you answer, please take into consideration that I have tortured myself for years, caused myself to have a nervous breakdown, destroyed my marriage and drove my husband out of my life—all because I be-lieved I was inadequate as a wife. I could not give my husband the baby he wanted so badly."

She stared hard, but Emma averted her gaze.

"Please look at me," she said, her voice trembling with emotion. Tears welled up in her eyes. She was desperate. "You slept with my husband for more than a year. Did he make you pregnant, or was it somebody else? Is he the father of your son, or is it somebody else? I need an answer! I need to know the truth!"

She sat back on her chair, staring at the bowed head of Emma across the table from her.

"The answer," said Emma lifting her head to look directly at Eleanor for the first time "is that I am not sure. Your husband and I had an affair that lasted more than a year before I became pregnant. I let another man make love to me one night and shortly after that I discovered I was pregnant. I never intended to be unfaithful to Kenneth—it just happened. I found myself alone with this other man; we got excited and ended up together in his bed. I am ashamed about it and I regret it, but what's done cannot be undone.

"I am almost sure that your husband was Mark's father. Up to the time Mark was born, it never occurred to me that he might not be the father, but after his death when I had time to think, it did occur to me that Krzysztof Walenski could have been responsible for my pregnancy."

Eleanor's heart skipped a few beats and she put her head into her hands, breathing heavily to avoid fainting. It was almost what she wanted to hear, what she hoped and prayed the answer would be. Now that she heard the words from the only person who knew, it took her breath away; she felt elated, as if a great burden had been lifted from her shoulders and womanhood restored to her body.

"In twenty years of marriage," she whispered, fighting back the tears, "I never suspected that there was any inadequacy on Kenneth's side. I let doctors and specialists probe my body and defile my womanhood looking for the defect that prevented me from having a baby. I tortured myself over my inadequacy as a woman while he hid behind false masculinity. After all my suffering and anxiety, it now appears that it was his fault all along—he was not capable of fathering a child."

Before Emma had time to reply, Eleanor got up from the chair, picked up her hat and gloves and walked out of the room to the hallway. While she was putting on her coat, Ethel came down the stairs carrying Mark. Eleanor stopped and stared at the boy, searching his face for some feature she could recognise, something that reminded her of her husband. But she could see nothing. The one outstanding feature he had was a wisp of red hair. She chuckled as she went through the front door. The only place she ever saw hair like that was on the blind man McKelvie in the witness box. Was it possible the prim and proper Emma had more than a passing acquaintance with him in the Sally Garden too? She shook her head in disbelief, more convinced than ever that whoever the father was, that baby had no blood connection with her husband. She walked unsteadily towards the waiting car and let herself in. Wheels grated on the pebble driveway as it turned sharply and disappeared through the front gate.

"The little English bitch!" she said aloud so that the driver could hear, "all she could manage was half-truths. After all that happened she could not bring herself to tell me the whole truth. But now that I have seen her baby, I know the truth."

Political stalemate reigned in Poland in the spring of 1945; nobody was sure what would happen with the Russians after the Germans pulled out. Stanislaw, sickened by the scale of the atrocities, got a taxi to the railway station to catch the train to Budapest to make his way West.

He arrived in England ten days after he left Warsaw with two suitcases that had never been opened and around his waist a cloth pouch containing a small fortune in gold and jewels.

Maria Kubinska, still using false papers with the name Walenski, became a Political Commissar in Poland and remained in that position until her marriage to an army officer six years later. She never disclosed to her husband that she was half-Jewish nor did she ever try to contact her father even though he got word to her that he had settled in England and was in business with Krzysztof.

She and her husband moved into the house in Lubiala that had once been her mother's restaurant, and the couple had three children. In the attic they found silver, antiques and paintings hidden there by her father but decided not to disturb them for it would only bring unwanted attention from the authorities. They left the hoard in the attic, hoping that someday they would be able to sell them and use the proceeds for their children's future.

Although a member of a group assigned to help the international inquiry team gather information about the concentration camps, she never found any trace of what happened to her mother after she was moved from the ghetto in Warsaw. The only thing she could be sure of was that Barbara was dead—otherwise she would have made contact after the war.

Lady Eleanor Montgomery, using her maiden name Eleanor Parker, sailed from Cobh, County Cork, for New York in November 1945 and settled in the state of Vermont. From the moment she arrived she let it be known that she was a wealthy woman looking for a husband and found there was no shortage of suitors.

She lied about her age, married Peter Wexford, a second-generation Irish farmer five years her junior and a year later she bore him a son. The following year she had another son and so excited was she with her new-found motherhood that she had to be dissuaded by her doctor from having more children as she approached 50 years of age.

When the two boys were old enough to go to school, the former Irish society girl realised her ambition to dabble in politics and embarked on a very successful career in the Democratic Party when she was in her sixties. Just when she was poised to contest the election for State Governor, the Kennedy brothers, President John F. and Attorney General Robert, were both assassinated within a short time and she became disillusioned with the political wrangling that followed. She left politics in 1965, retired to the family farm and died there in 1981 at the age of 83. She never returned to Ireland nor did she ever contact anybody from her previous life.

After Eleanor's death her sons found out about her life in Ireland before she went to America. They came to County Tyrone to visit the mill and talk to people who knew her. They perused newspaper clippings about the death of her first husband and the court case that followed and talked to families of people who had worked at Mill Brae. Most people still fondly remembered Kenneth and Eleanor Montgomery and expressed regret that the mill and their village and the Montgomery millions had passed to an English family, the

Johnstons. After all they read and heard, Eleanor's sons came to the conclusion that the Johnstons and the Irish courts had cruelly deprived their mother of her lawful inheritance.

The Wexford brothers instituted legal proceedings in the Irish and British courts in 1983 to recover the estate that they believed rightfully belonged to their mother. The case was based on evidence adduced from the fact that she was never barren, as had been alleged, and had children by her second marriage; that there was ample evidence to prove that Sir Kenneth Montgomery was incapable of fathering a child and that as a consequence Mark Anthony Montgomery could not be his son; that Emma Johnston had perpetrated a fraud in which she had misled Sir Kenneth Montgomery; that she had exerted undue influence on Sir Kenneth Montgomery to force him to change his will in favour of herself and her son.

Krzysztof Walenski, bitter at the way he was treated by Emma after the death of Sir Kenneth and still denied access to the boy, provided an affidavit for the Wexfords in which he stated that he believed he was the boy's father and was willing to submit to blood tests to provide proof of paternity. On the advice of their lawyers, Mark Montgomery and Emma Johnston refused to participate in the court proceedings or to submit to tests sought by the petitioners.

It took five years of hearings and appeals and judicial review before the House of Lords in England decided finally that the Wexford family action could not succeed. In the end the highest judges in the land came to the same conclusion as the trial judge in the original Probate Court action—that Sir Kenneth Montgomery, as was his right and privilege, had left the bulk of his fortune to Mark Anthony Montgomery. They affirmed that whether Mark Anthony Montgomery was or was not the testator's son, or indeed whether the testator had been deceived into believing that the boy was his son, was not relevant in this case.

Following the departure of Lady Eleanor from Mill Brae House, Emma moved in and thereafter played a large part in supervising the management of the mill until her son was old enough to look after his affairs. She was joined by the Colonel and her mother who came to visit and stayed. She installed them in Leyland House where they resided until their deaths in the early 1970's. She also had regular visits from her sisters, and they brought boyfriends and husbands and their children to enjoy the grandeur of Mill Brae and the new-found wealth of the family.

All three of her sisters married, but Emma did not. She had lots of admirers and a reputation for taking men to Mill Brae and bedding them until she tired of their company, but she had no desire to tie herself to any of them. She had such a reputation for promiscuity that it was said that in Sperrin even the Catholic curate had succumbed to her charms.

Emma treated Krzysztof with contempt and never once did she acknowledge that he was Mark's father. Disillusioned, he left Ireland altogether in 1950 for London to join his father in a new business of buying and selling property. Krzysztof tried for years to locate Kate and spent thousands of pounds with private detective agencies in Britain, America, Australia and New Zealand; he never succeeded in getting one scrap of reliable information about what happened to her after she took the train from Murrinbridge to Belfast, presumably to go to England. He kept in touch with her ageing parents for he found it difficult to believe she could walk out of all their lives forever. They both died in the 1960's not knowing whether their daughter was alive or dead.

Krzysztof never married; he died of a heart attack in 1989 at the age of 69, leaving a sizeable fortune to the man he believed was his son, but with the condition that he change his name to Walenski. Mark Anthony Montgomery, then a wealthy man in his own right, refused to change his name and so could not take the bequest under the terms of the will. It was subsequently claimed by Krzysztof's only living relatives, his half-sister, Maria Walenski of Lubiala, in a Poland emerging from Communist rule after half a century of Russian occupation.

In 1990 at the age of 73, Kate Reilly returned to Ireland. She booked into a hotel in her hometown and opened an account in the local bank to which she transferred more than 400,000 American dollars from the Bank of Argentina. Kate Reilly was back in town after all those years—and a millionaire.

She visited the graveyard where her parents were buried and asked them to forgive her for walking out of their lives all those years ago without even saying goodbye.

When she found out that Lady Eleanor Montgomery had lost a court battle over the will and emigrated to America where she married and had a family, Kate found it had to believe. All the trouble in Mill Brae between Lady Eleanor and Sir Kenneth was supposed to have been over Eleanor's inability to have a child. Why had so much changed after Kenneth's death?

She went to Mill Brae and re-introduced herself to Emma Johnston. After Emma got over the initial shock of seeing this ghost from the past, Kate was a frequent visitor to the big house. Emma even threw a party in her honour to which she invited her sisters and their families and Helen Flanagan and her husband and family.

Kate told Helen she was so hurt by Krysztof Walenski's betrayal that she packed her bags without even telling her parents and left for England. She stayed in London for a month trying to decide where to go. The war had disrupted relations between a lot of countries and she found it difficult to get a visa to America or Australia. When she applied to the Argentine Embassy she was advised by a friendly official to state on her application form that her reasons for leaving Ireland were political. She had her visa within two weeks and a passage booked by the Embassy to South America.

"All I could think of then was to get as far away from Ireland as possible," she said, "far enough to make sure that even if I got homesick, it would not be easy to return." She invested her savings in a cattle farm—she was advised that the demand for food in Europe after the war would push beef prices up. The farm turned out to be lucrative for a while but when prices began to fall she sold it and went into the business of breeding racehorses which was a great success. Kate never mentioned the fact that she had financed both her enterprises with £90,000 stolen from the mill.

On the long journey back to Ireland, she had given a lot of thought to her wealth, and particularly how she had acquired it.

In South America she worked hard with that money to make her own fortune. As the years passed and her wealth increased she convinced herself that the money that had fallen into her lap in Ireland belonged to her and nobody else. But when she decided to return to Ireland she made up her mind that she would return the stolen money to the Montgomerys—that way she could salve her conscience by saying it was only and loan which had now been repaid, that it was always her intention to give the money back.

But she discovered on her arrival in Murrinbridge that making restitution was not as simple as she thought it would be. So much had changed since she left. Eleanor Montgomery had emigrated to America and Emma Johnston and her son, Mark Montgomery had inherited everything. Kate did not fancy the idea of handing another £90,000 to people who already had more wealth that they would ever need.

She let it be known among her friends that she was home to spend as much as she could in the time she had left and hinted that she might even find somebody to keep her warm in bed at night in her old age; like Emma she had fancied a lot of men but never fell in love again after the heartbreak of Krzysztof.

"Stick with me, Kate," laughed Emma, "and there will be no shortage of men to keep you warm. This place is full of idle stallions—young and old—and your friend Emma will let you have the pick of the herd. We'll have a ball."

"I know a fine blind stallion...," quipped Helen Flanagan.

"That's enough," interrupted Emma, "I don't want to hear another word about your blind Valentino."

"My God, don't tell me he's still around!" said Kate.

Valentino never got his sight back. Even the most skilled surgeons could not repair damage to delicate membranes that detached that day on the bridge when fate rolled a dark grey curtain down over his youthful eyes.

Minnie confided in Helen that she was just as happy to see him the way he was.

"He is still a terrible animal in bed," she said. "The older he gets, the worse he becomes. If that man got his sight back, he would be chasing after every young girl in the town."

"And he would have his wicked way with them too," laughed Helen, "if past performances are anything to go by."

Valentino overheard them talking about him.

"Mind yourself Helen Flanagan," he called out, "or I might show you just how good I am. I heard you are still carrying that agreement around tucked inside your bra, and I might decide to take if from you by force one of these days"

"I'm too old for that kind of exercise," she laughed, "but I wonder if you would be interested in a fine filly just arrived from a South American stud farm? I hear she comes from top breeding stock—I could put in a good word for you!"

"For God's sake, Helen," said Minnie, "don't encourage him!"

Lightning Source UK Ltd.
Milton Keynes UK
UKHW011454100419
340803UK00001B/56/P